THE CASSANDRA BICK CHRONICLES

Tracey Sinclair

First published in 2014

Copyright © Text Tracey Sinclair
Printed by CreateSpace, an Amazon company

The author asserts the moral right under the Copyright, Designs and Patents Act 1988 to be identified as the author of this work.

All rights reserved. No part of this publication may be reproduced, stored in a retrieval system, or transmitted, in any form or by any means without the prior written consent of the author, nor be otherwise circulated in any form of binding or cover other than that in which it is published and without a similar condition being imposed on the subsequent purchaser.

Cover and text design by Red Button Publishing

PRAISE FOR DARK DATES

"I loved her humor and snark. I felt like we could be friends… I can't wait to see what she does next"

The Book Tart

"This book is fantastic. It should be a bestseller with an upcoming movie. Dark Dates is unique"

The TBR Pile

"I would say that any fan of earlier Anita Blake or Darynda Jones is going to love it. This pure joyful digging at ridiculous clichés of vampire culture... Anne Rice, LKH, mentions of Supernatural and Buffy… it was so much fun!"

Nocturnal Book Reviews

"Tracey Sinclair's talent for snarky wit comes through wonderfully in her lead character, Cassandra Bick. The dry British wit and humor shines, and I really enjoyed her unusual characters"

Jade Kerrion, award-winning author of the *Double Helix* series.

"I have to say that Sinclair has turned me into an out and out fanpoodle. I stayed up late reading this book because I simply could not put it down"

Fangs for the Fantasy

Dedicated to my mum, Marjorie Sinclair, my uncle, Bill Nellist, and my friend Cerwyss O'Hare.
Much loved and sorely missed.

Table of Contents

Prologue	7
Chapter 1	8
Chapter 2	14
Chapter 3	19
Chapter 4	29
Chapter 5	34
Chapter 6	36
Chapter 7	40
Chapter 8	44
Chapter 9	47
Chapter 10	55
Chapter 11	62
Chapter 12	68
Chapter 13	78
Chapter 14	85
Chapter 15	94
Chapter 16	102
Chapter 17	105
Chapter 18	110
Chapter 19	114
Chapter 20	125
Chapter 21	132
Chapter 22	140
Chapter 23	153
Chapter 24	160
Chapter 25	168
Chapter 26	176

Chapter 27	182
Chapter 28	189
Chapter 29	202
Chapter 30	205
Chapter 31	214
Chapter 32	226
Chapter 33	231
Chapter 34	241
Chapter 35	249
Chapter 36	256
Chapter 37	260
Chapter 38	269
Chapter 39	274
Epilogue	278
Acknowledgements	280
About the Author	281

Prologue

THE CRYPT was perfect: dark and dusty and smelling faintly of candles. I ran my fingers lightly across stone so old it remembered when the city was a child, and I could almost feel its memories stirring beneath my touch. This was stone that had survived wars, plagues, fires and bombs – all that man or nature could throw at it – and still it remained. We may have been in the heart of London, down an inconspicuous side street mere moments away from its shiny, commercial glory, but here the air was thick with history. I could Sense it as I moved, taste it in the air, feel it in the chill of the iron fixtures in the walls that were all they bore by way of decoration. Not far from here heretics had been burned, traitors tortured – brutalities committed that a civilised world had now disowned, but the stones had not forgotten.

I looked at my guide: a sly, careful glance that gave away nothing. He was sweating slightly, despite the coolness, anxious for my approval. I paused, not wanting to betray the depth of my desire. The silence stretched on, filled only with the sound of his breathing, quickened by nerves, until eventually I took pity on him and nodded my surrender.

"It's fine. I'll take it. Remind me, again, where will the caterers' tables go?"

Chapter 1

SO, WE'VE all seen Buffy, right? I mean, you didn't pick this up because the shop was out of Jane Austen and this looked like the next best thing. It's just that this story will go a whole lot faster if I don't have to spend too much time convincing you of the whole 'they walk among us' scenario, and we can all just accept it and move on.

Don't believe me? Just look around you. OK, not so much if you're sitting reading this on the sofa on a Sunday night – though that might not be a bad idea. Was that a shadow I saw there? (Made you look, right?) But if you're sitting on the bus or the tube or in the office canteen, take a good look around you and tell me, hand on heart, that everyone you see is 100% human. You're honestly saying you've never wondered? Look at them. *Really* look. Properly, go on, risk it, they won't be paying any attention to you anyway; they're too busy trying to pass as ordinary. Come on, don't some of them look a touch… undead, maybe? Witchy? A little less than normal? A bit… Other?

Of course, it's easier for me. I'm what you'd call – if you were in a generous mood and we'd got past all the denial and the labels like 'nutter', 'delusionist' and 'freak' – a Sensitive. With a capital S, if you don't mind, because I didn't go through all this crap for all these years to be lower case. What's a Sensitive? Well, it's probably easier to tell you what it's not. I can't give you the lottery numbers or put you in touch with your dead aunty Betty, and you won't see me doing mindreading tricks on TV anytime soon. But I can walk into a room and know it's haunted. I can look into someone's eyes and know they are a bad, bad person, even if I'll never be able to articulate why. What it means, in a nutshell, is that when *you* look at the woman with the saggy grey skin and the cracked fingernails and the slightly red eyes and you're wondering if, now that I mention it, there isn't something a little weird about her, or if she's just another zoned out commuter, one of life's lost losers with more on her plate to worry about than skincare and a manicure, I would *know*. Don't ask me how. I don't understand the physics or the history of it – as far as I'm aware, I come from a long line of Normals, with nary a sixth sense between them, but there's no one left anymore that I can ask. Like most people I've got my own backstory but I'm not sure I know you well enough yet to share. But trust me on this one thing – I'd know. It's not her, by the way. It's the guy at the back in the suit.

I'm in my office. As these things go, it's quite a nice office – small, of course, because I'm always on a budget, but well-located and tastefully if slightly blandly furnished. The windows may only look out onto the other side of the street, but they are large and let in a lot of light. Not now, of course, because this meeting, like most of my work, is taking place at night.

"So, tell me a little about yourself."

He's nervous, but that's not unusual: most first timers are. Scared of what they're telling me, scared of what I'll say, scared that this is all some elaborate set up and I am biding my time, waiting to spring a trap. He folds and refolds his pale hands in his lap, looking up at me through an unfairness of lashes that are as long and dark as a girl's.

"Um, I like the cinema. Westerns, action movies. I like Clint Eastwood. The older ones."

I nod, my professional smile glued firmly in place. Though my Sense is buzzing gently, it's not in alarm: there's nothing here to worry about except that, in his anxiety, he might knock something over and break it.

"OK, that's good. Anything else?"

"Books. History books."

I nod again, encouraging. I have his file open beside me – despite being a few months shy of my 29th birthday, I'm fairly old school in some ways and I like to do everything in hard copy first – and he's looking at my pen like it's some sort of weapon. Then again, it *is* silver, so that's not an entirely incorrect assumption.

"OK. How old are you, exactly?"

"Um, do I have to say… exactly?"

I try my best to look unthreatening, but I've been holding this 'harmless and professional' smile so long that my face is starting to hurt.

"A ballpark figure usually helps."

His head bobs, as if accepting the reasonableness of this, then he runs a slightly shaking hand over his face. He's not quite handsome – there's an almost crooked slant to his features – but he's not unattractive, with boyish looks and skin so smooth you could believe he had never had to shave.

"OK. Um… 60. About 60."

It's my turn to nod. I'm not surprised, that's the age I tend to cater for; not so old as to be stuck in their ways, not so young they don't need me. I make another note on my file, and he winces at the sound of the pen scratching on paper.

"And do you have a particular type of person you'd be interested in?"

"A girl, obviously." A short, embarrassed laugh. "Well, not obviously, these days, I suppose. But yes, a girl. Blonde, or brunette or… well, it doesn't matter. Colour… of skin, I mean… that doesn't matter, either. But maybe… a bit older? I mean, older than I look?"

I laugh kindly, still trying to put him at ease, though I am starting to think that particular task is beyond me. No wonder he needs my help.

"I'm sure we can find a nice cougar for you."

I'm not sure he understands my terminology, but like a puppy he is soothed by my tone, and he nods again in sheer relief that this part of his ordeal is over. Part of me is wondering how he managed to stay alive at all over the last few decades. He watches me fill in his form as if I am signing his death warrant – a not uncommon reaction. They tend not to like things being written down.

"Anything else?"

He pauses, frowns, then quickly licks his lips, before leaning forward slightly as if confiding a terrible, embarrassing secret.

"Um... O positive?"

I nodded and made a note.

So, you're probably wondering, who *is* this girl? What's so special about her that she has this insight into the underworld? Does she spend her spare time sharpening stakes and hunting down freaks? Well, that would be a no. Partly because, in my experience, most of the underworld is no more freaky than the overworld, and it's rude to murder something that did nothing to you but use up more toothpaste. You're going to laugh when I tell you – plenty of people do (not that I tell many people outside my target clientele, of course) – but I run a dating agency. That's OK, go on, I'll wait, get it out of your system.

Odd as it might seem to you, it makes perfect sense to me. I've always been fascinated by people – what drives them, what makes them tick, what makes them who they are. I did a little bit of psychology at university before dropping out (for reasons I don't need to go into here) and I loved it. Maybe it's the Sensitive in me, but I've always had good instincts, was always good at matchmaking, entertaining and throwing parties, so making a living doing those things seemed a natural next step. People just interest me – even those who, strictly speaking, don't qualify for the label of 'people'. So a few years ago when I was broke, unemployed and coming out of a bad relationship (the only kind I manage – ironic, yes, I'm aware) I realised there was a gap in the market I was uniquely placed to fill. I took all the lack of romance in my own life and put that energy into creating it for other people. And so, after a lot of work and a few false starts, Dark Dates was born.

But why monsters, you're asking? Why would any sane person pursue a career where they deal every day with the kind of nightmares that would send most people running away screaming? I suppose mostly – crucially – I don't think of them as monsters. Over the years I've had more than a few run ins with the Other Races, and once I got over the gigantic, screaming mindfuck that was discovering they existed at all, I came to see they weren't that different from anyone else. Some are bastards, some are sweeties – set aside by their nature they may be, but for the most part they are just like us, rubbing together alongside the humans in a world that isn't easy for anyone. Once I got used to the idea that they were different, but not that different, I realised that not only were they an underrepresented part of the community, they were also a great business opportunity.

Or maybe it was because – pop psychology time! – sometimes I felt like a monster myself. I'm human (though, in fairness, plenty of Others started out that way too) but I'm hardly normal. For a long time I was ashamed of what I was, scared of it, and that was after years of not even believing it to be true. That didn't make for an easy growing up. I was young and lost and wanted the craziness to go away, for the world to go back to how I thought it should be. Then I began to understand – with a little help, admittedly – that ordinary, if it even existed, was greatly overrated. My Sense was a gift. Yes, the world was bigger and crazier and scarier than I had ever imagined it, but I was also better equipped to deal with it than most. I could use the knowledge I had, I could befriend the other freaks and I could make my difference work for me.

Of course, I should have known better. I was young and naive and when I thought I'd looked into the darkness, I had barely even seen shadow. You can't control chaos. You can only hope to survive it.

Chapter 2

"THERE'S BEEN another murder."

Well, that wasn't the greeting I expected as I walked into my office. I put down the tray of coffees and pastries and scowled at Medea, my assistant, waiting for some further explanation. I realised that, far from imparting some cosmically divined information or making a psychic pronouncement of doom, she actually had the London news up on her computer screen, and indeed, another body had been found in a back alley near Covent Garden. It was the third in a fortnight, and the first two had already got the city nervous and wondering. Since both victims were men, the police were currently positing the theory of gang violence (London's current Big Bad) or robberies gone too far, while trying to strike the right balance of being concerned but not scaring the tourists, but the tabloids seemed keen to flog a more sensational angle and were darkly hinting at serial killing. It says something about the modern world, I suppose, that two murders on their own weren't sensational enough.

I looked over her shoulder at the screen: below that story, as if to back up the police's theory, there was an appeal for witnesses to a gang-related shooting that left a 12 year old in a coma, and a morally outraged op-ed piece about the lenient sentence given to two teenagers who had stomped on a gay man's head until he died. See what I mean? Never mind the monsters. It's people who suck. Despite this torrent of misery, I tried to keep my voice cheery.

"You shouldn't read the papers first thing, it's too depressing."

She gave me a small smile, reaching gratefully for the

pastry and the coffee. Maybe it was being the child of people who healed sickness for a living, but Medea had an ability to empathise with the everyday tragedies of the city that eluded me – and here was me, the Sensitive. Maybe she was just a nicer person than I was.

"That makes you sound old."

"The news makes me feel old," I conceded, and her smile warmed.

"Well, the good thing about this job is you're a spring chicken compared to most of the clients."

I laughed.

"Problem is all of them still *look* younger than me."

Most people I know have a witch or two in their office, but mine is one of the few who will happily admit to it. Strictly speaking, of course, she's a Wiccan, a white witch – I'm not having anyone into the black arts on my payroll – but Medea's equally at ease with the more common epithet. Then again, she's a woman who isn't put out by much. Her name, for a start. I know that's the name on her paycheques (the *only* name – sometimes I feel like I'm employing Cher), but I'm never sure whether the Greek tragedy moniker is self-styled or if her parents just had a very odd sense of humour, because Medea rarely lets slip anything about herself. I know very little about her beyond the fact that she is a little older than I am, and she has lived in London ten years, but was raised in Scotland: she is mixed race and the child of two doctors. What such down-to-earth careerists thought of their daughter's less than conventional beliefs I often wondered, but never dared ask, and though she spoke of them rarely, it was always with fondness. Her Indian mother presumably being the one bequeathing her the extraordinary beauty and skin you would weep for, her Scottish father the ability to drink most people under the table and the capacity for unexpectedly creative swearing – unless they were a much stranger couple than I assumed and it was the other way round – while their combined genetic smartypantsness no doubt contributed to the fact that Medea also has a fierce intelligence that often makes me regret my own abandoned education. Yes, she's clever *and* pretty: I know, I know, I'm a masochist. But we got talking one day when I went into the occult bookshop where she used to work – where I had gone in search of some texts that might illuminate my own condition – and there was something about her that made me like her instantly, and, more importantly, realise she could be a great asset to my then-fledgling business. She looks the part, certainly, though maybe not the way you're expecting. None of that hippy-dippy tie-dye shit for Medea: her look is pure Willow Gone Bad. If the short-lived union of Marilyn Manson and Dita von Teese had produced progeny, Medea might be it – tall, slender and corseted to emphasise her killer curves, she's Mad Men meets Bollywood meets burlesque, and she shimmers round the office with a poise and glamour I couldn't dream of aspiring to. Sometimes clients are so dazzled by her that they sign up to the whole package without even knowing what they are doing. My instincts were right – in the entertaining business it never hurts to hire a looker, and if you can get one who is also jam-packed with smarts and not likely to faint when she finds out who the clients are, that's even better.

None of which would be worth the daily dose of ego-destroying comparison were it not for the fact that she is also a lot of fun to hang out with. She might play her cards close to her chest, but she has a dry, sly sense of humour, a surprisingly dirty laugh and she always knows when it's time for a cake run. That's why I keep her around.

I watched her decant her coffee into the mug she kept in the office – you would imagine she would drink from fine china, but this was actually a big white mug emblazoned with the letters WWGWD (I was always scared to ask what they meant in case they stood for a spell that would turn me into something nasty). She took a mouthful of scalding hot liquid from this un-Medea-like incongruity and made a grateful sound as the initial shot of caffeine hit her. I took that as my cue to leave her to it for a while, and went through to my office. As ever, the first thing to do was sort through the usual pile of bills and fliers, and scan through my emails, leaving her to self-caffeinate. Neither Medea nor I are particularly morning people, but it wasn't long till Halloween – one of our busiest times of the year, of course – so both of us were putting in the extra hours, and I thought it diplomatic not to expect proper conversation as soon as I walked through the door. Normally I rarely spent time in my private office unless I was seeing clients, and even then it was about giving them privacy rather than imposing any boss-employee hierarchy: many of my clients are the sort who don't even want someone who looks like Medea to overhear their secrets. And, perversely, while beauty might be an asset at the front desk or a party, it can be a disadvantage when it comes to doing my part of the job – no one wants to admit to being a dateless loser in front of a smoking hot babe. But when I wasn't with clients, I mostly just hung around the front office with her: I hired extra help for parties or events, of course, but most of the time we were a two-woman band. When we're busy, we're really busy, but a lot of the time there are lulls when we have plenty of time to chat. Sometimes I think I pay Medea because it's cheaper than what I would spend on internet shopping if she weren't here to distract me.

So, having given us both a few minutes for that first, vital hit of caffeine and carbs, I was about to head back to the reception area when the main phoneline rang and froze me mid-stride. I heard Medea speak, her voice low and melodious, and despite myself my heart started pounding. I waited for a few moments, expecting her to call my name, and tried not to feel too disappointed at the sound of the handset clicking down, the call obviously finished. Forcing a smile, I headed back to Medea's desk, and saw her looking at me with an expression that was slightly too kind. I knew her answer before she even spoke.

"I'm sorry, Cassandra. That wasn't him."

Look, it's not like I'm a stalker or anything. I'm not obsessed. I'm a strong, independent, modern woman, and I deal with these creatures all the time. I know what they are like. Being Sensitive seems to make me more resistant to their charms, so I know I'm not in thrall. So why the hell couldn't I get this bloody man out of my mind?

Chapter 3

OK, BACKPEDAL, I'll explain. Like I said – yes, the short answer is that the things that go bump in the night are real. Vampires, werewolves, witches, ghosts, and plenty more besides, they all exist. Maybe not in exactly the way you picture them, maybe not anywhere near you, but they all can be found somewhere in the real world. And in the case of vampires, they are all around us. But while the Stoker-Rice-Whedon-Meyer club got that right, like all writers they tend to romanticise their subjects. So though you'll find plenty of vampires who seem a bit like they do in the books – usually because the vampires have read the books as well – there are some key things that are different.

For a start, vampires hardly ever kill anyone these days. In the era of forensics, 24 hour news and the internet, when everyone with a mobile phone is a journalist, gory murders on any sort of scale are hard to pull off, at least for long. I'm sure there are parts of the world where vampires still live like feudal lords and feed with impunity on beautiful virgins, but it's not happening here. Couldn't get the virgins, for a start. These days your average vamp is pretty assimilated. They survive by consensual feeding, hooking up with a willing human (or humans – from what I've seen, monogamy doesn't feature highly in their life choices), and they take only what they need, which is far less than you'd think. The humans are left a little giddy but most definitely alive, and they seem to get plenty out of the experience themselves. It's sort of like the blood donor service, only without the biscuits. Sometimes, of course, this feeding is done by stealth – a few too many drinks and how many people have woken up with some unexplained bruises and a headache that a hangover can't quite account for? But since vamps prefer not to feed on heavily intoxicated humans – gives *them* a headache, apparently – it's far easier and more pleasant to find a partner that's willing. That's where I come in. And while you might be feeling pretty judgemental about that right now, think about some of the more 'normal' relationships around you and tell me that I'm doing something wrong.

I set up Dark Dates a few years back, and it caters for straights (in the human, not the sexual, sense – I'm an equal opportunities arranger) and Others. I do individual introductions and parties, and some of my most popular events are my speed dating events, where vampires meet donors. Obviously that's not all I do – a big part of the day (or, more accurately, night) job is ordinary dating and singles parties – admittedly, usually with a slightly gothic theme – but the money is in what I like to think of as my niche specialty. And I'm very good at it.

I'd stumbled across the whole thing, really. I properly realised I was a Sensitive in my late teens, and in my youth I tended towards a bit of the goth myself, and that's a combination that's very attractive to a certain kind of man. The – how shall I put this – not entirely alive kind. I had a brief but illuminating post-university fling with what could most charitably be described as a much older man, and like many youthful affairs, while it didn't end that well (it's hard to be with someone who isn't interested in you from the neck down and the romance faded pretty quickly when he established that one particular kind of penetration was strictly off the cards), it did give me a refreshing new perspective on life. Or in this case, the afterlife. So I saw my opening. Vampires of fiction tend to be romantic ideals – beautiful, intelligent, sophisticated creatures whiling away the centuries in pursuits that are equal parts cultural and carnal. Hell, these days they're supposed to do all that and sparkle as well. (For the record, the only vampire I ever met who sparkled had been turned during the glam rock days of Marc Bolan and never quite adjusted his fashion sense). The reality tends to be somewhat different.

Because the problem with vampires is they were once people, and now in many ways they are just *older* people. So they're just like other, ordinary people: often stupid, or boring, or self-obsessed. Age just solidifies these characteristics – it doesn't suddenly turn them into Lord Byron. Most vampires simply aren't that interesting. They're not even usually that old. Or, at least the ones I meet – there may be a whole cache of aged, pale romantics out there, but they probably don't need my help getting laid. (Or fed, or whatever.) So I've never met one. Come on, looks, charm *and* brains were a rare enough combination in the past as they are now, so why assume all vampires possess all three? The brainboxes were too busy indoors discovering the theory of relativity or solving mathematical paradoxes to venture into the kind of circles vampires frequent, and beauty? Well, while it's true to say you rarely find an out and out ugly vamp, the problem with the most beautiful ones is after the first 10 years without a mirror, they tend to go a bit bonkers and from there it's just a short walk into the sunshine. And though vampires do indeed get stronger as they get older, they also, like people, tend to get more stuck in their ways. For anyone turned before the 1950s, the whole 21st century has come as a bit of a shock.

But progress brings advantages. It's easier to pass in a big city, where people are too concerned about their own reflection to worry about the lack of yours; the nightlife is more accommodating, and the lack of aging can be passed off as access to a really good plastic surgeon. Then of course, there was the arrival of the internet, the ultimate freak's best friend. And certainly mine, because without it there would be no Dark Dates.

So, background established. As I said, I cater for all sorts, but my vampire nights are the most successful, especially in these Twilight-True Blood days when everyone wants their own bloodsucker, whether for everlasting romance or just hot sweaty sex. So, my most recent party, a couple of weeks ago, wasn't unusual in being a sell out event. There was the standard crowd of humans; an eclectic and carefully chosen bunch, even if they did tend to wear a disproportionate amount of black. It was a mixture of regulars and newbies, the curious and the sceptical, the one-time-for-a-thrill and the full-on blood groupies. Some vampires like someone who knows what they're doing, some like a novice, and I don't feel it's my job to judge either side of the equation. I've organised full on fetish nights before and trust me, the things that humans in rubber can do to one another makes most supernatural interaction seem positively pale in comparison.

The vamps were obviously, for legal reasons, advertised as faux-vamps, but my Sense easily weeded out the wannabes and I did a B-list evening for fakes and donors whose taste for biting stopped at a nip from plastic fangs, and no one was any the wiser. These real vampires tended to be relatively young – mostly around the 50-80 mark. As I explained, old vampires are far rarer than you'd think – culture shock tends to hit them quite hard around the time they reach their first century. Give it 20 years or so and, with advances in medicine, we'll most likely be outliving most of them. Of course older vampires do exist – I'd never met them, but heard rumours and party chatter – but you don't live into the triple figures if you need help finding playmates. Tonight there was one I thought might be nearing a hundred – a young man with great posture, the slicked back hair and the kind of moustache that straight men don't wear any more. He had the air of a First World War Tommy – he looked like I should be viewing him in sepia, and I picked up a slight haze of power off him as I passed, marking him out from the crowd.

There was the usual pre-seating mingling, the humans making the most of the first of their three drinks (I have a strict limit, and it's small glasses only; I have to keep the vamps happy, but a drink or two helps the nerves), while the bloodsuckers cradled glasses of red that rarely got any emptier. I was in full on hostess mode, as was Medea, magnificent in her party regalia of a tight hobble skirt and corset, her eyes lined thickly with black kohl. She shimmered through the party like a mist, a head taller than most of the guests thanks to vertiginous heels, expertly balancing a tray of drinks with a smile that was friendly but strictly business: eyes might follow her hungrily, but no one ever approached her for more than a refill of wine.

My own glass was hardly touched: drink dulls my Sense, which was already close to being overwhelmed by the proximity to this much supernatural energy. I needed to keep alert; I'd vetted everyone carefully but you never knew. I had a purse spray full of holy water laced with silver in case anyone got out of hand and broke the 'no punctures at the party' rule. It had only happened once or twice before, but I couldn't afford to get that kind of reputation. Spray someone full in the face with some silver and word gets around fast that at a Dark Dates evening, you behave. So, all in all, I was set for a successful night. Then he walked in.

Even surrounded by a room full of vampires, I Sensed him before I saw him. A wave of power hit me like a blow, almost making me stagger, then receded quickly, as if being deliberately reined in. I turned, stunned, and even now I couldn't give you a proper description of him because, I swear, he was almost blurred. Most vampires have an amazing ability for stillness: this one, I felt, was in constant, almost imperceptible motion. I had a Sense of him being tall, pale and handsome – all the clichés – but there was also something else. Strength. Control. I felt I was seeing a lion in repose – all laziness and languor right until the moment it roared and ripped your head off. He stood with the deceptively casual stance of a hunter – one I instinctively recognised, and that sent a shiver through me, because the only other time I had seen it before was in the most dangerous man I'd ever met.

The vampire looked, I think, slightly older than the crowd, as if turned later in life, though of course physical age matters little to a vampire, and he clearly had the kind of power you don't pick up in a decade or two around the block. He scanned the room, an unmistakable expression of bitter amusement flickering across his features, and then walked slowly and purposely towards me. I almost flinched, prepared for another assault of power, but up close it was no more than a steady hum. He held out a hand in an almost courtly gesture, so I felt all I could do was allow him to take mine and bow into a kiss.

"So, this must be the fabled Dark Dates."

There was the hint of an accent in his voice – Eastern European, which I'm sure must have seemed exotic in his heyday, before there was a Polish deli on every high street. His diction, though slightly clipped, was perfect, but I'm guessing he'd had a long time to work on it.

"It is, but it's also a *private* party. I don't think you're registered, Mr…"

I let my sentence hang, but no name was forthcoming.

"No. No, I am not. I am just… curious, and wondered if I might be allowed to observe."

My Sense gave a short, sharp flare of alarm but I told myself I was just being foolish: this was a crowded room, after all. It might not be a request I'd had before, but what harm could it do? Besides, some part of me was thinking that it wasn't wise to needlessly offend something that radiated that level of power.

I nodded, and put on my professional smile. "Do come and join us then…"

Again, no name. It was starting to seem rude, and my inner sensible woman evaporated under the annoyance of my inner snark. I'm stupid like that: I get lippy under pressure.

"Well, make yourself at home, Lestat, and have a drink."

Which was a dumb comment, because at least three of the vampires near us turned round, assuming I was talking to them. Like I said: originality not a strong point. But Fangs McMystery ignored my sarcasm.

"So," he asked, leaning against the bar to watch Medea lead the people to their seats and hand out pens and scorecards, pretending not to notice the swift, wary glance she cast my way. "You introduce 'vampires' to their 'victims' and see if they 'hit it off'?" He made no effort to hide his incredulity, and I was impressed by his ability to actually pronounce the quotation marks without doing the annoying air quotes gesture. I'd seen this kind of scepticism before – I'd been scepted at by one of the masters of the form – so I just shrugged.

"That's the general idea, if not exactly the terminology I would use."

"Traditionally vampires would select their victims. The humans would get no choice in the matter."

"That's progress for you."

"And these people are all... willing?" He asked that like consent was a bad thing, and my Sense again prickled. I stared at him – which wasn't exactly a hardship, even though I'd be hard pressed now to tell you why not – and couldn't hide my surprise. How could he live to be so old, but be so naive?

"There's a thrill to it. You must know that."

He raised an eyebrow at me, and I could only shrug again.

"Hey, people do far worse for kicks on a Friday night." His look of thinly disguised horror made me laugh out loud. "Have you been in this country long?"

He paused for a moment before answering.

"I have spent some time in your coastal resorts."

Which made me think suddenly I was being played – I've read Dracula too, you know – but I was careful not to let my face show it, and kept my voice deliberately light.

"Well, you should know then. Seaside towns are the worst."

He took another look at the throng, then turned his full attention to me, and I felt a wave of giddiness at being the focus of that steady gaze.

"I can't say I approve of the idea, but I must admit to being impressed by the mind that created it. I'm afraid I still prefer the old ways."

"Where people are just food and have no choice?"

He tilted his head thoughtfully, in no rush to deny that.

"Where there was romance. Seduction. Where one took the time to select the right person, expended effort in pursuing them, overcame obstacles to possess them. Where you had not won until the one thing your prey desired above all was their own downfall."

"And where they ended up dead?"

"Some things are worth dying for."

"Says the one who drinks blood to have eternal life."

Despite his allure, I was irritated now, not only by all this 'creatures of the night how sweet their sound' bollocks, but by his very attitude: it's easy to romanticise something when it's not your race that ends up drained in a ditch. But somehow I felt that wasn't the argument that would sway him and I had the oddest compulsion to keep him talking. "We live in an instant society. Who has time for that?"

As if proving my point, the five minute bell went to change partners, and the vampires stood up to change places. Just for that moment, I saw it through his eyes: a graceless cattle market, the only difference being here the cows could talk. Then I shook off the thought, angrily, and blushed, annoyed with myself. The vampire regarded me coolly, as if reading my thoughts.

"No one here would be worth more than mere minutes," he scowled, and I got the impression it wasn't just the humans he was dismissing. Then he leaned in towards me, his voice low. "But some things, Ms Bick... or may I call you Cassandra? ...some things are worth spending time over."

Shaken by his tone, my hand fluttered to my name badge, and I was flustered to see I wasn't wearing it.

"You have given me much to ponder, Cassandra. For that, I am grateful."

Then he gave me another flash of that predator's smile and I blinked and he was gone. Simply gone. My Sense confirmed it, a sudden vacuum where his power had been, as if the air had been sucked out of the room. Medea was suddenly beside me, her face concerned.

"Who the hell was that? What did he want?" she

demanded, and I realised with a shock it was the first time I had seen Medea genuinely shaken by anything. I looked at the door, forlornly, as if staring at it would make him return.

"I have no idea. But I don't think we've seen the last of him."

I wasn't sure if that was a statement or a hope.

That had been a fortnight ago, and so far my prediction was proving woefully inaccurate, and I was driving Medea slightly nuts with my speculation as to why. He'd got under my skin in a way I couldn't yet clarify, and my Sense told me there was some unfinished business there. Besides, no one comes to a party and pulls a stunt like that unless they want to be remembered, right? You're not going to go to all that trouble and not follow up. Vampires love drama – that's the one thing the writers always get spot on – so this felt like an opening salvo, not a one-off guest appearance.

Of course, once I was over the initial shock of him, I had realised his appearance wasn't quite as clever as I thought; I have a website, after all, with my photo on it, so it's hardly difficult to identify me, and though I never advertise my venues online – I send the attendees personal invites – I assume it can't be that difficult to find out where they are if you know anyone in the vampire community. Which also meant that finding my office – finding *me* – would be child's play, if he wanted to. So why hadn't he? Why was I so convinced that he would? Maybe by this stage, I was so used to mysterious men with questionable purposes popping unbidden into my life that it had started to seem normal to me. But I should have also remembered that these mysterious appearances rarely ended well for me. I also should have known I was overdue another visit.

Chapter 4

I LOVE the social nature of my work, but sometimes – like when I've spent all day driving myself crazy wondering when a nameless vampire will make a reappearance in my life, while also trying to gear up for one of the busiest dates in my calendar – I'm just ridiculously glad to be home. I might not be much of a domestic goddess – I'm on first name terms with my local pizza delivery man – and there might be no one waiting for me but the cat (I know, I know, clichés abound) but it's my little corner of the world, and it suits me just fine.

It is a 'little' corner, too: my flat is what is politely called compact (estate agents might even say 'bijoux'), but it's well-located, right in the heart of Clerkenwell and a mere five minutes' walk from my office. I got some money from an accident insurance policy when I was younger and that, combined with some help from my parents and the fact that I bought the place long before the area got trendy, means that I own somewhere I couldn't dream of buying into now, and I could manage the mortgage without spending months living off soup and canapés. Not too many months, anyway. A couple a year, tops. Inside, it's nothing special: Ikea chic all the way, the only personal touches being more shoes and handbags than could be considered strictly necessary, a couple of framed vintage comic and sci-fi film posters to confirm to those who haven't already guessed it that yes, I am a geek. There are a handful of subtle touches that make it more mine, but I'm the only person who would recognise them as such. In the kitchen I have some of my mum's old cookbooks, filled with her handwritten amendments to my favourite recipes, although I never open them now for anything but sentimental reasons, and an old Le Creuset iron frying pan, too heavy for me to ever use even if I did cook, but a warm, orange presence that reminds me of my mum whenever I look at it. From my dad, there were the bookshelves: he'd built them for me when I first moved in, having answered my plaintive phone call after I spent the afternoon struggling with a screwdriver and realising independence was overrated and that a first aid kit was an essential ingredient in any home I planned to live in. Some of them still stood slightly crooked – there was only so much damage he could undo – but they are solid and reliable, like he was, and so I love them. No one is going to ask to do a feature on me in Interiors Monthly any time soon, but these things were part of what made up my home. Well, those and the loaded gun I kept in my bedside cabinet, and which I now had pointed at the figure wreathed in darkness that was standing at the foot of my bed.

He, however, didn't seem particularly fazed by this turn of events. He was probably used to it. Hell, I think he found it funny: I could hear the smirk in his voice when he spoke.

"So, what's a nice girl like you doing with a gun like that?"

My stomach flipped at the sound of his voice. Cain. Of course it was bloody Cain. No one else can short out both my Sense and my burglar alarm without even trying.

"I could have shot you!" I protested.

He didn't even bother answering that, instead stepping forward so that I could see him in the dim light that came from my window.

"You need to get a better security system."

He really was smiling. I was tempted to shoot him just for that.

"Would that stop you?"

He shrugged. "Might make it more fun getting in."

Cain. Bloody Cain. He was the one who bought me the gun in the first place, the one who taught me to use it, to shoot without fear or hesitation, because both of those sentiments were completely alien to him. Mainly because, whatever else he was – and I wasn't too clear on that point – Cain was insane. Not, 'hey, let's drink tequila and get tattoos' insane, but with the clear eyed insanity of a man who would plough a steamroller through a field of kittens if he was in a hurry and thought it would cut five minutes off his drive time. Cain was a stone-cold killer, and I knew this because I had seen him kill. He wasn't the kind of man most people want to see standing at the end of their bed in the middle of the night, especially when he was also holding a gun, and his was much bigger than mine. Fortunately – or, more likely, unfortunately – I'm not most people.

There was a moment that stretched out slightly too long. Clearly – *hopefully* – we weren't going to shoot, but the problem with two people pointing guns at one another is no one wants to be the first to put the weapon down. Then Cain took another step forward and raised his hands in a gesture of conciliation, as if to show he was only holding a gun because I'd pulled first, and his instinct was to respond in kind. Having done that, he slowly lowered his gun down onto the dresser behind him: it made a reassuring click on the wooden surface, the sound of a situation diffused and danger averted. Except it was a lie, because Cain didn't need a weapon to be dangerous.

"You do know that if I actually wanted to hurt you, the gun wouldn't stop me, right?" he asked, more in conversation than threat.

"You want me to pull the trigger on this thing and test that theory?"

Except we both knew that he was right, and only my innate stubbornness kept the weapon in my hands. Whatever else I felt around Cain – whatever scrambling job he did on both my Sense and my senses (including, clearly, my common sense) – I knew just how dangerous he could be. He smiled at me – a slow, lazy predator's smile that flashed me back to the mysterious vampire, and made me flush at the memory. He looked completely unbothered by the situation, as if a woman in bed pointing a firearm at him was all just part of a regular day for him. Being Cain, maybe it was.

"Are you going to put the gun down?"

"Are you scared I might shoot you?"

In answer, he kicked off his shoes, then shrugged off his jacket, and pulled off his t-shirt, dropping it soundlessly onto the floor. Part of me was outraged at the staggering presumption of it, the casual arrogance. But my mouth had gone dry at the sight of him: at the lean, tanned torso, the genuine muscle of a life of action, not the vanity of a gym regime. He unfastened the thick leather belt he wore and pulled it loose of his jeans, the leather slither against the denim almost folding me in lust. He tossed it beside his abandoned clothes, and smiled at me, quite aware of the effect he was having.

"I'm worried you might tighten your finger on the trigger by accident. Muscles can be unpredictable when you're nervous. Or excited."

His voice had lowered and it reverberated through my blood. I struggled to keep my own voice level, but my heart was pounding. I tore my eyes away from that ridiculously sculpted torso but his face offered me no relief, carved by the same steady artist that had made the rest of him: all strong lines and animal magnetism.

"Nothing's excited me so far," I lied, and he chuckled, leaning down on the bed, ignoring the gun that was now squarely – if somewhat unsteadily – pointed at his chest, and which was capable, if I wanted, of putting a fist sized hole in that muscle, no matter how impressive it was. Slowly, deliberately, he crawled on his hands and knees across the bed towards me, his eyes, darkening with desire, never leaving mine. He stopped, an inch away from me. At this range, I could kill him. At this range, he could kiss me.

In one smooth movement his mouth took mine and his fingers closed over my hand, steering the gun away from him and taking it from my suddenly weakened grip and placing it, useless, on the bedside table beside me.

"So, Cassandra .." he pulled back from me, smiling, his voice hoarse now. "Do you want me to hurt you?"

I didn't, of course. I don't roll that way and neither, to the best of my knowledge, does Cain. But he did make me scream a little.

Chapter 5

I WOKE up to the sound of children dying. I had a moment of breath-freezing panic before my sleep and sex-addled Sense kicked in enough to realise that the blood curdling screeches emanating from the street outside my window were nothing more sinister than the neighbourhood's urban foxes, engaged in one of their regular territorial spats with the neighbours' cats (my own cat, Dante, taking the eminently more sensible route of running away whenever there was trouble). Somehow being with Cain made me automatically fear the worst: despite the fact that he made me feel safer than anyone else alive, he rarely seemed to arrive with good news. I was never quite sure if he turned up in my life because he had foreseen a pending storm, or if trouble was something that trailed in his wake.

I lay still for a moment, waiting for the adrenalin surge to subside and my heartbeat to return to normal. Cain lay undisturbed beside me; somehow he had an inbuilt system that married an almost preternatural instinct for sensing danger with the ability to filter out anything that wasn't a threat. It's a talent I often envied, since as a Sensitive I regularly felt more than a little overwhelmed. Still, my wakefulness gave me a rare chance to watch him unobserved, and it was a sight I never got bored of.

Despite having a physique that could be used to sell underwear, Cain's body spoke of a life hard-lived. His skin is almost olive – not quite as dark as Medea, but more than a natural tan, the product of some indeterminate heritage that, like anything else remotely personal, he never even hinted at – but it is criss-crossed with scars, the remnants of a hundred different battles. Some I didn't recognise; new additions since I had seen him last, one or two still recent enough to be livid – but some I knew of old. Some were a mystery to me, some I knew only too well how he had come by, like the jagged lines across his forearms where he had smashed through a window frame too small to take a body; scars matched by the slash down my own side where he had pulled me, naked, after him to safety.

I didn't know, exactly, what Cain was, any more than I knew exactly who he was. My Sense could never get a hold on him; hardly surprising, given the effect he has on the rest of me, that he leaves my Sense equally baffled. I'm not entirely sure he's human. But I know he's a hunter. I know he spends a lot of his time in parts of the world where the bad things are really bad and the Others really are monsters. I know he sees himself as some sort of sheriff of the supernatural, and he's not afraid of getting as nasty as the things he hunts. He doesn't ply his trade in London for the same reasons the bad guys don't – it's too easy to get caught, to leave evidence, to give rise to questions that lead to answers you don't want the normal people to have. Or maybe he'd just think it was too easy.

Perhaps because of how he lived, Cain didn't see things quite the way I did. I knew that was the case, because it was a fight that would come up sooner or later, the way it always did, and always had, almost from as soon as we met. I believed the non-humans – the Others – in the dark places he visited behaved badly or evilly for the same reason as the people: poverty, fear, desperation, or simply because a lawless society allowed them to indulge their worst appetites in a way they couldn't in the more developed parts of the world. But did the existence of child soldiers in Africa mean children were born bad? Why should people be the result of their environment, but Others be inherently evil? But Cain just saw monsters, and treated them as such. It wasn't a job for him to kill them; it was a duty, and sometimes I worried it might even be a pleasure.

Frowning at the memory of too many similar arguments, I touched his chest and he sighed, turning over in his sleep, revealing his most ferocious scars. Over a foot long, they ran the full length of his back from shoulder to hip, two parallel lines that were still as rough and visible now as they had been when I first touched them nearly a decade ago. I had no idea how he got them, and was too scared to ask, afraid I would be stirring up a memory too terrible to share. Instead, I traced them softly with my fingers and then, moved by a tenderness that Cain awake could never stir, I leaned forward and kissed the ravaged flesh. Cain's breathing shifted, the merest fraction, and he reached behind his back, as fast as a snake, grabbing my hand. I almost winced at the swiftness, but he wasn't angry: he pulled my arm around him and touched my fingers to his lips for the briefest of kisses. Then, as if to make up for this uncharacteristically affectionate gesture, he muttered at me gruffly, "Go back to sleep. Tomorrow's not going to be a good day."

Because clearly I was going to manage to get back to sleep after *that*; but he was already dozing. Then again, Cain had a long history with me of making cryptic remarks.

Chapter 6

"YOU KNOW, you aren't actually crazy."

That was the first thing Cain ever said to me. And it was the one thing in the world I most needed to hear. I was 16 years old at the time, and I suppose you could argue that's what any 16 year old wants to be told – when else but in your teens are you so pinioned by those dual conflicting needs: terrified of being ordinary while desperate to be normal? Of course, my own case was a little more acute.

I'd always been a sensitive child, never realising that I was, in fact, a child Sensitive. I was subject to crying jags, to instantly formed likes and dislikes, seemingly irrational but passionate fits of emotion. I was the kind of precocious toddler who would point at strangers and loudly demand, 'Daddy, why is that lady wrong?' My parents were occasionally embarrassed but not overly concerned, and once I grew out of it – or at least seemed to – it retrospectively became charming and amusing. But of course I hadn't grown out of it. In my teens my Sense resurfaced with a vengeance, a seething mass of hormones thrown in for good measure. Not only did my body seem to be changing in a way that was completely out of my control, my mind was too. I'd see someone in the street and feel suddenly afraid – properly, wrenchingly, palm-sweating afraid – and certain places made me feel queasy. Just two nights before my first encounter with Cain, I'd mortified my friends by bursting into tears in a pub, thereby roundly breaking our covers and revealing us as the underage drinkers we were. All that had happened was that a boy had tried to talk to me, and I was struck by a terror so absolute I fled into the street. Even as I was sitting, then, in that cafe where Cain approached me, I could feel a familiar sense of dread creeping over me, triggered by nothing more outrageous than a glance at a woman who sat looking out of the window, but who unnerved me in ways I couldn't explain.

So when the handsome older man pulled up a chair next to me (looking, in retrospect, suspiciously similar to how he looks now), and offered me a smile and those kind, reassuring words, I was more than ready to listen. He was a dream come true – and the fact that he *looked* like a dream come true certainly didn't hurt his cause any either. You've seen the effect he has on the adult me: you can imagine how teenage me felt. Dressed casually in his timeless uniform of dark jeans and a black, v-necked t-shirt (not too tight or cut too low, but just enough of both), he emanated the kind of languid confidence that was alien to someone used to the gangly clamour of adolescent boys, and he spoke with a quiet authority that nailed me to my seat.

"You're really not crazy. You're just more… finely attuned to things than most people." He smiled at my obvious scepticism. "It may not feel like it now, but it's actually a gift."

I continued to gape at him like he'd just dropped out of the sky – I was a pretty gauche kid (compared, of course, to the epitome of coolness that I am now…). Encounters between mysterious mentors and awkward teens tend not to be that scintillating, apparently, unless they come from the pen of Kevin Williamson or Joss Whedon. In real life, there's a lot more stuttering and gawping. But Cain didn't look like he particularly expected a reply: he simply sipped at his coffee and continued to smile. This did give me a chance to notice just how *very* good looking he was (a move, also in retrospect, I don't think was accidental. Not that I've spent a lot of time analysing this, you understand. Honest.) He surveyed the room calmly, his green eyes settling on the woman who had so disturbed me.

"You're right about her, for a start."

"Right about what?" I asked, barely able to form the words, too nervous to look at the figure he was indicating.

"There's something off about her. Witch, maybe? Minor demon? Definitely Other." He paused, thoughtfully, his eyes narrowed. They really were extraordinarily green. "I'm thinking low level witch. Maybe did some accidental damage in her youth, scared herself, but she's pretty harmless now. You did well to pick up on it."

"I don't know what you're talking about," I protested, truthfully, but Cain's smile didn't falter. It was becoming clear to me that there was actually only one of us in this conversation.

"You'll get better at it, in time. You'll start understanding it more, controlling it. You just need to stop being so frightened of it."

With that, he stood, with the perfect timing presumably imbued at birth in those marked out to be mysterious mentors to gawky adolescents, then he gave me a long look that ended in a wink and strode quickly from the cafe.

The whole exchange had taken less than five minutes, if that. Which just goes to show that it really doesn't take that long to change someone's whole life.

Chapter 7

I WORK surrounded by blood and dead flesh, and I love it. Perverse as it sounds, the walk past Smithfield Meat Market, with all its gory bustle, never fails to lift my spirits. Even today, when I had woken from my uneven sleep feeling abandoned, if not surprised, by Cain's absence, the area cast its usual spell. Whether delivering dire warnings or no, Cain was always keen on the early morning flit; we'd spent a lot of time together over the years, but not much of it having breakfast, so it's not like I was shocked by his disappearance. Even listening to the news – with its slightly hysterical speculation on what it was now calling the Covent Garden Killings, and talk of yet *another* sodding tube strike – failed to mar the early morning walk for me, though that was also possibly the fact I was still giddy from the afterglow of exceptionally good sex.

If you've never seen it, the meat market at Smithfield is a thing of true beauty, despite a history as bloody as its early morning gutters, sluiced red with the juices of the butchers' trade. The covered part of the market is a 19th century building – listed, much to the chagrin of those who'd like to knock it down and build yet more ugly modern flats – and somehow only the Victorians would think to so elaborately decorate a place of death. But its origins go back much further – it has been a meat market for over eight centuries, but animals weren't the only things slaughtered here: even now the tourists lay flowers at the supposed spot where William Wallace breathed his last, the English defying the romance of Hollywood in managing to take both his life *and* his freedom, the latter not being a whole lot of use once the former was ripped from him. Not far from that is Charterhouse Square, where once a monastery stood, and during the time of the Black Death a massive plague pit had been home to the biggest mass grave in London. This was a part of the city with plenty of ghosts, for those who knew how to find them.

The Dark Dates office was only a couple of minutes away from all this, tucked down a side street you wouldn't know was there if you didn't know to look: we didn't exactly rely on passing trade. It's just one of the warrens of aged alleys that cobweb London's centre, but it's not accidentally located: a vampire arriving with the smell of blood already in his nostrils is more like to buy what I'm offering, so I consider the ridiculously high rent a sensible investment. But that's not the only reason why I like the area so much. I love the reality of Smithfield; the honesty of it. I love that in a city that makes its living on invisible trade, the electronic shuffling of money and jobs half of its citizens don't understand, that at the heart of it is a building that is testament to people's most basic needs. On the rare days I come into the office early, I always take time to walk around the market, simply enjoying the buzz. I love the men in white coats turned scarlet by midmorning as they wheel pallets piled high with carcasses with the casualness of someone pushing a supermarket trolley, their white rubber boots splashing up blood as they walk. I love the feeling that here *real* work is done: I love the motorbike couriers and delivery drivers parked at the roadside where they smoke and drink coffee from polystyrene cups; I love the pubs that open at 8am so that men finishing a shift can enjoy a hard-earned pint. It may be increasingly surrounded by espresso bars and trendy eateries – and, hypocrite that I am, I am a frequenter of them all – but it still felt like London in a way that nowhere else did to me.

So as I made my leisurely way into work my mind fizzed both with Cain's arrival, and with thoughts of my mystery vampire: could those two things be related? What of that vampire, anyway? He was clearly old – much older than I had encountered before – but how old? Was he just one of many? Were they out there, all over London, creatures who had frequented the same inns as Dickens, who had hunted in a Cheapside populated by Falstaff and Hal? Did they look around here now – with half the streets under plastic as buildings were demolished to make way for a new, efficient cross-town railway that may or may not arrive, depending on the vagaries of funding and politics as it did – and marvel at our progress? Or did they yearn for the days of fire and torture?

Trying to shake off these uncharacteristically weighty thoughts, I nipped into Prêt for a couple of coffees and some pastries, on the off chance Medea would have managed to get in before me, and steeled myself for a busy day at the office. If Cain was intent on doing his elusive hunter routine, and the enigmatic vamp was still AWOL, no matter; I still had plenty to do. Not that I minded; my job could be a lot of hard work, but I enjoyed it, and my office was as much a sanctuary as my home could be. Though not, apparently, today.

It didn't take a Sensitive to realise something was wrong. Even had my Sense not given off a sudden, dark flare the moment I walked into the office, one look at Medea – her face set in a brittle welcoming smile – would have warned me that something was amiss.

"There's a man waiting in your office to see you," she said, her voice sounding artificially bright, and despite her obvious nervousness, I felt my tension leave me.

"You let him in my office?"

I sighed, inwardly. Honestly, bloody Cain, coming in here like he owned it, scaring my staff. I thought vampires were drama queens, but he could give them lessons.

"He really didn't seem the type I should say no to."

This time my sigh was audible. "No, you're probably right."

Medea's hand, I noticed, had closed around a letter opener and she was holding it like a weapon, and her aura had the metallic tang of magic, a spell brewing. Wow, he really *had* shaken her.

"Shall I come in with you?"

"No, that's alright," I smiled, handing her one of the paper mugs of coffee and doing my best to sound reassuring. "I'm pretty sure I can handle this one."

Medea looked at me sceptically, but I refused to be intimidated by a man I had so recently seen naked, whatever he was up to. Cain could be scary, sometimes – OK, a *lot* of the time – and he could also be a first class prick, but if he'd come to my place of work in full daylight I doubted it was to cause serious trouble.

"What's the matter, hotshot, still feel like you need a date?" I laughed, nudging the door open with my hip, balancing coffee and pastries in hand – so not really paying attention to what my beleaguered Sense was telling me. "Maybe I can show you something you'd like?"

"That rather depends on what you're offering," said the tall, smiling, heavily armed man waiting for me in my office. The man who was most definitely not, in any way, shape or form, Cain.

Chapter 8

"CAN I help you?" I asked, trying to sound calm, and not for the first time cursing my Sense for being as much use as a candyfloss umbrella, too easily thrown out of whack by the low-level supernatural ambience my office had picked up over the years. Though probably, in all honesty, the night of incredible sex with a possibly non-human lover had more than a little to do with that, too. Still, it was the second time in 24 hours a man had pointed a gun at me, so I wasn't ready to panic *just* yet. I switched my weight to my back foot and shifted my grip on my cup, hoping that a well-aimed throw of hot coffee might at least buy me some time if necessary. Not that the best Americano in the world is any match for a bullet, but you work with what you have to hand.

But heavy weaponry aside, my visitor didn't look that threatening. He was leaning insouciantly against my filing cabinet, looking around as if he'd bought the place and wasn't yet quite certain that he hadn't been sold a dud. Gingerly, I let my rattled Sense roll towards him; focused, now, it would be more use to me. He was as human as I was – though clearly he spent a lot more time in the gym – and then I almost started back in surprise as I realised he wasn't actually armed. Or at least not visibly so: he had his hands in his pockets and his jacket was cut loosely enough to hide any tell-tale gun bulge. Either I had been hanging out with Cain too much, or my self-maligned Sense had actually been trying to tell me something after all – or show me, at least, a visual warning to take him seriously. The man was clearly in no hurry: he calmly watched me making my assessments, and from the way his eyes flickered briefly to my cup, he'd guessed that thought, too. But when he smiled I was pleased there was half a room and a potentially scalding liquid projectile between us.

"I rather liked your original offer."

I struggled for a second to regain my composure in the face of that smile, but luckily my first resort in times of crisis is always lippiness. I'd interviewed vampires and I worked with a witch; I wasn't going to let some bruiser in a suit throw me.

"Well, tell me what you're after and I'll see if I can help. Do you prefer men or women?"

He flinched slightly – ha! – and I strolled as casually as I could manage to my desk, as if this were any other meeting. "If you'd care to let me know your preferences, I can consult my files and see if we have anything suitable."

"Ah, yes, your files. I don't think I'd be happy with having my details written down."

"I'm very discreet. My business depends on that."

"That's really not the point. But I didn't come to avail myself of your services, Ms Bick. I came to let you know that your activities have been noticed."

"Well, good to know my marketing budget isn't going to waste," I trilled, and his smile was like a guillotine.

"Ah, yes, the clever retort. All very amusing. But I'm not here to trade tedious banter with you, Ms Bick." Who was he calling tedious? Once I stopped being scared, I would be seriously offended. "I'm here to warn you. You've had your fun. You've thrown your parties. Now it's time to stop."

My throat was suddenly so dry I took a gulp of coffee, and then spluttered as I nearly burnt off the lining of my mouth. Trying to regain some dignity, I forced a smile and tried to keep my voice light.

"And why would I want to do that, just as my business is taking off?"

He leaned forward, and his jacket fell open: and I noticed his gun, exactly as he wanted me to. My Sense had been right after all.

"Because the people I work for don't like the kind of attention you're getting, and they only give one warning. The next time I see you, Ms Bick, I won't be so polite."

With that, he turned and slammed out of the room.

"No wonder you can't get a date, you fucking thug!" I yelled after him. Admittedly a couple of minutes after him, when I was sure he was well out of earshot – I'm lippy, I'm not an idiot. Medea frowned at me from the doorway.

"Who was that?" she demanded, the Scottishness thickening her voice as it did when she was anxious or angry. "What the hell is going on?"

Not for the first time, I didn't have an answer.

Chapter 9

MEDEA, BEING almost unflappable – it's one of her most annoying characteristics – recovered quickly, and soon we were back at work. Because what else could we do? Call the police? "Officer, a man with a gun said he didn't like my vampire parties, and unfortunately I'd left my own illegal gun at home so couldn't fight him off". You could imagine how well that conversation would go. But I was finding it hard to settle: this was a few too many mysterious visitations, even by my standards, and Cain's sleepy warning echoed in my brain. Was the gunman working for a vampire? I could imagine they might hire people for their daywork, and charming as he had been, my gatecrashing mystery vamp hadn't seemed keen on my parties: it was surely not possible that these two things were unrelated? But he struck me as the type who would approach me directly, not send a thug with a gun to threaten me. I thought we'd made some sort of connection, but maybe I was kidding myself. Or was it just that after a couple of years of building up my business, it was reaching a size when people – and Others – were noticing it, and some of them weren't happy? Where did Cain fit into all this? History had shown me that although his appearances usually seemed without motive, they never turned out to be quite that random after all.

All this uncertainty was making me nervous – a large slice of cake and a double shot latte nervous, since you asked. And as anxiety eating is one trait Medea and I don't share (which is possibly why she has the body of a goddess and I… don't), I decided to take myself off to the local Italian deli to indulge in private. I should have remembered, of course, that an inviolable law of the universe is if you're doing something you don't really want anyone else to see, someone you know will appear in front of you just as you're doing it.

"Glad last night gave you an appetite," Cain grinned, plonking himself in the seat opposite me. I scowled at him, and hoped I didn't have cake stuck to my teeth.

"Actually, being threatened by a thug with a gun gives me an appetite."

If I'd expected a rush of sympathy, of course, I was talking to the wrong person. Cain just raised an eyebrow a fraction of an inch, as if filing a potentially useful piece of information away. Perhaps he thought I was referring to him. When it became clear he wasn't going to swamp me with concern for my well-being, I changed tack, though couldn't keep the annoyance from my voice.

"How did you find me, anyway?"

He gave me an amused look.

"I spend my life hunting things, Cassandra. Things that don't want to be found. You hardly hide yourself: I could probably find you in five seconds using Tweeter or MyFace."

"Or whatever the kids are calling it these days, granddad." I smiled, despite myself. He gave me a faux stern look.

"Now, now. Don't mock your elders."

"Or what? You'll spank me?"

His eyes darkened.

"Are you asking?"

Well, OK, I'd rather set that one up for him, but his grin did strange things to my insides. Luckily – or unluckily – at that moment the waitress appeared, looking just as flustered as I was by Cain's raw magnetism. And she hadn't even seen him naked, so you can forgive *me* for blushing a little. Cain flashed her a quick smile, and ordered a double espresso. She giggled as if this was somehow hilarious – honestly, some women – and fluttered off to get his order, while Cain cast one of his trademark assessing looks around the venue. I knew if I asked him, he would be able to tell me exactly how many people were in the place, and just where all the exits were. It was a Cain thing.

"You know, they used to burn heretics here," he said, which for Cain, I think, counts as an effort at small talk. "They used to torture them until they admitted whatever heresy was fashionable at the time… at St Paul's… what *was* St Paul's… If they felt merciful, they'd tie gunpowder around their necks, so they'd die more quickly, or pile them on greenwood so the smoke would kill them. If they weren't, they'd let them burn, and their friends and relatives had to pick up the scrapings. Or they'd hang, draw and quarter them…"

"Good morning to you too, sunshine."

He gave an unoffended shrug. "I'm just fascinated by how cruel people can be in the name of morality. All those priests trying to save people's souls by tormenting their bodies." Another shrug. "Call it professional interest."

I wasn't sure I wanted to touch on *that* point, but I felt I should say something.

"That was a long time ago." I sounded more stiff than I'd like, but sometimes Cain made me feel like a reluctant witness for the defence of the whole human race.

"Try spending some time in Darfur or Afghanistan and saying those things no longer happen."

Something about the way he said that made me think he spoke from practical experience.

"Yes, fine," I sighed, audibly impatient at yet another rehashing of this argument. "I pay my direct debit to Amnesty International. I'm aware there are mean people in the world."

His mouth twitched into a smile.

"*Mean people*? I love how you can mix with monsters on a daily basis yet the worst you can say about the evil that walks the earth is that there are 'mean people'?"

The evil that walks the earth? You see what I have to put up with?

"Well, that's the whole thing with you, isn't it?" I retorted, taking his bait, the same way I always did. "You don't hunt the bad guys. You hunt a very *specific* set of bad guys, because you've decided their very nature makes them 'evil', so you're going all Winchester on their arses."

He looked at me blankly. "I don't carry a Winchester. I carry a Glock."

I sighed. Honestly, this is the problem with the supernatural crowd: they never watch TV. If they did they might not so readily turn into such bloody clichés.

"What would you like me to do, Cass? Throw them parties?"

Damn, I was hoping he hadn't known about that. He snorted at my expression.

"Don't think I've spent ages researching you, Cassandra, but you have a website. It's hardly a secret." He took a breath, as if willing himself to control his temper. "Did it ever occur to you that the purpose of your gift was to help you to stay away from these things? To stay safe? To avoid the monsters, not... socialise with them?"

Seriously, what was it with everyone and my job today? I knew I was taking my frustrations with the gunman out on him, but I didn't care.

"You really want to know? Then, no, it didn't. Not for one minute. And it's not as if my 'gift' actually does me any good most of the time. What do you think I should be doing?"

"You could use it better. Learn to focus it. You could help

me hunt them."

I almost choked on my drink. This was new. "For fuck's sake, Cain, do I look like bloody Buffy to you? And they're not simply creatures. They're not vermin." I couldn't believe we were having this argument *again*. "Some of them have jobs. Families. They're just Others. They're more like us than they're different."

"Only they have no souls."

"Well, you could probably say that about bankers and politicians. Why don't you go and kill all them?"

"They're evil!"

"That's what I just said."

"Not the bank... you're twisting my words. I'm not talking about bankers and politicians."

"But why not? That's my whole bloody point! You think the supernatural nasties have caused more damage, created more misery? If you're hunting bad guys, why stick to the vampires and the demons and the ghouls or whatever *you* have decided is monster of the week? Why not hunt the bankers who ruined the economy or the politicians in their pockets who let them get away with it? Why not try stopping the 13 year olds stabbing people on buses, or the thugs mugging old ladies? They probably worry more people than a handful of bloodsuckers no one knows exist."

"That's why it has to be me fighting them. Because I *do* know they exist, and I can do something about it. I know what they're capable of. "

He took another deep breath, clearly trying to calm himself down before we both went nuclear. Why did we always do this to one another? Sometimes he made me feel like a stroppy child, but we never seemed to be able to avoid falling into the same patterns. Obviously, he was thinking the same, because he leaned back, took one more long breath and rearranged his features into a conciliatory smile.

"If it's any consolation, if a 13 year old pulled a knife on a bus, I'd take him down too."

I nodded, not quite sure I was ready to be mollified.

"Well, that'll help me sleep better at night."

Cain leaned forward, and now his smile really was genuine. "Babe, I have absolutely no interest in helping you sleep better…"

Oh my. I had to hold onto the table a little, there. It was probably a good job the waitress chose that moment to reappear with Cain's drink. Bitch.

Cain looked down at his espresso like he'd forgotten ordering it, but nevertheless flashed the briefest of smiles at the waitress, who reacted like he'd thrown her a bouquet of flowers, and hovered frankly way too long before retreating back to the counter. Still, her interruption had given me a chance to regain my composure.

"So, intrigued as I always am by your fifth horseman of the Apocalypse routine, why are you actually here?"

"To see you?"

It says much for our 'relationship' that at no point would I accept that as an explanation. "You managed without seeing me for nearly the last three years," I pointed out, trying not to sound bitter – not that he would notice. Emotional nuance wasn't exactly Cain's strongpoint. He drank down his coffee in one swift gulp – an asbestos mouth clearly being another one of his superpowers – and set the cup down slightly too carefully. There was a pause that dragged on just a fraction too long.

"I think something bad is happening in London."

"Well, I know you're out of the country a lot, but that's not exactly a newsflash. Read the papers. There's always *something* bad happening in London."

He shot me one of those 'don't be obtuse' looks I was painfully familiar with, and I scowled at him. A shiver of realisation prickled on my neck. "You think... *I* might be mixed up in it?"

"I honestly don't know, not yet. I just know something is up. Look, I might not like the status quo in London, but I like the fact that there *is* a status quo." He looked so serious I refrained from making a joke about the band. He wouldn't have got it, anyway. "But I've been hearing things. Nothing more than rumours and whispers at the minute, and it's not like the supernatural community is lining up to talk to me – but something is up. And I think it's going to get worse." He sighed, heavily. "I just hate that you're so involved in this world, Cass."

"Well, I hate being unemployed and homeless," I frowned, trying not to show how pleased I was by this uncharacteristic expression of concern. "I have to work, Cain, and you might be on a great crusade to save humanity but I live in the real world, where mundane things like money actually matter. I need a job, and I'm good at this one, and while the hunting evil trade might be booming, you might want to look around and see the rest of the economy isn't. I have a business, now, and responsibilities, and I can't walk away from them."

"No matter what it costs?"

"It hasn't cost me anything."

"Are you sure?"

"I'm a Sensitive, aren't I? I'm sure I would have noticed."

He scowled at me, and stood with his usual feline swiftness, pulling enough money from his wallet to cover both our orders and throwing it on the table with a gesture that couldn't have looked more weary and annoyed had he tried.

"Just be careful, Cass. Something is coming, and I'm not sure if even I can stop it. You don't want to be in the way."

And with that, as usual, he left.

Chapter 10

UNFORTUNATELY, THREATS, mysterious strangers and cataclysmic prophecies of doom, fun as they are, don't go towards paying the bills and, as I was getting a little bit tired of telling people, I had a business to run. So I spent the afternoon interviewing clients – humans, obviously – and tried to put as normal a slant on my day as possible. I was worried, and from the slight metallic tang that still clung to Medea's aura, she had been working on some defensive spells, so clearly she wasn't quite as unruffled as she appeared, but luckily none of my visitors turned out to be gun-wielding maniacs, just the usual crowd of the curious and lonely, and one thirtysomething divorcee who had been finding slightly too much solace in Robert Pattinson fantasies and who was firmly steered onto the plastic fang list.

The evening was taken up by a site visit. Normally I love this part of the job; in how many other careers do you get to visit posh restaurants and party venues and chalk it all up to expenses? But tonight I could have done with a pass and a night in. I'm sure the question of whether that would be a night in *alone* wasn't at all what was making me wish for my flat. Honest. Still, by the time I had changed – I'd had a shower installed in the office bathroom, and both Medea and I kept spare clothes at work, albeit hers were considerably more glamorous than mine – I was feeling slightly better for it. I did a fair number of these visits, as I get a lot of repeat custom at Dark Dates and I'm always on the lookout for new venues to keep things interesting. London is a treasure chest for that: from art galleries to crypts to old guild meeting halls and museums, it had a wealth of venues that, whatever their day job, now bowed to the lure of the corporate dollar and rented out for events, and I had become smart at picking those with a suitably Dark Dates vibe. Tonight it was a burlesque club in a basement just inside the Square Mile, and though burlesque was now so mainstream as to be almost passé, I thought it might fit the bill for me. My clients may often be sharp of fang, but they tend not to be cutting edge, so this was a way of injecting some old school glamour without scaring the horses, and let's face it, a night in a dark room while women cavort in their underwear never really goes out of fashion.

I was wearing a dress that was probably too short and heels that were definitely too high, and had decanted my belongings into one of those cute little box-clutch-on-a-chain bags that look super elegant, but only hold your phone, keys, lipstick and credit card, so are useless 90% of the time. But at least I looked like I'd made an effort. Of course by the time I got there, my dress was riding up, my feet were killing me and the sharp metal edges of the clutch bag were digging into my hip while the chain was wearing a groove in my shoulder, but it was nothing a couple of dirty martinis and some quality girl talk couldn't soothe. I was meeting a couple of fellow female entrepreneurs I knew from a women's networking organisation: both in their thirties, so a few years older than me but good fun and, as I may have pointed out earlier, I am tragic and don't have a lot of friends. Still, there's actually something pretty refreshing about hanging out with people you don't know that well, whose problems you can be sympathetic about without engaging with, and who take your life exactly as superficially as you give it. Who, for instance, think you run a normal dating agency and don't have any idea you spent last night in the arms of a possibly non-human lover who you suspect is a sociopath, and the morning being threatened by a gunman who may or may not be in the pay of supernatural forces. Plus they drink like fishes, which always helps.

So despite everything, I was having a pretty good time. Of course, that was when my Sense went off. It's hard – as you may have noticed – to explain exactly how my Sense works (or, quite often, unfortunately, *doesn't* work). Trying to describe it is like trying to draw a picture of a smell. For the geeks in the audience, the Spidey Sense comparison can be a good one, but it doesn't work in quite the same way, unless everyone's favourite web-slinger got visions of guns when he was threatened and I just happened to miss that scene in the movie. Sometimes it feels like a literal sixth sense, other times a taste, a feeling, and it responds the way my other senses do to external stimuli. Right now, even slightly numbed by alcohol and the proximity of 100 other people in a very old building, it started screaming at me. To get back to the smell analogy, I reeled as if someone had just let off a stink bomb under my nose. Then, just as abruptly, it stopped, the stench vanished, and I was left wondering if I'd experienced it at all.

"Are you OK? You went a bit pale there. You look like you just saw a ghost!" Jenny, one of my companions, frowned at me in concern and it took me longer than it should have to process her question, as if I were hearing her words through a translator. I shook myself – literally – and forced myself to smile.

"Oh, I think someone just walked over my grave."

Both she and Sunita were looking at me in alarm, but Jenny rallied quickly.

"Well, you know what the cure for that is? Another martini!"

Which seemed like an excellent idea.

That was a really *bad* idea, I thought to myself, as my stomach gave another worrying lurch, thus taking my attention from the fuzziness engulfing my head. It was an hour later and my drinking companions had tottered respectively to their homeward bound tubes and buses and I was heading home myself. I was more than a little unsteady, regretting both alcohol consumption and footwear choices, or at the very least the combination of both. My flat might only be a 15 minute walk from the venue, but in these heels that was starting to seem like a marathon, and in accordance with the universal rule of all cities, anywhere, the availability of cabs was in direct inverse proportion to my desperation to find one – this being a part of the City that was relatively empty of bars, and the hour being well after the offices emptied, the roads were as empty as the pavements. All I needed now was for it to bloody start raining. Or to discover that I was being followed.

My Sense flared and my scalp prickled, my stomach protesting this time from nerves, not alcohol. It took me a moment to realise that, though I couldn't hear a sound, I knew with absolute certainty that there was something out there on the streets with me, and that it wasn't human. Straining both my Sense and my hearing, I finally made out its presence: a steady, wary pace far back enough away from me that it shouldn't really be a threat – but of course that only applied to anything moving at human speed. So definitely Other, but not vampire – I would have Sensed a vamp, the same way I was Sensing whatever this was, but vampires are virtually silent; if this had been a vampire, I wouldn't have heard a sound until it was on top of me. After the day I'd had, it was far too much to hope that this was simply a coincidence. I sighed to myself, cursing my teeny bag: not that I ever carried a weapon, but I really could have used that gun right now. Or, you know, the company of the heavily armed, ruthless demon killer who, whatever his flaws, did at least take an inordinate interest in my welfare. Instead I was walking down a deserted street, drunk and in stupid shoes. Fear, though, acted like a cold shower and a hot shot of coffee combined and I suddenly felt a lot less muzzy than I had moments before, though quite how much use that would be, I wasn't certain. I tightened my grip on the chain of my bag, so that I could, at last resort, swing it as a weapon (a ridiculously lightweight and flimsy weapon, but beggars can't be choosers) and I tried to put as much purpose into my stride as possible, praying to any god that would listen in the hope that a cab would appear. Predators of any ilk like easy victims, so I straightened my back and made myself think 'lion', all the time painfully aware that my glamorous but deeply impractical shoes were making me much more a limping gazelle.

But I wasn't completely helpless. I rolled my Sense out around me – one advantage of the quiet street was that there were no distractions – and so I Sensed the ripple of movement an instant before it came, giving me a fraction of a second to dodge the blow that, had it connected, would have probably taken my head clear off my shoulders, delivered by a pile driver of a fist that less than a minute before had been a whole street away. I ducked and spun as the arm above me drove through dead air, and as I did I swung my bag as hard as I could at where I Sensed rather than saw my assailant was. The Other gave a yelp of surprise – gazelles aren't supposed to fight back – and I used its confusion to strike again. I could barely see what I was hitting – it looked human, albeit a human put together by someone who had only been given the sketchiest of instructions – but it radiated Other, and possessed a strength that should have meant the fiercest of my blows bounced harmlessly off it. But it gave a howl of pain as my bag connected again, and I smelled sulphur and heard a sizzle of flesh. I realised that the same metal corners of the bag that had given my hip such punishment all night had burnt a gash an inch wide in the thing's forehead, and even now it was swatting helplessly at the bag, blinded by the blue-black slime of its own blood. Confused, in pain, it staggered back, and I lashed out with my foot, driving my stiletto heel as hard as I could into what I thought was a foot – or possibly a paw – and was rewarded with another howl and a satisfying squelch. I wrenched my foot free, leaving my shoe impaled where it was, pulled off the other shoe (giving the monster another whack in the head with the heel, for good measure) then took off down the street as fast as my adrenalin-fuelled legs could take me.

I don't know how long I ran for. It was probably less than a minute, though to my burning lungs and pounding heart it felt like a lot longer. I had no clue where I was – I could get lost in these alleys in broad daylight so now, drunk and disoriented by fear, I had no hope. So I had no idea where I was, no idea what I was running from – or if it was still after me – and, of no little importance on the less-than-spotless streets of London, I didn't have any shoes, so it was probably only a matter of seconds before I added either injury or at least unpleasantness to the equation. Folded over, panting, I tried to reach out with my Sense, but came up empty: whether because I had actually got clear of the thing, or I was just too addled to Sense it, I wasn't sure, so that wasn't much of a comfort. I heaved for a few moments, trying to get my breath back – honestly, I'm sure this never happens to the women in the movies – and then a noise in the street startled me so much that vomiting seemed a strong possibility. But as my terror abated I realised that it was actually a cab. And because – occasional evidence to the contrary – there really must be a

God and He doesn't hate me – it had its light on. I almost threw myself in the road in front of it, gesturing wildly for it to stop and hoping that the driver would slow down to help a damsel in distress rather than put his foot to the pedal to avoid a screaming, shoeless drunk.

Thank God, thank God, he stopped. I hurled myself inside and slumped against the seat, all of my energy evaporating. The driver cast me an openly curious look.

"You alright, pet? Where are you going?"

I paused, not sure of an answer to either question. Could I go home? I somehow didn't think this was a random attack, so if they had followed me here, it wasn't inconceivable that they knew where I lived. Admittedly, if Cain was *in situ* any monster come calling would be met with very short shrift and some serious automatic weaponry, but so far he was proving to be fairly adept at being wherever trouble wasn't, and I didn't want to stake my life on him being around now. I was pretty much out of options. I hesitated for a moment, then gave the driver Medea's address.

Chapter 11

SHAKEN AS I was, I still paused at the door of Medea's house, knocking three times carefully and slowly on the front door and stepping back. Medea might well be a white Wiccan, but only the terminally reckless go charging into any witch's home unannounced, and it would be the perfect end to the perfect day to be turned into a frog now. I'd called, of course, on the way here, and after a brief burst of shocked expletives – her Scottish side showing again – Medea's normal calm had descended and she was all steady reassurance.

"Of course, come over, I'm right here."

But there was still a long moment before she answered. I heard a bell chime three times in response to my knock, and the door opened. Medea, her face softened and creased with sleep, frowned out at me. Part of me – the non-gibbering with terror part – was mildly annoyed to see that even roused from her bed in the middle of the night, she looked sensational. It *must* be a spell.

"Thanks for letting me come over."

She nodded, cautiously, and stepped back from the doorway. Very carefully *not* inviting me in. I strode across the threshold with all the confidence I could muster, and felt my Sense prickle in reaction to all the latent magic in the house – not an unpleasant feeling, but an unmistakable one. I saw some of the tension leave her eyes as I entered: clearly I wasn't the only one rattled by recent events.

"Come through to the kitchen. I'm making cocoa."

I followed her as instructed, giving her a quick summary of the attack as she moved purposefully around her compact kitchen. The fact that she was in her own space amplified her usual grace, making her movements almost hypnotically fluid. With practised ease she put a pot of milk on the stove and spooned chocolate into mugs. Three mugs. Oops. Had I interrupted something? I realised guiltily that while at work I prattled on endlessly about my own life, Medea rarely gave anything away about hers. I liked her enormously – and I thought the feeling was mutual – but we didn't socialise outside of the office and it was suddenly plain to me I had no idea what her life was like beyond work. If I'd ever thought about it, I would have imagined her spending her evenings reclining on perfumed silks in an exotic boudoir, so it was somewhat disappointing to see her pottering around the kitchen of a South London semi, her hair scraped back, her enviable figure clad in pastel boyshorts and a t-shirt emblazoned with the incongruous slogan Willow Is My Nation. The kitchen, as well, was spectacularly unmystical: it looked like the whole place had been furnished from a catalogue from Normals R Us. Cookbooks rather than spellbooks packed the shelves (though, somewhat worryingly, there were a few anatomy textbooks scattered amongst them – I was glad I hadn't come for dinner), and there was the standard collection of photos, notes and postcards that decorate most people's houses stuck to the fridge and a cork notice board on the wall. An artfully arranged display of flowers stood in a vase on the windowsill, and while a bowl for cat food might have hinted at the presence of a Familiar in the house, it was labelled with the decidedly non-eldritch name 'Timmy'. In fact, the only remotely witchy thing about the place was that the windowsills were all adorned with small mirrors, and crystals hung in every corner. That and the witch who stood calmly leaning against the counter, listening to my story, of course.

Medea didn't speak as I recounted it all, her attention

soothing in itself, and it was only when I stopped talking that she asked her questions.

"And the metal on your bag burned it? Do you know what the metal is – silver, iron?"

"Topshop." I shrugged. "I have no idea."

She cocked her head to one side. "Well, we know that certain metals have negative effects on Others, but without knowing what exactly…"

She broke off, distracted by the arrival of the owner of Mug Number 3, who chose just this moment to walk into the kitchen.

If Medea was a study in the exotic, this woman was just the opposite. She had the kind of fresh-faced, rosy cheeked looks that could have put her age as anywhere between 20 and 35, a friendly if sleep ruffled expression and copper red hair that was cut into a shaggy bob. She was slightly plump, in that way that suits some women, and wearing checked pyjama bottoms and a t-shirt that proudly bore the slogan Nurses Make it Better. Which explained the anatomy books, at least. I hoped.

"Katie," the new arrival smiled, extending a hand, her voice carrying a slight lilt of Scotland. "Are you OK? Meds said you'd been attacked. Should we call the police?"

'Meds?' I boggled, as Katie ambled towards the counter, picked up her mug and gave Medea a light peck of gratitude on the shoulder, unselfconsciously answering the question I hadn't realised I had mentally been asking.

"Um… I'm fine, really, it was nothing. I'm just sorry to have to disturb you this late."

Katie gave an amiable shrug.

"Don't worry, I'm a nurse, I'm used to odd hours. But at the risk of *sounding* like a nurse, are you sure? You could be in shock."

I shook my head.

"Honestly, I'm fine, I wasn't bitten or any…" I broke off, my hand to my mouth, but Medea – I'm sorry, she just could never be a 'Meds' to me – gave me a small smile.

"It's OK. Katie's well aware of what I am, and what we do. You can speak freely in front of her."

Katie gave me a "hey, what can you do about it, that's life" kind of shrug, and nodded encouragingly. I hesitated, but only for a second: if Medea trusted her, then that should be good enough for me, too, especially since I was in their home.

"OK, then, it didn't bite me, or scratch me. I'm not even sure what it *was*. Maybe it just wanted to scare me, I don't know."

Katie gave a rueful smile towards my now very battered handbag.

"Motto of the story is never go out with a bag you can't fit a stake into, right?"

Despite myself, I laughed, and nodded towards Medea.

"I'm guessing the t-shirt came from you, then?"

Katie grinned. "You fall in love with a gay witch, you might as well accept the fact that you're living the cliché."

Medea rolled her eyes, slipping an arm around her girlfriend.

"Gods, I knew there was a reason I hadn't introduced you two. I'm going to be drowning in geek speak from now on, aren't I?"

"Hey, I don't think watching those shows is geeky, it's research. Right, Cass?" Katie gave me a broad wink, and I laughed again. I was going to like this girl.

With one final enquiry after my health, Katie excused herself, leaving Medea and I to chew over the events of the day. One thing was painfully apparent to me now: for all my Sensitive nature, for all my dealings with Others, I actually had little idea how they lived and how their society was structured – or even how many of them were in London. It was not, after all, a question that came up much in the day-to-day business of my job: "So, as well as describing your ideal woman, could you tell me if you have a supreme leader?" It had never affected my business, so it had never really mattered to me, and I had been happy to remain in relative ignorance. From what I had gathered from the few conversations I'd had on the subject, I knew that vampires in London were only loosely organised: some aware of one another, some not, some living independently, some clustered together in cabals of varying casualness. Medea couldn't shed much more light on it, either, her supernatural connections being fairly restricted to the Wiccan community, who tended to avoid contact with any Others. Beyond that, I didn't know much, which made it so much harder to figure out what was happening here. Was I being targeted by some random vamp with a grudge (and some fairly impressive hired help), or had I inadvertently offended someone higher up the food chain (which might explain said impressive hired help)? Was I up against a couple of nutters or an army? And how did this fit into Cain's arrival and his dark mutterings of doom?

But there are only so many ways you can rephrase 'I have no idea what is happening' and eventually Medea and I ran out of them all, and she showed me upstairs to a small but cosy spare room. Katie – who had clearly departed for reasons of diplomacy rather than tiredness – emerged from their bedroom as she heard us, and issued a smiling but stern warning to wake them both if I felt "the least bit unwell". Given my martini intake, that was probably a self-inflicted inevitability, but I nodded my agreement. She laid a hand on my shoulder and for a split second my Sense reeled back and I almost flinched, but the feeling disappeared as quickly as it came, though a flicker of a frown on Katie's face told me she had noted my reaction. I opened my mouth to apologise but, with a brief kiss to her girlfriend, Katie retreated, Medea's face softening with affection as she watched her go.

"Nurses. On the one hand, they worry, on the other you never get any sympathy for anything but a gushing head wound. In fact, probably not even then."

"She's nice," I said, and I meant it. I was sure my Sense had just picked up on the residual magic contact with Medea would bring. "And it's nice of you both not to mind me barging in on you."

"Don't be silly, you're not barging in. Besides, where else would you go?"

I tried not to wince at that – after all, Medea was right. I was pretty short of friends. She noticed my expression and misread it as fear.

"You're safe here, you know. I have wards on all the entrances, no vampire could come in uninvited, and…" she hesitated, as if about to say something else, but stopped, thinking better of it, and my Sense flickered at the pause. "You'll be safe," she reiterated, slightly awkwardly, which really hadn't been what she was going to say at all.

"Thanks. I appreciate it." And of course I did. Cain had said something bad was going to happen – but I hadn't thought he meant so soon. I hadn't thought he meant to *me*. Medea nodded solemnly and gave my shoulder a gentle squeeze, an echo of Katie's gesture.

"Just try and get some sleep. It'll look better in the morning."

I nodded, grateful for her kindness, and her assurances. I would have taken less solace in her words had I known how wrong she was.

Chapter 12

I DREAMT of fire and smoke and shattering glass, and woke up crying, clutching at the sheets for a saviour that wasn't there. Because, after all this time, I still expected Cain to save me...

I was nearly 19 years old and I'd never been more excited in my life. My two closest friends and I had been invited to a house party at Halloween – a proper, 'drive to the country, get as drunk as you like and stay overnight' house party, held by some moneyed friends who had hired an old farmhouse for a weekend of spooky fun. To add to the frisson, we were assured the place was actually haunted, and though none of us really believed in all that (well, OK, I sort of did, but I was keeping quiet on that score) we were all willing to go along with being scared for the sake of a good party.

By then it was years since I had last seen Cain. In the immediate aftermath of our meeting, I had spent days, if not weeks... OK, maybe months... fantasising and obsessing about him, expecting him to reappear in my life. But when, after all that time, he didn't, even I couldn't keep a crush going indefinitely, so he went from being a source of potential excitement to something weird that once happened to me, and then something I pretty much forgot, even if I had taken his words more to heart than he could know. I got into university, and everything became new and shiny and fun and, while my Sense gave the occasional flare, it was never anything too worrying and was nothing I couldn't control. There were no more crying jags or random hysterics and, as I was yet to meet the vampire with whom I would have my youthful indiscretion, I was willing to believe there were things that went bump in the night but was also content that they had little or no interest in, or connection to, me. My parents were delighted; they thought I'd simply outgrown a troubled adolescence, and I was happy to let them think that. And now I had proper friends and mixed in circles where I got invited to overnight parties in haunted houses. As far as I was concerned, life was good.

The hosts were a couple of students a year or so older than us and a couple of income brackets higher, so by that virtue alone were impossibly cool, and they had gone to some trouble to create a suitably spooky atmosphere with the house. It was probably a perfectly lovely building in the daytime, but driving up to it in my friend Tina's battered Beetle, through deserted country lanes illuminated only by our own headlights, as we approached it the place appeared like something from the Blair Witch Project. Sam, the female half of the hosting couple, tottered out onto the gravel to meet us at the sound of our car pulling up. She was gothed up to the eyeballs – not much of a stretch for Sam, who naturally favoured a lot of black lace and kohl in her look – but she had ramped it up to 11 for the occasion. She had a cigarette in one hand and a bottle of vodka in the other and she pulled us into a boozy and potentially flammable embrace before waving us up the stairs to our rooms. We were lucky to be in the main house, rather than one of the outbuildings that would be accommodating many of the guests – a result of Sam being protective of our relative youth, I think. We'd drawn straws for rooms, and I'd won: Tina and Pav would be sharing a tiny room that housed little but a double bed, whereas I had the equally small but, importantly, single bedroom in the eves of the thatched roof. This demarcation was carried out with the tacit understanding that if anyone got lucky they would automatically get the single room, and such was my current romantic hit rate that I was fairly certain it wasn't going to be me. At the time, of course, I couldn't have realised just how lucky I would get.

Once ensconced in my room, I changed quickly into my outfit, anxious not to miss any of the fun. I was wearing more make up than I had worn in my entire life, and I almost felt like a different person. Eyes heavily lined with kohl, lipstick the colour of blood and straightened hair teamed with a basque that did serious things to a cleavage that was, with the perkiness of youth and my natural curviness, already pretty damn impressive. Proving I can never be accused of underkill, I combined this with a skirt consisting of acres of taffeta threaded with rhinestones over fishnets, and insanely high heels. Needless to say, I probably looked an utter fright, but I went down to the party convinced I was *It*.

Once downstairs, though, I realised my efforts were fairly tame compared to many of the other partygoers, who had fully embraced Sam's steampunk goth ethos. I grabbed a drink and tried not to goggle at the costumes, hoping that I looked worldly and sophisticated rather than as young and gauche and out of place as I felt. I was quickly reunited with Tina and Pav, who both wore variants on my own outfit, though Tina had emphasised her enviable slenderness with trousers that made her legs look like she had been skinny dipping in oil, and Pav had woven her lustrous black mane into a towering beehive, a white streak of fake hair inserted for true Bride of Frankenstein effect, and she was wearing enough magical symbols to start her own coven. We laughed at our own audaciousness, and knocked back our drinks to a soundtrack of the Cult and Sisters of Mercy and lots of other shouty anguished bands I didn't recognise turned up so loud the floor vibrated, and we assured ourselves that this was going to be the night of our lives.

We headed through the crowds, in search of more drinks and giggles and people we knew. I automatically rolled out my Sense around me, in the way that I'd taught myself to do over the last few years and which had become something of a habit whenever I went somewhere new. I was used to the reassuring burr of it being undisturbed. Tonight there were a couple of buzzes, but nothing that alarmed me – it was probably just the age of the house, which I imagined *was* a little haunted after all, and the effects of the alcohol and adrenaline, both of which could have a slight distorting affect. Nothing that could stop me enjoying myself. Then, without any warning, I went deaf. It was only for a moment, and it wasn't real, but for a second I felt like my Sense had hit a solid brick wall and taken the rest of me with it. I stood, frozen, helpless, unaware of the music or the lights or the press of people, and then the world returned in a flood.

"That's a new look for you. I like it."

Cain was standing so close to me that I felt his words on my cheek as much as I heard them. I jumped, startled by his sudden proximity, and the glass tumbled from my hand, only to be caught by his a millisecond later, without a single drop spilled. He handed it back to me wordlessly, with a slightly smug smile.

"Are you following me?" It was a ridiculous question, I know, but I couldn't help but blurt it out. He looked amused rather than annoyed by such an accusation.

"If I am, I'm not very good at it, am I? It's taken me long enough to catch up with you." Since that was precisely what *I* was thinking, I said nothing. Cain continued to watch me with that lazy smirk on his face, enjoying my discombobulation. "I do have friends of my own, you know. I get invited to things."

I nodded, foolishly; at the time I had no reason to know he was lying. Besides, I was distracted. I had forgotten how good – how really, *really* good – he looked. His appearance was virtually unchanged since our first meeting (as I said earlier: in retrospect, suspiciously so). Like almost everyone else here, he was wearing black, though on him it looked so casual that it gave him the air of having wandered in from somewhere else rather than having dressed especially for a party. A black t-shirt cut in a slight v at the throat clung to that impressive torso, and he wore black jeans and boots, his one concession to the occasion being a silver belt buckle in the shape of a skull, which I looked at for slightly too long before realising I was basically ogling his crotch. I averted my eyes hastily, my cheeks aflame, but when I caught his gaze the slightly cocky expression he wore really didn't help any.

"I never really imagined you as the socialising type," I managed, which was of course nonsense; I'd met him for five minutes at a cafe more than two years ago – how could I imagine him to be any 'type'? But he nodded as if conceding a point.

"I'm not here to socialise. I'm here to hunt."

And with that he raised his glass in smiling salute, kissed me on the cheek and, in the time it took me to recover from the shock of that, melted into the party. Stunned as I was, I couldn't help but laugh at his brazenness: who else would admit they had come just to pick up girls? Though a small voice in my head couldn't help but wonder why one of those girls wasn't me.

The party carried on, as parties are wont to do. I mingled and chatted – there were plenty of fellow students I knew there, with enough people I didn't to make it an interesting mix. I even managed some mild flirtation, though to no great result, and as the night wore on I found myself back where I always ended any party, with Tina and Pav, the three of us huddled together, laughing, critiquing the scene. My friends were entertainingly scandalised by the behaviour of one of the other guests, and desperate to share.

"Honestly, he must have been on the super hardcore stuff. He went completely bonkers. Total freak out!" Tina exclaimed, gleefully. "'I saw a real vampire! It tried to bite me! It crumbled to dust in front of my eyes!'" She raised her hands in mock horror. Pav chortled, joining in the tale.

"I think he got a bit *too* much into the Halloween spirit... Sam had to take him upstairs for a lie down."

I stared at them, forcing myself to smile, because something in their story caused my Sense to flare, and I realised with sudden, unshakeable clarity the real nature of Cain's prey. I got a couple of odd looks from the girls as I launched myself unsteadily to my feet, but with a muttered explanation of 'bathroom' I staggered back towards the body of the party, which was now in full swing. I got a few comments as I pushed my way through people dancing, or snogging, not caring what anyone thought, gripped by a panic I couldn't explain or shake, frantically searching for the gap in my Sense where a person should be. I followed it through to the kitchen and the attached pantry, and was on the step leading out to the back garden before it occurred to me how monumentally stupid I was being. I had just committed horror movie mistake number 1: unarmed and alone damsel rushing to investigate the mysterious noise, anyone?

"Shit," I muttered, about to turn back, but a flicker of movement in the shadows froze me to the spot.

"I didn't expect that kind of language from a lady." There he was again, emerging from the darkness like a spectre in a dream, a faintly ironic smile on his face. I stepped back, nervously realising I couldn't see his hands... or what might be in them.

"You know this whole 'appearing from nowhere with a clever remark' thing is really creepy, right?" I snapped, adrenaline making me bold. He inclined his head, his smile unshifting.

"A little bit sexy, though, come on, admit it."

Well, he had me there, but I had no intention of agreeing.

"Did you kill someone tonight?" I blurted. I had no idea where that came from, but he looked less surprised at hearing it than I was at saying it.

"I killed some*thing*."

"Like what? Define 'something'. A rat, a cockroach, what?"

He shrugged. "Either of those metaphors works for me."

"You can't just murder people!" He looked at me blandly, like I had just said something so irredeemably stupid it was pointless to argue. "Is this what you do? You kill people?"

"I take issue with the word 'murder'. And with the term 'people'. I *stopped* some*thing* that was planning to feed on you and your pretty little friends in there. You should be grateful."

"But... you just *killed* someone." I was repeating myself, I know that, but he really didn't seem to be picking up on this rather important key fact.

Another shrug. "That's what I do."

I stared at him, aghast. "I... I don't know what to say to that."

"Good. Because I've been waiting for you to shut up long enough to let me kiss you."

And that really did render me speechless.

He leaned in, slowly, and kissed me, and for a second I

thought he had staked me too and I was bursting into flames. He pulled me close, too easily, and the heat and the hardness of his chest against mine was an almost physical shock. I couldn't help but respond: I pushed myself against him, my arms snaking around his neck, and as his embrace tightened and his kiss became more urgent, my own desire flared. Desperate to touch him, my hands sought the bare flesh under his t-shirt, only to freeze for the slightest of moments as I felt the thick welts of scar tissue on his back – scars that I'm now so familiar with, but at the time made me reel backwards in shock. He stepped away from me, his eyes meeting mine. It was a question; an opportunity to stop. Instead I pulled him close again and kissed him like my life depended on it. It was only later that I realised it probably did.

There's nothing graceful, attractive or classy about having frantic, sweaty and slightly drunken sex in someone else's back garden, so I'll spare you the details for the sake of my own blushes, if not yours. I'm also more than a little aware that my moral outrage seemed to have dissipated rather quickly under the onslaught of my hormones. What can I say? I was young and impressionable, and Cain had that effect on me. As opposed to now, of course…

So let's fast forward a little to upstairs, and suffice to say by then I was tired, quite sore and possibly in a state of shock. We were both now naked, but at least there was a duvet. I was lying with my head on his chest, luxuriating in feel of him, strangely soothed as he softly stroked my hair. I had finally recovered my senses enough to ask a proper question.

"Why didn't I know the vampire was out there?"

I felt his body move in a shrug. "A room full of people, alcohol… you're still pretty new to this. What are you, not even 20? The vampire I killed was at least 10 times your age, maybe older, judging from the way he crumbled when I staked him." He must have felt my confusion, because he shifted slightly so that I could see his face. "Only the older vampires disintegrate, the younger ones don't. I guess I should be grateful, or I'd have been spending tonight with a shovel." He gave me a light kiss. "And this is a *much* more enjoyable form of exercise." My insides purred at his smile, but he hadn't answered my question. Seeing my expression, he continued. "He's probably learned to hide from a Sensitive. I had trouble enough tracking him down myself... by that age most of them get good at hiding, and at damping down their power if they need to. Makes it harder for people like you to find him."

I wasn't sure whether I was worried or consoled by the prospect of 'people like me', but I had a more immediate concern.

"Why would he think I'd *want* to find him?"

"Your Sense works both ways. He might have wanted to find *you*. Sensitives often stand out to vampires, it can attract them. To be honest, it did cross my mind that he was here after you."

Well, that was a heartwarming thought, but somehow with Cain's arms around me, it didn't seem one worth pursuing. Instead I curled into his chest and smiled.

"So how did I attract *you*?" I asked. Alright, I was shamelessly fishing for a compliment, but wouldn't you? I was young and quite pretty and I had great tits, but I wasn't delusional: on a scale of hotness I was Scotland on a sunny day; Cain was a midday stroll in the Sahara. But he didn't answer my question, instead just kissed my hair. I twisted to look at him again, but his expression was unreadable.

"You're going to vanish again, though, right?"

He held my gaze steadily, not bothering to deny it. I sighed for a moment, but I'm not sure which of us was more surprised that I took this as my cue to sit up and swing myself on top of him.

"Well, since you probably won't be around in the morning, I suppose we better make the most of tonight."

Cain let out a low chuckle that vibrated through his stomach to the tops of my thighs.

"And you ask me why I'm interested…"

So that was the night that Cain and I first 'got together'; that was the start of whatever this relationship is, and it set a pattern for us that has remained fairly unchanged since then. That was also the night that someone burned the house down and killed all of my friends.

Chapter 13

I WOKE up in Medea's spare room the next day, shaken and sweating. The dream, always so vivid, never failed to leave me feeling low, a sort of weary sadness that seemed to emanate from my very bones. Coming on top of everything else that had just happened, it added up to a pretty crappy start to the day. I lay there, for a while, reluctant to leave the soft sanctuary of bed, thinking of that night, which was still fresh in my mind nearly a decade later, no hazing of the memory to soften the pain.

So many things had changed so quickly that night, and my life wasn't ever quite the same afterwards. I'd never had friends as close as Pav and Tina again – some capacity for openness in me died with them, and in losing them I lost a part of me that never came back. I never even found out exactly what killed them, or why. Cain pulled me out of the house, and saved my life, but there was nothing he could do for the rest of them – of the 20 people sleeping in the house that night, only four survived – the other two, our hosts, had been sleeping in a room on the ground floor, near the back door, but their lives were as scarred by guilt in the aftermath as surely as if they had been caught in the flames. No one could pin down the cause of the fire: they blamed faulty wiring or a stray cigarette or the thatched roof – fingers pointed everywhere but at the real culprits. Cain, of course, fled as soon as the alarm was raised, not being a man who wanted to tangle with the authorities. Having ascertained the ragged cut on my side wasn't serious, he gently but briskly kissed the tears on my cheeks, murmuring a goodbye and disappearing into the flame-streaked darkness even as the other guests rushed out to the scene to find me safe but dazed, bleeding and naked, unable to properly answer the questions of those who huddled around me with blankets and solace.

It was six months later when I saw him again; six months in which my life had fairly comprehensively unravelled, as my studies failed and I spiralled into grief. Is that why I didn't question his reappearance, his uninvited presence at the foot of my bed? The memory of that night, too, remains vivid and raw: of pulling him, unspeaking, into my arms, as if we could exorcise the memory of pain and death with sweat and passion. It was morning before we even spoke, when he fixed me with that steady green gaze and told me he had killed the thing that set the fire. That was all he told me; all he was willing to share. He didn't even tell me *what* it was – was the house really haunted by some malevolent destructive spirit? Was it another vampire – someone after Cain, seeking revenge for the vampire he'd killed? Were they after me, drawn to the Sensitive the way Cain hinted they might be? Was it a random slaying or a targeted attack? Cain didn't offer me answers, because he couldn't comprehend why I needed them.

"But why did they do it?" I pleaded, when he told me it was over, and he looked at me strangely, not understanding the question.

"I didn't ask," he shrugged, and that, to him, was the end of it.

For me, of course, the fire was the beginning. My studies failed, despite the understanding of my tutors, and I eventually dropped out, realising the world I was studying bore no resemblance to the one I lived in. Cain had shone a light onto a part of life I had only dimly been aware of, even though the results weren't at all what he hoped they would be.

His stubborn refusal to give me answers just made me more determined in my questions. This became my new study, my new assignment, and what I found astonished me, because it wasn't Cain's world of hunters and victims, of terror and prey. It was actually, for the most part, fairly ordinary: its inhabitants as varied as those of my own. I realised that to be Other didn't mean being a monster – yes, there were bad things that weren't human, but not everything that wasn't human was bad. My motives may have stemmed from denial as much as desire, but I let myself date a vampire. I hired a witch. I built my life and my business on the belief that we're defined by what we do, not what we are: a belief I had clung to for as long as I could remember. But waking up scared with my mind full of the terror of a supernatural attacker, I was wondering if I had been wrong all along.

Medea, always adept at reading a mood, was as quiet as I was, silent company on the commute as we made our way into work. Our sombreness wasn't helped by the fact that we'd picked up a paper at the station: another murder, the same as the others. We glanced at one another, our fear unspoken. There was nothing to imply these killings were supernatural in nature – in fact, the police were doing everything they could to suggest they weren't even connected – but the papers were hardly likely to pick up on anything that fell into the realm of the Others, and it was starting to seem like an awfully big coincidence. What if the attack on me last night wasn't personal at all – what if it were part of this larger pattern? Just how lucky had I been?

So we weren't exactly singing when we reached the office – and then it just got worse. My Sense roared as soon as we approached the doorway, and I stopped so suddenly Medea careered into the back of me. The lock on the front door was warped, the door itself looking closed but, when I examined it more closely, I could tell it was no longer secure. Realising something was wrong, Medea reached into her bag for a charm sack she carried, and I felt the air around her thicken as she pulled in energy for a spell. I wasn't sure how much mojo she could conjure with no prep time, but it had to be better than anything I could currently bring to the party. I really needed to start carrying that gun.

I rolled my Sense forward, trying to block out the feel of Medea's aura, and after a second I almost sagged in relief as I realised nothing was there. Whatever had been in the office had left its mark – the air felt oily, as if some taint or residue had been left behind – but the perpetrator had gone. I nodded to Medea and felt her flare of magic dampen, but not extinguish – wisely, she wasn't winding down completely until she knew for certain we were safe. Gingerly, we nudged open the door and crept inside.

The main reception wasn't as bad as I had feared: a few desk drawers pulled open, a chair overturned and some broken glass where a vase had been knocked over, scattering flowers over the floor. But my office... I felt my eyes well up. The door had been kicked so hard it had splintered, and was left hanging by only a sliver of one hinge. My computer was smashed to pieces, a jumble of plastic and wire, the hard drive missing, torn from its casing. My steel filing cabinets had been ripped open with such force the metal had twisted, the drawers left gaping empty. Papers were strewn everywhere, the whole room carpeted in white.

"I'll call the police." Medea frowned, digging out her mobile, because one glance showed us that the landlines had been ripped from the walls.

"The police won't be able to help you."

"For fuck's sake!" I wheeled, terror making me furious,

and Cain was so shocked by my anger he actually took a step back. There are times when mysteriously appearing out of the ether is charming: this was not one of those times. "Did you do this?"

Part of me was gratified to see I could startle him, but though he had stepped away from me, Cain's face remained infuriatingly calm.

"Why would *I* do this?"

He cast a glance at Medea, and for the briefest of seconds their eyes met – I saw hers widen, and he looked away quickly, though something in his posture stiffened. I didn't have time or inclination to process that little mystery just yet, because I was still too bloody angry.

"Because you hate what I do! Because you want me to stop doing it! Do you think this will stop me? Trashing my office? Destroying my files?" I cast around angrily for more damage. "Stealing my bloody diary?"

Cain glanced around the room, assessing the wreckage, and when he spoke his voice was glacial.

"You know this wasn't me. Because I know this… this *inconvenience* wouldn't stop you. I know how bloody stubborn you are, remember? If I thought you needed to be stopped – if I *really* thought that was a necessity – you know this isn't how I'd go about it."

"What would you do?" I demanded, my voice tipping into hysteria. "Kill me? Kill us?" At that moment, I wouldn't have put it past him. And he looked like he was genuinely considering the question, the bastard.

"I might. Possibly. If there was no viable alternative." He ignored my expression at this charming revelation, his manner eerily nonchalant. "But if that's what I had to do, I'd go to one of your parties, wait till everyone was inside and firebomb the place. That way I'd kill you, her, and all of the monsters you so delight in socialising with."

I was so shocked by the steel in his voice – and the memory of smoke and fire clinging to me from my dreams – that my anger disappeared in a moment, wiped out by the cold clamour of fear. Beside me, I felt Medea's scent change, her aura darken, and I struggled to keep my voice level.

"You'd be killing a lot of innocent people," I managed, feebly, but Cain just shrugged, as if that were the most minor of considerations.

"For a greater cause. God's always been fine with collateral damage. So am I."

"So now you're *religious* all of a sudden? You're with God?"

"I'm just saying He set a reasonable precedent to follow. One your own government follows much of the time, don't forget."

"Well, God says a lot of bollocks, are you going to follow that too? Bomb Oxford Street to stop people shopping on a Sunday, kill people for eating shellfish or…" Not being religious at all, I was quickly running out of examples. "God says don't suffer a witch to live, are you going to kill Medea here, too?"

"Hey, leave me out of it!" Medea exclaimed in a panic, and Cain's eyes flickered towards her in interest. I realised I possibly shouldn't have brought that up, so hastily tried to change the subject.

"And don't start me on the bloody government…" I paused, my anger having returned. "Are we honestly going to have this fucking fight every time you show up, Cain? Because seriously, I'm so fucking tired of it. And if you must do your international man of mystery routine, how about turning up in time to *stop* people attacking me or robbing my office, rather than just showing up after the event to make gnomic bloody pronouncements and veiled threats?"

"You were attacked?" he frowned, and the shift from aggression to concern startlingly abrupt. "Are you alright?" He took a step towards me, reaching for my face, but I stepped sharply out of his way. It was a bit late now to wheel out the concerned boyfriend routine.

"I'm fine, no bloody thanks to you! You *weren't there*. And when you finally are here you're... mean to me!" OK, that ended less strongly than it should have, but I was feeling a bit fragile by then. Cain scowled at me.

"I'm trying to help, if you'd just stop being so bloody difficult for two seconds and listen to me for once!"

"Some help! Too bloody little, too bloody late!"

We glared at one another for a moment that threatened to stretch out too long, until Medea, ever sensible, stepped between us.

"Perhaps we should all calm down and have a nice cup of tea?"

Chapter 14

WE DID, in the end, call the police – my insurance wouldn't be valid without a crime report – and though they were polite and sympathetic, they didn't exactly fill me with hope. In a city with London's problems, a non-violent burglary with minimal theft isn't going to be high on anyone but the victim's agenda. Cain and I had managed to come to a reluctant detente – whatever issues I had with him, there was no denying he was a handy man to have around when there was heavy lifting to be done. My filing cabinets were a write-off, as was my computer, but it took him less than an hour to clean up the mess and leave my office looking serviceable and tidy, if somewhat bare. Medea and I tackled collecting and reorganising my paperwork, and while Cain was working I filled him in on all the events of the past few weeks: my mystery vampire and equally mysterious gunman and the attack on me the night before. He agreed with me it sounded like they were connected, but that didn't get us any farther forward. Once his part of clean up was done, Cain vanished, only to return with impressive speed with a new door: as he hung it, I realised this one came with steel reinforcements.

"I'll pick you up some new filing cabinets tomorrow," he said, as he sat with me surveying his handiwork. I was oddly touched by his thoughtfulness, though it didn't help shake my gloom.

"If only I had some files to go in them." Because despite the papers that had been scattered in the break in, it was clear that a huge amount of my notes were missing.

"But everything must be backed up on your laptop, right?"

I averted my eyes, guiltily. Like I said, I was always a bit old school about my record keeping – paper is so much nicer than computers – and now it was coming back to bite me.

"Some of it. But a lot of my client records – all my questionnaires, my notes from the parties – are on paper. It's easier to get people to fill them in than to put stuff on the computer. I'm not exactly dealing with the iPhone generation here, am I?" Because obviously, it was their fault, not mine.

"There's something else," Medea chipped in, tapping a newly-sorted stack of files.

"Isn't there always?" Cain sighed.

"As far as I can tell, they only took the vampire files. All of the human ones seem to be still here."

Cain turned to me, scowling.

"Surely, though, they were coded?"

"Of course they were!" I protested. If writing a big 'V' on the corner was considered a code, that is. Cain read the truth in my face and let out a sigh. "So someone stole half of your files, and your diary? That tells them an awful lot about a lot of the monsters in this city." I bit my tongue so as not to correct the 'monsters' gibe. It seemed like the wrong moment to protest.

"You think that's why someone broke in? For my records? Who on earth would bother doing that?"

"Maybe a journalist?" suggested Medea, a trifle too hopefully. I thought of all that twisted metal, my kicked in, ruined door.

"Not unless the tabloids have the Incredible Hulk on their payroll. So you think someone came here looking for information?"

Cain shrugged. "It's what I would do."

"I thought what *you'd* do is firebomb my party." I wasn't quite ready to let that one go, yet. His expression didn't flicker.

"Well, the files would be plan A."

He smiled at me then. I didn't smile back.

"Someone has taken my files so they can hunt vampires?"

"Or stop someone else hunting them."

"To stop you?" I couldn't *not* ask. After all, if Cain's reappearance hadn't exactly kick-started all this craziness, it certainly seemed to have escalated it. He seemed unperturbed by the thought.

"Maybe. That would be a misinterpretation of my motives and a gross underestimation of my skills, but it's possible."

Medea raised her eyebrows at that, but I shrugged at her. It's not bragging if it's true.

"So how do we find out which? Obviously the police are no use, but someone has to know who all these visitors are, how they're connected."

"I can ask around," Cain said. "Knock some heads together if need be. I have some sources in town. Someone must know something."

"What if they won't tell you?"

He flashed me that familiar wolf grin.

"I'll ask harder."

He leaned in and kissed me on the forehead with a tenderness that surprised me and, nodding curtly to Medea, he strode out. OK, the man has his flaws, but procrastination isn't one of them. Medea watched him go warily, as if she were eyeing a tiger in retreat.

"I don't like him."

"Most of the time, I don't like him much either," I sighed, but she wasn't smiling.

"I'm not kidding, Cassandra. He… he scares me."

I tried not to let her seriousness rattle me.

"Well, he can be plenty scary."

She frowned, as if struggling to articulate herself, which in itself was uncharacteristic for Medea. Eventually, she spoke, her voice small. "He smells like death."

I laughed. Cain never smelled like anything but Cain to me, and that was a pretty good smell. "Come on, Medea, we work with vampires in the middle of a meat market. Everything here smells a little bit of death."

She shook her head. God, she really *was* actually scared. "He doesn't smell a little *bit* of death. He smells like the fall of Troy."

This time I did laugh, rolling my eyes. The fall of Troy? You see what I am surrounded by? This was back to 'the evil that walks the earth' territory. It's amazing she and Cain didn't like each other more, given their joint love of the overblown metaphor. Medea frowned at my sceptical expression. "Can't you Sense it?"

"Look, I know Cain's not exactly little Mr Sunshine, but…"

"Sunshine? Cassandra, the things that we work with… we see squalls, and light rainclouds. Cain is… Hurricane Katrina."

"He's probably the best chance we have of finding out what happened here!" I snapped, finally unnerved. Medea paused then gave me a slight, reluctant smile.

"I may be able to help a little with that one."

I'd rarely seen Medea do anything but the most basic of spells – although, as I've said, I have my suspicions she doesn't *naturally* look that good all the time – so even if her offer hadn't seemed like the best chance we had to get fast answers, I would have agreed out of sheer curiosity. Clearly she hadn't wanted to do this in front of Cain – I really should have steered clear of the whole 'don't suffer a witch to live' thing –

but was she happy enough to get magical now he had departed. It was sort of fascinating.

She paced the room, slowly, first clockwise then counter clockwise, her face set in concentration, trailing a circle of salt around her. I tried not to think about the fact that we'd just hoovered up the glass and were now making more mess.

"What are you doing?"

She didn't look at me. "This keeps the magic focused, and stops anything bad coming in or out."

"Bad like a bullet?"

"I'm rather hoping you won't feel the need to shoot me," she smiled. "Nothing physical, no, but anything magical or spiritual. It might not stop it completely – it depends how strong it is – but it should at least slow it down."

"Salt really stops it? Like off TV?" I paused. "Does it have to be salt, or will any condiment do? Bath crystals? Talc?" OK, I admit it, I gibber when I'm nervous, and magic makes me slightly nervous.

Medea rolled her eyes.

"Mostly it's the spell that stops it. The salt is just a conduit."

A worrying thought occurred to me. "You're not summoning anything, are you? It's just I feel like I've had enough unexpected visitors lately…"

She sighed.

"I'm not really strong enough to summon anything – that takes a huge amount of energy, and then you have to control it when it's here. I'm more… reading a trail. Conjuring a shadow, if you like – the residue of whatever was here last night. It's similar to how you can Sense things after they have happened, only hopefully much clearer."

"And if there's no residue?"

"Then it was a couple of junkies looking for cash and

being disappointed by how cheap our computers are."

I frowned at that. We were a start up business: I wasn't made of money. But both of us knew in our hearts already that it wasn't a couple of unlucky druggies. I watched her for a moment more. "So it's a telescope rather than a telephone?"

This time her sigh was much heavier. "It really works so much better if I have quiet in which to concentrate."

I took the hint and shut up. Boss or not, there are times when you have to hand over to the experts. Medea took a deep breath, did another circle, and then muttered something I couldn't make out before freezing stock still in the centre of her salt ring, her eyes closed.

For a moment, there was nothing, and then the air shimmered and thickened: I saw colours flicker around Medea's head, though whether I actually saw or Sensed them I wasn't sure. Medea was no longer just a lovely young woman, she was a throbbing column of power and light, the line of salt glowing bright at her feet. Then her eyes and mouth flew open and she gasped and staggered, and the lights disappeared as she almost toppled.

"What was it?" I rushed forward to catch her but stopped, not sure whether breaking the circle would do more harm than good. But she reached out and grabbed my arm, and stepped outside the salt ring, sagging into my arms.

"I… I couldn't make it out. Not properly… it's protecting itself. But, oh, Cass, it's strong. So strong. And evil. It means us harm. It means all of us harm…"

Her voice was shaken with fear and there were tears in her eyes: I'd never seen Medea in such a state and it alarmed me almost more than her words. I guided her to a chair, fetched a glass of water and held it while she drank. After a few sips the colour returned to her face and she nodded her thanks, her hands now steady enough to hold the glass herself.

Never the most impressive person in a crisis, I flapped rather uselessly at her side.

"I seem to have come at somewhat of a bad time."

We both looked up in shock at the voice. Seriously, was I running a bloody drop in centre? Then I remembered that actually, yes, I did run an office that encouraged visitors – it was on the website and everything – so I put on my professional face and tried not to look annoyed at the intrusion. I straightened up, subtly kicking over the ring of salt, though not so subtly that the man who had spoken didn't notice it, even though he politely pretended not to. Still, at least this one didn't seem to have a gun.

"No, not at all… my colleague was just feeling a bit faint."

Medea, bless her, gave a feeble nod at this, and the man inclined his head in a nod. Or rather, the *vampire* did. I realised with a start that twilight had arrived; so much of the day had been taken up with the police and clearing up I hadn't noticed it was now early evening. I tried not to panic: if I started being scared of every vampire that walked in, I might as well pack up now – and though this tall, solid block of a vamp radiated a steady pulse of power, I got no Sense of threat from him. Though I have to say that if he was here to deliver an eldritch warning, I was going to be very, *very* pissed off: I would have to start giving out appointments, at this rate. The vampire watched me calmly, aware I was taking his measure and not offended by it. After a moment I smiled – assessment over – and nodded him towards a seat. He didn't move.

"How can I help you?"

"I'd like to arrange a meeting."

"That's what I'm here for."

He shook his head slightly in an 'ah, no,' gesture and gave

me a thin lipped, civil servant's smile.

"Apologies, Ms Bick, you misunderstand. My... employer would like to arrange a meeting with you."

"To... um, what purpose?"

God, I was talking like him now.

"To share information. To make your acquaintance. It has come to his attention that you are becoming an influential figure in this city..." That was news to me. "And he feels an introduction is overdue. Especially as he is aware that some of his... colleagues... have already taken the trouble to make themselves known to you."

My Sense prickled.

"Is this where I turn up alone at a deserted warehouse and he kills me?"

This got another smile, albeit one that illustrated how completely unfunny he was finding me.

"Please be assured, Ms Bick, that if my employer wished you dead he would not have bothered with such a charade. I would have simply killed you a few moments ago, while you were engrossed in helping your... fainting colleague."

"Well, that is reassuring," I muttered, though of course it was anything but. But I was sick of people trying to scare me, so I was damn well not going to show him that he had. He simply nodded at my remark, and handed me a business card. My hand didn't shake when I took it. Not too much, anyway.

"7.30. You will be expected at the doorway."

"I'll see if I am free."

Another incline of the head.

"Just so."

He turned on his heels and almost glided from the room, a vampire's silence unnerving in such a big man. I looked at the embossed card in my hand, wondering how something so flimsy could feel so heavy to me. I turned it over and read the words spelled out in exquisite calligraphy: "Side entrance. The Crypt. St Paul's Cathedral."

Holy fucking crap. Was I ever going to have a normal day again?

Chapter 15

ST PAUL'S Cathedral is one of the most famous buildings in Britain, if not the world. Though the current iconic dome was built by Sir Christopher Wren to replace the building lost to London's Great Fire in the late 17th century, there has been a St Paul's on that spot since the 7th century. That's well over a thousand years it's been hallowed ground, a space dedicated to God. And now I was being summoned there… for what? By whom? Was I supposed to believe that a nest of vampires lived under one of London's biggest landmarks? I'd been to the Crypt at St Paul's before – it was beautiful, and historic, but not exactly a space where monsters lurk. There's a gift shop and a cafe, for God's sake. Was this some elaborate joke?

Medea didn't want me to go, or at least, not to go alone, and she had a point – annoying as Cain was, I wouldn't have been averse to some company from a cool-eyed monster slayer. But he wasn't around, as usual, and I couldn't ask her to come with me on a jaunt she so clearly disapproved of. I wanted to know what the hell was going on, and if this would get me some answers, I would have to go, that was all there was to it – and as the vampire messenger had said, it seemed a little too convoluted for a ploy to kill me, when clearly there were plenty of other opportunities. But I wasn't stupid, and after the last few days I wasn't taking any chances, so I went in armed for bear.

Though when I arrived at Paternoster Square, very conscious of the gun, silver-laced spray and wooden stake weighing down my handbag, I felt more than a little ridiculous. This wasn't some isolated rendezvous: the whole area around St Paul's – always a tourist spot – had been redeveloped recently, so now housed a bustling shopping centre and some of the busiest bars in the City. The night was young but there were plenty of people around: late night shoppers laden with bags, smokers huddled outside the pubs, the sound of their chatter loud in the evening air. It takes more than a recession to stop the English drinking, and in this part of town there was still plenty of money to go round. I watched them for a moment – sorely tempted to give up the whole thing and go for a beer myself – but instead I steeled myself and went in search of the door I had been directed to.

The main entrance to the Crypt was, as I expected, closed for the day. It took a few moments of fruitless searching before I found a smaller, unmarked side door, tucked away in the garden of the cathedral, partly camouflaged by greenery and hidden from the main glare of the tourists. Old, weathered-looking wood was set back slightly in the stone, and even touching it sent my Sense buzzing. It's hard to describe the sensation exactly: the nearest I can give you is the feeling you get walking past a nightclub when you can feel the pulse of the music, knowing that inside it must be deafening. Suddenly this seemed like a really, really bad idea. I turned to retreat, but before I could take a step the big vampire was before me, his eyes oil black in the dimness.

"Ms Bick. I do hope you haven't been waiting long."

He held out his hand in an old-fashioned gesture of courtesy and, not knowing what else to do, I took it. I knew in that instant what Cain had meant about power held in, because my Sense almost recoiled: I could feel it, an ocean of strength dammed up inside him. I tried not to shake, but I knew that my heartbeat would already have betrayed me to his vampire senses. He knew just how terrified I was – and, as if in recognition, he turned and gave me that thin-mouthed smile again, nodding politely, as if he expected my reaction and was neither offended nor gratified by it. Then he pushed open the heavy wooden door as if it weighed nothing at all, and led me into the devil's lair.

I tried to stay both calm and sharp as I was led down several sets of worn stone stairs into the darkness. The vampire at my side didn't speak, just matched his pace carefully to mine as he guided me down barely illuminated twisting staircases, punctuated by small, narrow landings, that took us far deeper into the earth than I knew the crypt to be. For a few moments, I just concentrated on not losing my footing on the uneven stone, barely able to see my feet beneath me. We emerged, eventually, into a cool, low-roofed room, a small antechamber lit only by candles and decorated with a large tapestry illustrating the grisly end of St Sebastian – perhaps as a dark joke, or maybe the vampires genuinely felt an affinity with a saint who was impaled to death. With a curt bow, the massive vampire disappeared through another wooden door, but before I even had a chance to wonder at what lay beyond, he reappeared.

"He's ready for you."

A flash of distaste flickered across his face, though I couldn't tell if it was for me. I nodded, mutely, and followed him through the entrance, and then all I could do was gape. The room he led me into was pure dungeon chic: the low stone roof gave it a sense of closeness, but it was immense, and looked all the more so for being so sparsely furnished. A couple of well-padded leather chairs sat in the foreground, some screens and tapestries dotted the walls, but what grabbed the attention was the massive, wood-framed bed that was set into an alcove, its ornately carved headboard pushed back against one of the walls. A bed, I couldn't help but notice, which was currently occupied – or at least, was being sprawled over – by a *very* naked couple. It was hard to notice much else after that, but my Sense was less easily distracted and pulled my focus to the far wall, where a compact Asian man dressed in the traditional outfit of a Samurai warrior stood so motionless it took me a moment to realise he wasn't a statue – only the steady pulse of power coming from him gave him away as a vampire of some age. With the merest nod to me, my guide slid into position beside him, taking up an equally silent sentry stance, with a stillness so absolute I could barely believe he had ever moved at all. Which left me face to face with my host, who had emerged smiling from behind one of the heavily brocaded screens that stood near the bed. And when I say face to face, I mean… sort of. Because he was also naked. And handsome. Very, *very*, 'put someone's eye out' naked. And handsome. Did I mention handsome? Even in my head I was gibbering.

"I'm actually up here," he chuckled, and I felt his voice thrum in my blood. My Sense quivered, and the rest of me nearly followed. The vampire put a finger under my chin and tilted my face towards his, his hand slightly warm from the blood he'd clearly just consumed, his lips as full and flushed as if I had kissed them. Did I just think that? Speechless, I cast a panicked glance at the figures on the bed, but they were definitely alive: whatever had just taken place here, it hadn't been murder. He watched my gaze and flashed me a lascivious smirk.

"Does that disgust or excite you?"

I shrugged, feigning a confidence I didn't feel. "Oh, the debauched bisexual bloodsucker routine is always a classic," I said, and nodded to the surroundings. "And you've got the decor for it."

He looked vaguely amused by my answer.

"What makes you think it's a routine?"

"Well, you knew I was coming – you invited me, after all – so it's not like I caught you by surprise. What makes *you* think I care one way or another?"

He stepped back, slightly, as if I had surprised him, and he was appraising me anew.

"You'd be amazed by how little labels matter after the first hundred years or so." Another grin, his teeth white and sharp. "Besides," he added, conspiratorially, "most people think it's hot."

"I'm sure they do, but if I wanted this sort of thing, I have satellite TV. And in your circles it might be considered polite to greet people without your pants on, but most of my meetings aren't clothing optional."

This time he looked properly amused. "Really? Most people find *this* hot, too." He stretched his arms out by his sides, as if inviting me to examine him. It took every inch of my willpower to keep my eyes on his face.

"Some people find Justin Bieber hot. We live in a crazy world."

He barked out a shocked laugh, and it took him a fraction of a second too long to put his face back into the look-how-enigmatic-and-sexy-I-am expression for me to believe it wasn't at least partly an act. He nodded in a gesture of conciliation, looking more amused than chastised. "My apologies. I'll only be a moment."

He stepped behind the screen. I stood rigid, waiting, trying not to look either at the couple on the bed or the stony-faced sentinels watching the whole thing. A moment later he returned in – oh, no, I kid you not – leather trousers. That's not even the worst part: the awful thing was, he actually suited them. He looked *great*, in fact, like the love child of Jesus and Jim Morrison, all lean, sculpted torso and soft hair hanging in dark waves to his shoulders, a contrast to the pale marble of his skin. It was an... affecting image, to say the least, made all the more so by the fact that he clearly knew it.

He gestured to one of the chairs, and waited until I was seated before taking the one opposite me.

"Can I have someone fetch you a drink? Some champagne, perhaps?"

"Can they bring you a shirt?"

He smiled at me. "Come, I can't do all of the compromising."

"Perhaps you could do some of the explaining?" I paused. "And, alright, I'll have a glass of champagne."

OK, that might not have been smart, but frankly by this stage my mouth was a little dry and I felt like I needed a drink. Barely had I spoken the words than some flunky appeared with a chilled glass filled to the brim, then disappeared into the shadows as quickly as he arrived. Clearly we weren't quite as alone as I'd thought: there must be rooms beyond this where they kept the non-gothic furniture and the boring things like cupboards and fridges and washing machines. Judging from what I'd seen so far, they would get through a lot of laundry – if not a lot of clothing, then an awful lot of sheets. Champagne or not, I was sobered to think I didn't have a clue how many vampires were actually in here. The one I was currently concerned with watched me curiously for a moment, then arranged his features into friendliness.

"So, you are Cassandra Bick?"

"Apparently so."

"Do you know the legend of Cassandra?" he asked, mildly. "She was doomed by the gods to be able to see the future, but for no one ever to believe her prophecies. Imagine the torment of always knowing the truth, but never being able to communicate it."

I shrugged.

"Well, not really a problem for me, since most of the time I have enough trouble understanding the present. Like what's happening now, for instance. Or knowing who I am talking to."

"Ah. My apologies. I am Laclos."

"Of course you are. Louis and Lestat being taken."

He shrugged, a half smile, either unbothered by my sarcasm, or planning to eviscerate me, I really couldn't tell.

"Yes, obviously that's not my real name, but sometimes it can be useful to play to the clichés, and it has served me well for long enough. Besides, I liked the book. He was a quite charming man, actually."

I frowned, until the tiny part of my brain where what remains of my education lives flickered into action. Choderelos de Laclos – the Frenchman who had written Dangerous Liaisons, a book of debauchery set just before the French Revolution. I'm not sure if he wrote it before the Revolution, or after it, I was hazy on that part. I could only really remember the film. But I knew it wasn't written yesterday. Laclos watched the wheels turn in my head, smiling at my expression.

"You were alive during the French Revolution?" That meant he was what, 250? 300? That would make him one of the oldest – and most powerful – vampires I had ever met.

"I was already centuries old at the time of the Revolution."

Gulp.

"Doesn't that make you a bit too old for leather trousers?"

Again, a laugh, but I felt a flicker of disapproval emanate

from the statues on the back wall. Clearly taking the piss out of the boss wasn't allowed, even if Laclos himself seemed immune to my mockery, or even actually rather enjoying it. And why should he be bothered by my opinion? He really was in *exceptionally* good shape. And fast, too, because there was a blur of movement and he was behind me, leaning down over the chair, his mouth at my ear. My hands gripped the leather of the armrests tightly as if to steady myself, trying to calm down my heartbeat as my skin prickled at his proximity, but the husky laugh against my suddenly flushed cheek let me know how completely I had failed. With a feather-light gesture, he moved my hair aside and laid the briefest of kisses on my neck, but I barely had time to register the shudder of terror and desire his touch elicited than he was back in his chair, poised and still, as if he had never moved and I had imagined the whole thing. He cast a fake contrite glance down at his clothing, or what little of it he wore.

"Something tells me you secretly quite approve."

I opened my mouth to speak but for once my gobbiness failed me. I raised the glass to my lips and realised it was empty, only for it, a split second later, to once again be full. Though frankly, fast as the hand-servant vampire was, I managed to empty it again at a pretty impressive speed. Laclos was watching me, smug as a cat, and it was his self-satisfied expression that eventually stirred me into speech.

"I'm sure you didn't bring me here to get my opinion on your wardrobe," I snapped, and his face turned instantly serious.

"You're quite right, Ms Bick. I brought you here to find out what you know about who is killing London's vampires."

Chapter 16

I SUDDENLY wished I had said no the champagne. My stomach lurched, and I was aware I was doing a very bad job of not pulling an expression of goggly-eyed shock.

"I... don't know what you mean."

Laclos looked at me coolly for a long, quiet moment, and my Sense felt the air in the room thicken – he wasn't the only one scrutinising me. I tried not to let my gaze go to the back of the room, where I knew at least two vampires of considerable age and power were standing.

"You don't?"

"I... honestly don't. I work with vampires, I'm sure you know that, but that's *all* I do – I arrange parties. They're my customers. Why would I want them dead?"

"I'm not saying that you do. However, not wanting them dead doesn't preclude you standing by while someone else kills them."

"I wouldn't do that either!" I protested. Then I paused – I had no reason to lie, and maybe honesty was my best bet of getting out of here unperforated. "I actually have no idea what I *would* do if I knew someone was killing vampires, mind. I don't suppose I could exactly call the police. But if you have some super secret cadre of fangy feds you want me to call if I hear anything, feel free to give me their number."

Laclos raised an eyebrow, and I couldn't tell if I was annoying or amusing him. Then again, I get that a lot.

"Really..." I insisted. "I don't know anything about any killings."

"Not even those that have been all over your newspapers?"

"Those were *vampires*?"

I felt an icy trickle of shock run down my spine. Suddenly a lot of things were starting to become worryingly clear. Laclos paused, as if not sure how much to tell me.

"Some of them were."

"How do you know?"

He waved his hand in a gesture of exaggerated modesty.

"I'm not sure if you're aware of how we… function in this city, Ms Bick. How we organise, for want of a better word. But please be assured when I tell you that I am not without… influence in London. Or without friends."

"Well, you do seem like a friendly guy."

He smiled, completely without humour.

"If they're vampires… how are the police finding bodies? I thought you turned to dust when you were killed." Even as I asked the question, the answer came to me, springing from a conversation I'd once had in the dark. "Wait, they're *young* vampires? Because it's the old ones who disintegrate, right?"

He nodded, as if I had passed some sort of test.

"That is correct. Whoever is targeting vampires is picking off the youngest, and therefore weakest, of our race."

"Then if there are bodies, how does no one… know about you?"

Another smile, this one slightly tighter. "As I said, I am not without influence. But it is becoming… worrying. There are only so many bodies that can be lost and so many autopsies we can fake before people start to ask inconvenient questions. So far not even all of the murders have been reported, but I'm not sure how long we can keep that the case. The police are very sensitive about accusations of bribery, these days; there have been one too many scandals to make it as easy as it used to be. Frankly I'd prefer it if they were killing elders, it would mean a lot less paperwork." He sighed, and for the first time I saw genuine concern behind that flippant facade. I actually felt sorry for him.

"I wish I could help you, but I don't know anything."

"Perhaps you don't. Perhaps not yet."

"I don't think the killer is exactly planning to pop up and tell me his plans." I laughed, nervously, but my pulse jumped, and something in Laclos' face told me that my reaction hadn't gone unnoticed. What if the killer already had told me his plans? Maybe not specifics, but didn't I know someone for whom 'kill vampires' was pretty much a mission statement? Laclos looked at me, hearing my heartbeat, and his voice grew colder.

"You really do need to know how badly I will take it if you withhold information from me."

There was a pause, and then his expression changed, and he was abruptly all smiles, a politician glad a difficult meeting was done. "Well, I am aware I have imposed on you long enough. The Counsel will show you out. I must attend to my other guests."

Barely had he said the words, than the large, dark eyed man who had originally guided me here was at my side. He took my arm as he led me towards the exit, Laclos watching me go, his expression an odd mix of predatory and pleased.

Chapter 17

THE SURGE of fear and adrenalin I'd felt in the crypt (I was ignoring the fact that a worryingly significant component of that feeling might have also been lust) had left my legs shaking so the walk home was more of an effort than it should have been. My Sense was still overwhelmed by the proximity to so many strong vampires – Laclos and the Counsel weren't the only ones in that room with centuries under their belts – and Laclos' news of the murders had left my mind in a dither, too. However, having learned my lesson, I was careful to stick to a well-lit and populated route – I wasn't sure what the hell I'd run into last night but I wasn't taking any more chances.

What had I just witnessed? I had contacts and clients, if not exactly friends, in the world of the Others, and I knew the vampires in London weren't in some rigid hierarchy, but I had always assumed they had some sort of structure that reflected our own. I knew some vampires were older and stronger, and had followers, or progeny, or perhaps even just companions – human or vampire – but if there was some sort of vampire king or council, no one was telling me. So who was Laclos and how did he fit into their society? I had to think that, if real estate was as much an indicator of wealth and power in undead circles as it is in the human world, then he had some serious clout – after all, you couldn't get a more prime location than under St Paul's. Yet he'd come to me. Why? Was he connected with the attack on my office? My mysterious party crasher? Did he know about Cain? Even just thinking about it was giving me a headache, so I was seriously pleased to get home.

Like many people who are sociable for a living, I like to spend time with just my own company. My favourite way of unwinding is a night in with DVDs and the cat, and that's on those days when I *haven't* been cavorting with a psychopath or been lured to ancient crypts by erotically overcharged vampires. Perhaps it was more than that, as well. I had always wondered if Cain and I had brought death to that burning house, and it made me wary of opening my new home – and my life – to anyone else. Now I wondered if that curse was following us still.

I tried to shake off *that* cheery thought as I opened the door, calling for Dante and wondering if – and, yes, half-hoping that – Cain would be waiting for me as well. Instead, unsurprisingly, not even the cat could be bothered to come and greet me, so I took off my coat, dumped my bag on the hallway table and schlepped through to the kitchen. Too tired to even think about cooking, I stuck a couple of slices of bread in the toaster and poured myself a generous slug of red wine. The champagne lay heavy on my stomach, churned by nerves, so I thought the combination of carbs and a nice red might calm me down a little. Slumped against the kitchen counter, I heard a thump from the living room; was Cain making his usual entry, never using a door like a normal person when there's a window to break into? Then another clatter. Definitely not Cain, then, he never made a noise.

"Dante! Dinner!" I called, in a half-hearted effort to stop my cat knocking things over by distracting him with food. Then I paused. My Sense was dulled – like hearing after a loud gig – but I wasn't deaf, and it was trying to tell me something. And almost as important as my Sense was my lifelong geekiness – because there's one thing any geek can always tell you…

It's *never* just the cat.

I clutched the knife in my hand tighter, but it was a butter knife – not exactly a machete in terms of self-defence, so I decided the bottle of wine might be a better bet and hefted it into a swinging grip. Really, someone had picked the wrong day to mess with me. I peered into the living room, anger buzzing in my veins – then instantly turning to terror as I saw what was waiting there. It was the biggest, nastiest... *thing* I had ever seen. It looked like the offspring of a tiger that had been raped by a T-Rex, and as it reared up on two legs, all muscle and claws and teeth as long as knives, it was clear that it knew I was there. With a roar it dived towards me, and I did the only thing I could do. I screamed like a baby and fell backwards, my cowardice at least saving me from having my face slashed off. I kicked the coffee table at the monster's legs to try and slow it, but it swiped through the wood as if it were paper. The bottle, hurled at its head with all my strength, fared no better, bouncing off its skull harmlessly, though spraying an arc of red across the walls and carpet as it went. I couldn't help thinking, in terrified irrelevance, that if I lived I'd have a hell of a cleaning bill.

Pushing such unhelpful thoughts aside, I scuttled backwards in an ungainly shuffle as the creature advanced towards me, drool dripping from its ferocious looking jaws. I kicked out as I went, sending anything in my way towards it in a desperate attempt to slow its progress. A toppling stack of glossy magazines went over and, proving against all odds that fashion mags can do something other than make you feel fat and depressed, they won me a valuable moment as the creature's hoof landed heavily on them only for it to lose its footing on the shifting pile, sprawling to the floor with an inhuman howl. I leapt to my feet and fled to the kitchen, frantically searching for something, anything, I could use as a weapon. My knife block was empty; the victim of my sloppy housekeeping, all my knives were still in the dishwasher. Whoever said an untidy house never killed anyone might be proved wrong tonight. My eyes blurring with tears, I threw the wooden block at the monster as it appeared in the doorway, but it was as useless as the wine bottle, and didn't slow it an inch.

Then Dante really was there, darting past the creature with a hiss, his ears down and his fur up, claws out and teeth bared. He slashed at the intruder, drawing something that looked more like oil than blood, before the monster reacted in pained irritation and swatted my poor pet away as if he were a fly, Dante's mewl of distress as he was thrown through the air bringing a sob to my throat.

"You better not have hurt my cat, you fucker!" I screamed, but that was about as effective as you can imagine. I swear, the bloody thing actually smiled. I was going to die, here, alone, and this thing was going to kill me. I sank to my knees, and wondered if I'd see my murdered friends again, if I'd once more be reunited with my parents. I didn't believe in heaven, or think there was an afterlife, but at that moment I wished with all my heart that one existed. Then at the thought of my mother an idea struck me, and as the creature lunged towards me I ducked under it, grabbed my mum's Le Creuset frying pan from its stand and swung it with every ounce of my strength right into the thing's face. There was a hiss of burning flesh and the sickening splinter of teeth and the monster let out a howl of agony, rearing back. It hadn't been lovely before, and now, flattened and fractured and seeping black blood, it was even more grotesque.

"Want some more, you bastard? Come and fucking get it!" I yelled, stupidly, hoisting the pan as if it were a baseball bat, ready to take another swing. The creature paused, then looked at me, and I saw something like fear flicker in those inhuman eyes. Then it let out another howl and spun on its heels, hurling itself out of my window, taking most of the now-tattered frame with it, and suddenly I was alone again.

Shaking and crying, I slumped to the floor, hugging my life-saving iron pan as if it were my mother herself, so desperate was I for even that comfort. I'd never felt so scared or alone. What was happening here? Why was everything and everyone suddenly so interested in me?

Chapter 18

IT WAS much, much later. Dante – mercifully unharmed, if clearly not best pleased by his monstrous encounter – was curled up sullenly beside me as I lay on the bed, both gun and frying pan lying within easy reach, when I heard the tiniest of noises. My Sense knew almost straight away that it was Cain, but I felt a surge of anger so hot that I nearly picked up the gun and shot him anyway, just to see if a bullet would at least dent the fucker. Where had he been? Why hadn't he been *here*, when there were monsters to be fought? And if he couldn't manage that, couldn't he at least be here when there were emergency glaziers to be called, and extortionate fees to be handed over for boarded up windows? If nothing else, he could have picked up a hammer and made himself useful.

I saw him come into the room, undressing silently in the dark like an errant husband stayed out too late and scared of waking up a nagging wife. That's how sure he was of his welcome in my bed, and for a moment I hated him for it. I tensed as he slid in beside me: he must know something had happened – the flat was in a state of disarray that even my shoddy housekeeping couldn't explain. How could he be so calm? I was going to give him a piece of my mind; he could just sod off to wherever he had come from if he thought I was putting up with this. But when I turned over in bed to face him he was looking at me with such a sad, earnest expression that my anger died in my throat.

"Why weren't you here?" I demanded, though it came out the whine of a petulant child. He gently pushed the hair from my face, as if scared that he might break me.

"I'm sorry. But I'm here now."

That wasn't an answer. I knew that. What good was that? But then he leaned forward and kissed me, slowly, and I felt myself melt, reacting as I always did to the heat and comfort of his embrace. As his kiss hardened my own became more fierce, his hands on my face, holding me. He pushed me firmly back, moving on top of me, his familiar weight trapping me, but somehow earthing me: he was my shield, my safety rail, and I felt nothing could hurt me with him in my arms. Softly his mouth moved over my throat as he made his way down my body. I was dissolving, blurring, but he brought me back sharply with a delicious sliver of pain as his teeth pulled gently at the silver crucifix in my nipple, just hard enough to hurt, a delightful contrast to warm pleasure of his hand, his fingers now moving deftly between my legs. His tongue was rough as it outlined the tattoo on my hip, and as his head dipped lower all my fear and anger was forgotten, drowned out by desire as I bucked beneath him.

Finally, eventually, he pulled away from me, retracing his route up my body, a man in no hurry at all. I clung to him as he entered me, wrapping my legs around him. Pinned by his weight, his strength, I felt weightless, and free, and I could do nothing but give into him, letting him hold me tightly as my body twisted and glowed.

Again, it was later. I lay dazed and sated, my mind a happy blur, my body a sweaty, trembling mess as I curled up like a cat against Cain's chest, nuzzled into the crook of his arm. He had one palm flat on my stomach, a warm, steady and somehow calming presence. It was a contradiction that never ceased to puzzle me – that despite being the craziest person I knew (at least until this week) Cain always made me feel so safe. Maybe when someone pulls you out of a burning building, you tend towards the hero worship – though, even in my giddy state, a tiny part of me couldn't help remembering that he hadn't exactly excelled himself on the hero front lately.

"You know that something bad is happening."

I felt rather than heard his words, but right at that moment it seemed that nothing bad could really happen, not when he was here. I stretched back against him, luxuriating in the warmth of his body, the latent power of his embrace. His hand moved idly across my belly, stroking me absently as if I was a pet, and it was an oddly soothing gesture. Frankly, it was all I could do not to purr.

"What?" I managed, eventually, when my hormone-addled brain registered he'd spoken.

"I said that something bad is happening."

"Yeah, well, I'm starting to realise that." I frowned, not sure what I wanted to hear from him. "But... honestly, is it really? Is something worse than normal happening, or is it just the usual stuff but this time I'm involved?"

He kissed my shoulder, gently.

"It's worse, trust me. And we haven't even got to the really bad parts yet."

"Well, someone killing vampires is bad enough, isn't it?" He snorted and I smacked him lightly. "And don't start up with the 'you could be living in Rwanda' lecture."

He laughed, a throaty chuckle that I felt rumbling through his chest against my hair. "Well, since you mentioned it... or London, 150 years ago. This isn't bad. You don't want to see it when it's bad."

"So what can I do?"

"You can leave. Take Medea with you, go away for a couple of weeks. I can't function when I have to split my attention between protecting you and trying to find out what is going on, never mind when I'm trying to stop it."

I refrained from pointing out that so far he hadn't done a

whole lot of protecting.

"So I just leave?"

"You're clearly a target. Take yourself off the playing field for a while, leave it to the experts."

"And what will you do?"

"Whatever I have to."

I paused, almost scared to ask my next question.

"Will there be a town for me to come back to?"

"That depends on what I have to do." He said it with no menace, no emotion, and it terrified me all the more for that. Because I suddenly knew – knew as clearly as I knew that he was here beside me – that the man who was so tenderly caressing me and speaking so calmly would raze this city to the ground if he thought it was the only solution. And what's more, it wouldn't be the first time he had done something like that.

Sometimes I really hated my Sense.

Chapter 19

SOMEHOW, THOUGH, suggesting the 'pack up and get the hell out of Dodge' option to Medea just didn't seem possible. It felt, well, just a bit silly. Not that telling her I'd been attacked in my flat by a monster felt particularly normal, it has to be said, though of course she took it a lot more calmly than I would have had our situations been reversed. She once again listened to the whole story without comment, only asking me questions when she was sure I was done.

"So the iron in the pan hurt it, and it fled?"

"Yes. That means it's mystical, right? I mean, it looked like nothing that I can imagine existing on earth."

"Well, either that or you hit it really, *really* hard."

I pulled a face at her.

"Seriously. Does this mean it was... summoned? Conjured? Could someone do that?"

She considered the question. "Someone with enough power, certainly. But it would have to be a lot of power, to summon a creature like that from one of the hells."

"Um, *one* of the hells?"

Medea cast me a look of patient pity.

"There are multiple belief systems that posit that every time you summon a spirit, you are summoning it from one of an almost infinite number of alternate dimensions, many of which would be classed as 'hell'."

"So... are you saying I fought off an actual... demon?"

"We can assume so."

"Do you think it was the same person who broke in here, then? You said they had a lot of power."

"I think that's likely. I hope so, anyway."

"*Hope?*"

"Do you want *more* than one extremely powerful supernatural entity after you?"

I sighed. "Good point. Can it come after me again? What it I put salt around my windows and doors?"

Medea frowned at me. "Um, you'll make a mess of your windowsills and carpets?"

"It works on TV," I pouted, and this time she really did look like she pitied me. "And you used it the other day!"

"As a conduit for a minor spell," she corrected me. "Look, I don't know how much I can do, but I can try and lay some protective wards down. They may not help much in terms of stopping things, but they might give you an indication if your home has been breached, act as an early warning system."

"Even that would be useful, trust me. Since the demon – or whoever conjured him – somehow managed to bugger my burglar alarm and Cain seems to be remarkably lapse about arriving in time to save the day lately, I could do with all the help I can get."

I tried to ignore her sceptical expression at the mention of his name. I thought back to that creature, and what a lucky escape I'd had. "Honestly, Mey, it was like nothing on earth."

"Well, precisely," she murmured, though not unkindly. Then as she reached across to refill the coffee, she frowned at me in alarm. "Your arm! If it scratched you, Cassandra, I should look at those wounds, they could be infected… I know some healing spells."

I looked down at the vivid criss-crossing of red lines that currently latticed my arm.

"No, that was Dante. After the creature vanished, he was covered in gunk so I had to give him a bath."

"Ah." She nodded, and I could see she was trying not to

laugh. "Perhaps just some TCP from the First Aid kit, then?"

"Super."

Medea's hard-to-ruffle serenity was catching: even better was her instinctive ability to know when it was time to do a cake run. She left me in the office, smelling faintly of TCP and huddled over my laptop – I couldn't afford to replace the main computers until the insurance money came through – and fretting over the loss of my diary and paper files. Still, there are few things in the world that can't be improved by a big slice of cake. Then Medea came back into the office, her face ashen and her hands shaking, and it seemed that this was one of them.

"Have you seen today's paper?"

"Too busy recovering from my own news," I shrugged, trying to make her smile, but she wasn't to be distracted. She leaned over me, and switched my browser to a local news site.

"Look at the top story. The Covent Garden killer has struck again."

Something about the way she said it made me snatch the laptop away from her, to get a better look at the story on screen. Two murders, both within a few yards of one another. The police were trying to blame gangs, but the papers weren't buying – and rightly so. My blood froze as I saw that the bodies had already been identified.

"The names… oh, my God."

"They were our clients, Cass. Both of them. Someone *is* using our files to pick their victims. To kill vampires."

My stomach plummeted. Laclos had been right. So had Cain. But could he actually be the one behind it? The timetable would certainly fit – the killings might have started before he showed up at my place, but I had no way of knowing how long he had actually been in town – and it would certainly explain all of his mysterious disappearances.

"I need to go home. I have to find Cain, find out if he knows anything about this."

Medea scowled at me.

"I think that's the *least* of what you need to find out about Cain."

Well, whatever Cain was doing, he wasn't hiding from me. I found him where I left him, naked in my bed, half-covered in my duvet and half-covered in my cat, who lay stretched across him like blanket of fur. It was such a cosy, inviting picture that I almost forgot what I came home for and just climbed in beside him. Plus, if my cat liked him, how bad could he really be? Then I sighed. Dante was just a typical feline: he'd merrily snuggle up to Jack the Ripper if there was a tin of cat food in it for him.

Cain, clearly having been alerted to my arrival by the sound of my keys in the lock, gave me a lazy smile as I came into the bedroom, which was nearly enough to distract me from noticing that he was reaching over to put his gun back down on the bedside table. Nice to know he wasn't planning to shoot me, anyway.

"I didn't expect you back this early."

"I need to talk to you."

Whatever Cain's true nature – human or Other – he reacted to that sentence the way that all men are programmed to; with a frown. He sat up, gently pushing aside Dante, who gave a mewl of annoyance and then reformed himself into a fluffy puddle in the warmth Cain left behind him.

"Do you have any food?" Cain asked, by way of answer to my statement, climbing out of bed and padding, naked, into my kitchen.

I followed him patiently. I'm not particularly domesticated

– you're shocked, I can tell – so I knew this wouldn't be a long distraction. I know there's some fantasy that us single ladies live in white-walled oases with fluffy towels and scented candles and fridges full of salad, but my flat wasn't much to write home about even before the demon got there, and, as Cain was discovering, it wasn't a place rife with foraging opportunities.

"Don't you ever shop?"

He was staring into my fridge, as if that would magically make food materialise there, replacing the current contents: an open tin of cat food, a bottle of prosecco and a packet of those individually wrapped cheeses that always seem a good idea at the time but never look quite so tempting once you have them home and which had been there for longer than I cared to remember. Still, he wasn't wearing any clothes and the whole bending over routine was doing very nice things to his arse and arms, so I said nothing and left him to look, which was pretty much what I was doing.

"Seriously. There is *no* food in here." He said this as if it were news to me.

"I eat out a lot."

"Clearly."

Disgruntled, he opened the freezer, but unless he fancied vodka for breakfast, there wasn't much solace there, either. He shook his head and sighed, presumably in despair at the ways of modern womanhood, and started opening all my cupboards. Honestly, what is it with men when they do that? What do they expect to find?

"Your cat has more food here than you do."

"He finds it harder to pay for takeaways. Cain…"

Catching my tone, he turned, but his smile was wolfish.

"So, you get me all starving then you don't have any food in. What kind of host are you?"

"Most of my guests give me more notice. And don't break into my house."

He ignored that, still smiling, and reached out to grab me. Tempted as I was – he really was *very* naked – I stepped back sharply.

"I really need to talk to you."

He sighed again, disappointed, and turned back to the fridge and pulled out the mini-cheeses, sniffing at them dubiously. It would be beyond ironic if my mysterious gladiator got felled by out of date dairy, but I left him to it.

"Why would you want to wrap cheeses individually?" he asked, holding one aloft in sceptical examination.

"I don't know. To make them feel special?"

I was losing my patience fast. Cain unwrapped a cheese and popped the whole thing into his mouth, grimacing slightly as he bit into it.

"Please, can you put some clothes on so we can talk?"

He looked at me in amusement.

"I'm perfectly capable of talking without being dressed."

Honestly, I don't see any naked men for ages, then suddenly I'm surrounded by hotties who won't put their pants on.

"Well, it's distracting for me."

He leaned forward and planted a light, slightly cheddar-flavoured kiss on my mouth.

"That's a comfort."

And with that he chuckled and headed off to the bedroom, taking the packet of cheeses with him.

Cain was fully clothed and frowning at me. I realised I liked him smiling and naked so much better.

"You're really asking if I'm doing this?"

"Yes. Yes, I am. I need to know."

He paused, looking at the newspaper I'd picked up on the way home.

"No. No, I'm not."

"Do you promise?" It was a child's question, a whine, but I couldn't help it. He sighed.

"Honestly, Cass, do you think if I were doing it, I'd bother to lie?"

And of course that was true. Why would Cain lie about killing vampires – or killing anything, for that matter? I'm not sure if it's because he doesn't think it's wrong, or if he doesn't mind if it upsets me, or both.

"Why do you even care?" he asked, genuinely puzzled.

"Because it's murder!"

He looked sceptical.

"And because someone is using my files to do it. It can't be a coincidence that only the vampire files were stolen, Cain. I'm involved and I don't know how or why, but I feel like I just handed someone a loaded gun and showed them where to point it."

"But why does that bother you? Besides, the killings started before your files were taken. Admittedly, you've probably made the killer's life a lot easier by giving them a handy list to tick off, but that hardly makes it your fault."

"Gee, thanks." I sighed. "Can we just pretend for one second we're on the same page when it comes to murder being a bad thing?"

"I don't see it as murder. I see it as pest control."

"I **knew** these people, Cain! I met them, I talked to them, I asked them about their favourite films, and what music they liked, and what they wanted in a lover. They had jobs. Some of them had families. They weren't just nameless monsters. There are people in the world who will miss them. How can you be so cold about this?"

"How can you be so stubborn?"

I struggled to maintain my composure against his chilly calm. "Can't we just agree to disagree and move on?"

He shrugged.

"OK. So you know it's not me, now."

I paused. Did I believe him? I did, though if I was completely honest, I had no idea why I did. So now came the real question. "Will you help me stop them?"

For once, his composure cracked.

"Help you? You can't be involved in this!"

"I'm already involved in this! We both know that."

He frowned, but since we were sitting in the ruins of my demon-ravaged flat, he could hardly argue with that.

"So, basically, you're saying that you want my help to stop a bunch of killings that, when it comes down to it, I actually quite approve of?"

I nodded. "That pretty much sums it up, yes."

"Why?"

I hesitated. Here was the gamble, and it scared me more than anything else that had happened to me so far.

"Because I'm asking you to."

There was a pause that seemed to last my whole life. Cain gave me one of those long, steady looks that felt like he was stripping me down to my bones. Then he nodded, slowly, and his lips twitched into almost a smile.

"OK. But for the love of God, if I'm sticking around to help you, you've got to promise me you'll buy some proper food."

So, of course, we went back to bed. Look, it's not like I get so much action that I can afford to pass up the opportunity when I have a hot, horny man in the house, and whatever our disagreements, the bedroom was one place that Cain and I were always perfectly in accord. I woke from a pleasant daze to the sound of running water and the small, domestic sounds of someone having a shower – those notes of a shared home life that I was all too unfamiliar with. I lay there for a moment, revelling in that pleasantly achy afterglow of fantastic sex, but then Medea's words drifted unbidden back into my mind, an unwelcome intruder into my post-coital haze. Other than the fact that he was a great lover – and I mean, a really, really, *really* great lover – what did I actually know about Cain? He popped in and out of my life without explanation. I had no idea where he was when he wasn't with me, what he did, where he lived. I didn't know how old he was, where he was born, what his parents did – I didn't even know if Cain was his first or last name. So, stirred on by curiosity and the knowledge that, if I didn't at least try this, I'd have Medea to answer to, I tiptoed into the bathroom. For a moment, the sight of him – naked, wet, oblivious – distracted me so much I almost lost my resolve. He was someone I'd never get tired of looking at: all that lean muscle and power, the scars emphasising rather than distracting from his attractiveness, a network of lines delineating his life. He sensed me looking and turned to me with a slow, lazy smile, an unmistakable offer.

I felt a surge of heat from my thighs to my hairline. It was extremely tempting, and as Cain rather deliberately ran his lathered up hands across his chest and down the front of his body, enjoying my transfixed gaze, it was obvious that whatever our earlier exertions he wasn't out of energy just yet. Why the hell did I need to know, anyway? He had agreed to help me, we'd just had some rather amazing sex and he was clearly – and, ahem, *visibly*, now, in a good mood – so why spoil it by risking finding out something I didn't want to know? But Medea had shaken me with her overblown talk of death, and besides, what harm could it do? I couldn't believe I had never even thought to try it before. So I closed my eyes – much as it pained me to block out that slick, soapy vision – and leaned back on the sink, clearing my mind of everything and just letting my Sense gently expand, rolling out in front of me like a mist, embracing Cain, caressing the lines of his body in my mind, and slowly, slowly, probing deeper…

The world tilted, a wave of blackness washing over me as I fell. I could hear screaming, far away, and only slowly realised that it was me. Then my head hit cold enamel, my legs folded beneath me and the world went dark.

"Cass? Cass? Cassandra? Are you OK?"

I was shivering, and naked, and it took me a while to understand that this was because I was lying on my bathroom floor, a still-damp-from-the-shower Cain cradling me in his arms, his face creased with concern. But when I looked up at him, it was in unaduIterated horror.

"My God, what *are* you?"

"You fainted," he said, after a pause that went on a moment too long.

I stared at him. "That's not what I asked you."

"Have you eaten today?"

I sat up sharply, then regretted it as the world took a spin, and I sank back down dizzily.

"Stop stalling and answer me!"

"I just want to make sure you're alright."

"*I'm* fine. What are *you*?"

He sat back, helping me sit up, propping me carefully against the side of the bath as he draped a towel around my shoulders in an effort to try and stop me shaking, but as he stood, I could see the impatience in his face, together with something I'd never seen before: worry.

"You know who I am."

Annoyance made me articulate. "Even you know that's not true. I see you every few years when, remarkably unchanged by age, you drop into my life at a suitably dramatic moment then disappear without warning. I know you spend your time in horrible places hunting what you see as horrible things. But I have no idea who you really are, Cain. And that's not what I'm asking. I'm asking *what* you are. What did I just Sense?"

He gave an awkward, almost nervous and very un-Cain like laugh.

"How am I supposed to know what you Sensed? I'm still going with too much sex on an empty stomach, which is no wonder given the state of your cupboards."

Suddenly furious at his attempts to fob me off, I shut my eyes tightly and tried again. This time I was forewarned, and this time I would be careful – now I knew what to expect.

It didn't matter. It couldn't protect me – nothing could. Knowing fire burns you won't stop it hurting, and this was fire and ice at once, a maelstrom of hurt that I was drowning in. It was a blackness so deep it was blinding, a vacuum that was endless, inescapable, the coldness of eternity and the vastness of space and I was lost, trapped, alone and so very scared. Then Cain was holding me, shaking me, the warmth of his body an almost visceral shock, and when my vision cleared I could see a face that was equal parts concern and annoyance.

"You really need to stop doing that," he sighed.

Chapter 20

I WAS in bed again, though this time it wasn't in any loved up hazy sex glow: I felt like I'd been hit by a bus. Cain had had to carry me in, as I could barely walk: even putting one foot in front of the other was too much for me. He sat beside me, holding a cup of water from which he made me take slow, regular sips, his face settled into the sternly pained expression of a man who knows there is a conversation coming that he really doesn't want to have but can't see a way of avoiding.

"I can't believe you're such a bloody hypocrite." As an opener, it certainly got his attention. He frowned at me, puzzled. "All this bollocks you spout about monsters and you're no more human than they are!"

He let out a *very* weary sigh.

"You might be stubborn and you might be reckless, Cass, but you're not stupid. You've always known on some level that I'm not exactly human… whether you wanted to admit it or not."

I stared at him. He was right, of course, but it wasn't something I'd ever let myself think about, not properly: it had always been a sore spot I'd been simply too scared to prod.

"But… if you're one of them, why do you hunt them?"

He looked vaguely offended by the question.

"I'm not one of the Other races."

"So what are you?" I demanded, impatiently. "A bloody Martian?"

He looked away from me.

"Does it really matter?"

"Of course it matters!"

"You're not going to believe me."

"Try me. I'm pretty much ready to believe anything after the week I've had."

"OK." There was a long, uncomfortable pause, and I had the unnerving feeling that Cain was steeling himself. "OK. I'm... OK, there's really no way to say this that doesn't sound insane."

"Well, 'crazy' is the one thing I already know about you."

That at least got a small smile.

"OK." He inhaled, deeply. "OK. If you really have to know... if it really matters to you..."

"Stop stalling!"

Another weary sigh, like he was dragging the words from the deepest part of his soul.

"I'm an angel."

I was ready to believe almost anything. I wasn't ready to believe that.

Eventually, I stopped laughing. Cain sat with an air of exaggerated patience waiting for my hysterics to subside. I stared at him, boggled. An angel? A freaking *angel*? Now I'd heard it all. There surely couldn't be anyone less like an angel on this whole bloody planet. Trust me, the way we'd spent the afternoon hadn't exactly been angelic.

"You're kidding."

Another deep sigh. Clearly, this wasn't an unusual reaction to his news.

"I'm really not."

"An angel? And actual... *angel* angel?"

"As opposed to all those non-angel angels?"

"Like... immortal? From Heaven?"

"Yes."

"A... servant of God?"

"In a manner of speaking, yes."

"So... there's actually a God?"

Wearily: "Yes."

"Have you spoken to Him? Seen Him? Met Him? What's Heaven like? Does that mean there's a proper Hell…?" Cain looked slightly stunned by my barrage of questions. "Answer the God ones first. There's really a God?"

"I'm sorry, I'm a bit lost as to what I'm answering."

"Have you met God?"

"No."

"So you don't actually know there is a God."

"Have you met the Queen?"

"That's hardly the same, is it? Besides, I've seen her on TV. I know she exists."

"I know God exists. But, no, I've never spoken to Him. Or seen Him. Or been in the same room as Him. But I do know He's real."

"How?"

"I take it on faith."

"That's not *knowing* though, is it? It's hardly convincing."

"It is to me."

"What if you're wrong?"

He sighed. "I'm not wrong."

"So you think… you're doing God's work?"

"I *am* doing God's work."

"What if you're wrong?"

Cain gave me a look. "I'm *not* wrong. Look, this could go on forever, and we're just going around in circles. Some things you're just going to have to accept as true. Or at least accept that I believe they are true."

This conversation was a lot less satisfying than I'd expected it to be. Then a terrifying thought occurred to me.

"But I don't believe in God. Or angels."

"But you believe in ghosts and vampires?"

"I've seen them. It's not '*believing*' in them when you've

sat across a table from them, any more than you 'believe' in the sea, or the ground. They actually exist."

"Obviously, so do I."

"But I don't know you're an actual *angel*."

Cain sighed again. He really wasn't having any fun with this. Then again, it was hardly a basket of kittens for me, either.

"If you'd prefer to think of me as a deluded Other with a religious complex, that's fine with me – I honestly don't care."

"But I don't believe in God!" I was starting to feel hysterical again. He gave me a small smile and took my hand, gently.

"I really don't think God cares."

"Am I going to hell?"

The smile turned into a smirk. "I have no idea."

"Stop looking at me like I'm asking stupid questions!"

He took a breath, clearly trying not to laugh. I wanted to hit him, except I was suddenly worried that would be blasphemous and I'd be struck by lightning. Also, it would most likely hurt.

"Go on, then," he sighed. "Ask the rest of your questions."

"Can you fly?"

He swallowed a snort of laughter.

"What?"

"Or… I don't know, teleport or materialise or something?" He gawped at me. What, now, I was the crazy one? "Do you have a flaming sword?"

Cain sighed again. "This is why I never tell people."

"Oh, *this* is why? Not the fact that, ooh, I don't know, they'll think you're freaking mental?"

Cain rubbed a hand across his face, looking suddenly

tired. Then he turned back to me, and took my face in his hands, his green eyes fixed on mine. I'd never seen Cain look so serious.

"Do *you* believe me?"

I avoided that one. How could I answer? He seemed completely serious – or at least completely convinced – but I wasn't sure I was quite ready to abandon a lifetime of atheism. "Why couldn't I Sense it?"

"It's shielded. Always. It's too much for humans to process, Cass. For all your abilities, you're still only human."

I reached out and touched him, that face I was so achingly familiar with, that suddenly looked so strange to me.

"Is this… how you look? Is this your real body or just… a meat suit?"

"A meat suit?" he snorted. "You really do watch too much TV. But yes, to all intents and purposes, this is my actual body. This is how I look, on this plane of existence."

I wasn't sure that was actually an answer.

"Where are your wings?"

"I think they might draw some attention, don't you?"

"Can you… pop them out? Like Wolverine's claws?"

"I'm not even answering that."

I thought of those long, jagged scars, and realised that was a question I was too scared to ask. I paused, for which Cain looked grateful, but there was no way this was over.

"How do you even have scars?" I asked, confusing him, as I'd been working to my own internal dialogue. "Don't you… heal, or… regenerate or something?"

Again, he gave me a look, and I slapped lightly him on the arm, feeling defensive.

"I don't know, do I? I don't know what I should be asking, what I should be saying! This is a big thing to take in! It's not like you have a police record or got some girl pregnant in college, Cain. I don't know where I am here, how I'm supposed to react."

He gave me a sympathetic but slightly pained smile. "Possibly with fewer questions taken from the annals of science fiction?"

"Well, excuse me, if I'd known this was coming I would have swotted up on my Bible a little more! Though presumably you know enough about that for the both of us!"

Cain stood up, angrily, as if he was going to go, then sat down again, abruptly. His face wore an expression I didn't recognise. I think it was a look of apology. There was a long moment before he spoke.

"Look, Cassandra, I'm not trying to be difficult or opaque. But there's a lot I simply can't answer, a lot you simply can't know. You have to understand that. This *is* how I look. This *is* me. I have... powers, and abilities, but far less and far more limited than you'd think. They aren't infinite, and I'm immortal, so they're stretched a little thin, and I try not to waste them healing the odd stupid scar." He took my hand and placed it on his chest, on a faded lined that I had traced only hours ago with my tongue. "Besides," he smiled, the old Cain back again, "I thought you liked my scars."

I ducked my head, not quite ready to be teased out of my bewilderment.

"Is Cain even your real name?"

"No. You couldn't pronounce my real name."

A terrible thought occurred to me.

"Are you a *fallen* angel?" Because *that* would make a lot of sense.

"No. I'm... earthbound."

"What's the difference?"

He looked thoughtful, as if trying to find an explanation I could comprehend. "It's the difference between not paying a parking ticket, and being Hitler."

"But… I don't understand!" I wailed, suddenly overcome, and he touched my jaw, gently, but I almost winced, scared now of the power that could be in those hands.

"You don't need to understand. You won't ever be able to, not truly. You're not expected to. You're only human."

"If that's going to be your get out clause for everything from now on, I am not going to be happy."

He laughed at that. Then another question occurred to me, though I hesitated before asking it. It was a bit presumptuous, after all.

"Are you… *my* guardian angel, then?"

"Oh, babe, the life you lead, I don't think one guardian angel would be enough for you!"

"So you're not?" That thought was oddly disappointing. Cain leaned forward and gave me a very human leer.

"I can be if you want me to be."

But this prompted another thought, and this one *really* scared me.

"If there is a God… doesn't he mind…" my voice dropped to a whisper, as if I didn't want this new found deity to hear me. "… all the *sex*?"

Cain leaned in even closer, his throaty chuckle sounding anything but angelic. He reached forward and kissed me, his eyes darkening. "I never asked. Shall we see if we get smited?"

Chapter 21

IT WAS the next morning, and Cain and I had managed to get through the whole of the day – and a fair amount of seriously ungodly activity – without being struck down by a vengeful deity. I thought I was handling the whole thing well, but the look of horror on Medea's face when I came into the office told a different story.

"What the hell happened to you?" she demanded, the minute I walked in. I frowned, not sure what to say, and propped myself up at her desk.

"So… I looked into Cain. With my Sense. Like you suggested." I tried to keep my voice light, but Medea's expression was shrewd.

"And…?"

"And… he's not human. He… he says he's an angel."

There was a long, long silence.

"I see."

I looked at her, helplessly.

"I don't believe in God!"

"Does that matter?"

"When someone's telling you they think they're a frigging angel? A little bit!"

Medea gave a uniquely Medea-like smile.

"Really? My mum is a Hindu and my dad is a Scottish Presbyterian. I'm a Wiccan and my girlfriend is an ex-Catholic who thinks all religion is nonsense and doesn't believe in anything that can't be dissected on a laboratory table. I'm not sure it matters whether you believe in what your lover believes, as long as you believe in them."

"This isn't a debate on where we'll send our kids to

school, Mey. He says he's an angel. A freaking *angel*."

She frowned, as if considering this.

"A fallen angel?"

I sighed. "You'd think so, right? But apparently more… mildly lapsed."

Medea gave me a long, slow look. I felt like she could see the last few hours played out on a screen in her head, and I flushed a deep and unbecoming shade of red. She tilted her head to one side, and smiled.

"Well. That actually makes quite a lot of sense."

She stood up, with a briskness that threw me.

"Where are you going?" I demanded, alarmed. I wasn't through talking about this yet!

"I thought I might pop out and get us some cake."

I paused.

"Yes. Yes. Cake. Good idea."

We had thought about cancelling the party, but where would that lead? We cancel for one reason today, another tomorrow, and the business we'd spent the last few years building up would vanish in a matter of months. And, as I kept reminding people, I had a living to earn. Plus, I was a Londoner. I kept flat shoes under my desk in case of tube strikes or bomb attacks; I lived in a city that refused to be bowed by Al-Qaeda, the IRA, the Nazis or its own looting and rioting inhabitants, and if it took invoking the spirit of the Blitz to get through this, I would. (Cain, most unhelpfully, frowned at me when I said this. "It wasn't at all like it looked in the newsreels," he muttered. I ignored him: the revelation of his immortality was already irritating me, as it just made him even more self-righteous.) Still, plucky as I liked to think of myself, stupid I wasn't. Cain agreed to case the joint in advance – just knowing that he wasn't planning to firebomb us was consolation of sorts, and I think he was relieved to be doing something that got him away from my endless questions about God and heaven (I think it was when I asked him if Dante, my cat, would qualify for eternal afterlife that he reached some sort of breaking point) so I could entrust him to do a thorough job, even if I was nervous of him scaring off my guests. Still, I couldn't help fretting. Something was out there, and it was targeting my clients. Was I making things too easy for it by putting them all in one place?

I watched the door nervously. Cain was around outside – somewhere – I knew, and Medea was walking the room, clipboard in hand. She looked more pensive than usual, and there was a tang to her aura that told me she had been using her magic, even if I couldn't tell exactly what for. The party itself was quieter than I liked it. We'd had more than the usual number of no-shows, and it was making me anxious. Of course, it was London, and the vampires lived in the same city as the rest of us, so were subject to the same transport annoyances, work deadlines and simple can't-be-arsedness that the rest of the populace regularly succumbed to, but whereas usually I'd have only a handful of cancellations with a couple of no-shows on top, here it felt like a good half dozen, and no one had called me to say they wouldn't be coming. I couldn't help wondering if that was because some of them were no longer in any condition to get to a phone. But the threat simply wasn't here, no matter how hard I looked for it. My Sense was rolled out to breaking point, I was trying to be everywhere at once, but there was nothing more than the usual minor tensions tweaking at my nerves.

Of course this was the part of the job I was good at: the ability to work a room, to smooth out anxieties or unhappiness, to look at a client – human or Other – and to see not just what they said they wanted, but what they *really* wanted, what they needed. It also allowed me to weed out the real freaks and the dangers, the hunters and the sadists on both sides of the tables, the ones who never got past my first interview. I wasn't putting sharks among minnows here, whatever Cain thought. When those kinds of people came before me, I closed my books firmly and apologised that I had no vacancies. The next time Cain nagged me about facilitating monsters, I should give him some statistics about how many women were killed each year by human partners, let him get riled up about that, go attack some *normal* dating agencies. No, this room held plenty of hunger, and desire – even deep and desperate need. But full-scale wickedness? Not even close.

Consoled by my findings, I allowed myself a drink – but no sooner had I reached the bar than my Sense felt the force of a heat wave and I turned, stunned, to the door, half expecting the return of my mysterious critic, finally back to play the rest of what was turning into a very long game. But then the heat reached my face and I was suddenly glad that Cain had chosen to stay outside of the venue. Because there, smiling, delighted, and giving off enough sexual energy to light up the whole of London, was Laclos. At a cautious distance behind him, stony-faced and solemn, was the solid, unsmiling mass of the Counsel.

Laclos moved like a man who knew exactly the effect he was having on the room. His head tilted, a slight sway in those hips that was almost feminine, in contrast to the unbridled masculinity that was coming off him like a scent – it was an intoxicating, arousing combination, and I wasn't the only one who noticed. While the Counsel positioned himself against a wall, eyes on the exits, Laclos slipped through the crowd like a rock star at an aftershow party thrown solely in his honour. The occasional friendly word or half-lidded smile, the lightest of touches on an arm, the small of a back, a buttock, as he passed. You could see the slight slump in everyone he visited the instant he moved away, the subtle disappointment he left in his wake, the way each pair turned to one another in his absence, suddenly fuelled with anger and the unshakeable, crushing knowledge that they would never be, or possess, half the man that he was, but tantalised by the fantasy of a chance, the lure of the hint of his availability that danced in his touch. I saw people lean towards him, yearning, sunflowers stretching to the light, but already he had moved on, and was always just an inch out of reach. My God, he fucking *loved* it.

He should have looked ridiculous. The long hair, the leather trousers, the white, v-necked t-shirt revealing a little too much chest: he should have looked like the most hackneyed of clichés. But instead he looked magnificent, and he knew it, and he was basking in it, drinking it in like blood. In the midst of it all, he turned to me, his eye catching mine across the length of the room, and he gave me the slightest of winks. Now it wasn't just my face that was feeling hot.

He was at my side without seeming to move, the subtle chill of his skin making me shiver. At least, I think that's why I had goosebumps.

"This really is a rather splendid gathering," he purred, leaning close to me. "I'm impressed."

"Well, this is what I do for a living."

"And only one of your many talents, I'm sure."

He was, at this stage, rather blatantly looking down my top, but doing it so obviously that it was hard to be offended. Besides, I was sort of returning the favour.

"I think you're supposed to twirl your moustache when you say that."

He smiled and took a lock of my hair and laid it across his

upper lip. He really had a very sensual mouth.

"Mwah hah ha. Like that?"

I tried not to smile. "It suits you. Goes with the 1970s trousers."

His head snapped back with laughter, and he gave me a look of genuine amusement. I was gathering that he probably didn't get a lot of cheek from his minions.

"You really aren't afraid of anything, are you?"

"Actually, I'm pretty much terrified of everything, so it makes it hard to differentiate."

He smiled again at that, as if this was all oh-so amusing to him. He was only millimetres from me now, and he still had hold of my hair. I found myself tilting towards him, as if my very blood was drawn to his: this close, my Sense was almost overwhelmed by his presence, and I felt suddenly drunk. Taking control of myself, I stepped back from him and, still smiling, he let my hair drop.

"Can I get you a drink?" I asked.

"That rather depends on what you're offering."

"Just wine or prosecco, I'm afraid."

He gave a half shrug and inclined his head slightly, as if listening to something that I couldn't hear.

"Then that will have to do for now. Perhaps there will be something stronger on offer, later."

I returned his shrug. "That depends on how lucky you get, but it won't be from me."

"Ah, well. Hope, like blood, springs eternal. Now, if you'll forgive me, I really must… mingle."

He gave a small bow, and merged back into the adoring crowd. As if summoned by his departure, the Counsel made his way towards me, deliberately slow in this mixed party, not wanting to give himself away to the humans. I suspected this would be a much less fun encounter.

"You must forgive Laclos. He enjoys the drama."

And you like hiding behind it, I thought, but didn't say it. When I spoke, I tried to keep my tone neutral.

"He makes my party more interesting, so I can't complain."

The Counsel gave a slight nod of acknowledgement, but his expression said that agreeing with me cost him something.

"Yet, you have guests missing."

I felt myself flinch. What did he know? But his face gave nothing away: it was just the usual stern glare.

"You've seen the newspapers," he hissed, his voice low. "You know what is going on that isn't in the news, the stories that never reach the masses. So you feel responsible. Guilty."

I waited for the consolation, but his scowl simply deepened. "Well, that is only natural. You *should* feel guilty. It is, after all, your fault."

I opened my mouth, shocked, but he held up a hand to stay my protests. His voice was clenched in fury.

"Listen to me, you stupid, reckless child. We have survived for centuries… for millennia… among a race that, despite its sporadic infatuations with our kind, fears and despises and ultimately destroys anything different to itself. And we have done that by keeping hidden. By being secret. And one of the ways in which we have maintained this secrecy, amazingly enough, is by *not writing things down*."

I almost reeled from the intensity of his anger, the force behind his words. I wanted to argue, to protest – after all, as Cain had pointed out, the killings had started before my files were stolen – but I couldn't find the voice to interrupt.

"And then you come along with your little parties and your forms and you ask all your little questions and you take your little notes. You keep *records*." He couldn't have put any more venom into 'you skin kittens'. In fact, he would probably have approved of that more.

"They were in code," I managed, but that sounded feeble, even to me.

"A difficult code?" he sneered.

We already knew the answer to that one.

"So *you* did this. You handed them the names, you even marked up the ages so they could pick off the young ones, the weak ones. You and your frivolity and your ridiculously intergrationist ideas. So you are correct to feel guilty. I hope that you are wracked with guilt. I want you to feel the agony of that responsibility, that knowledge, tearing at your insides like a spike through your guts. And then I want you to get over your wallowing and I want you and your little Wiccan bitch and your cocky celestial consort to get together and to *make it stop*."

He glared at me again and then, his message delivered, he stalked angrily back to Laclos' side. Laclos, true to form, greeted his companion – his servant? – with an arm slung around his shoulder and a tongue down his throat in a kiss that raised the temperature of the room by about 10 degrees. Whatever risks I had exposed my clientele to by having this party, I could console myself that they were getting their money's worth. This display over – and it did take a few minutes – the two vampires pulled apart and strolled to the exit, and like everyone else in the room my eyes were glued to them until the door swung closed behind them. It was certainly one way to make an exit. As I watched them leave, I couldn't help thinking that, bisexual rock god posturing aside, Laclos was more than aware of his bruiser's message, it just didn't suit him to be the one delivering it. But what the hell did either of them expect me to *do*?

Chapter 22

OTHER THAN mild flirting, vampirically enigmatic warnings, a floorshow I could have sold tickets for and – presumably unrelated – someone throwing up in the toilets, the party passed without incident. Cain was (surprise!) nowhere to be seen as Medea, the caterers and I did the clean up, though if I pushed my Sense I could pick up a trace of him, hanging in the air like a scent. I wasn't sure of his absence was a good sign (that he was bored by the lack of action) or a bad one (that he was currently engaged in plenty of it) but I trusted him enough to know he'd keep his promise that he wouldn't be picking off my guests as they left, and I was too tired to worry about anything beyond that. These parties were always tiring; having my Sense ramped up all evening wore me out, but add to that the week's stresses and the vast amount of sex, both of which had seriously deprived me of my sleep time, and I was even more knackered than usual. I saw Medea into a cab with a hug and a peck on the cheek – not something I would normally have done, but I felt that now I'd stayed in her house and seen her in her PJs we had definitely passed into the 'friends who hug' stage – and we swapped promises to text when we each got back to our respective places, neither of us quite managing to hide our relief that the evening had gone without major incident, or our worry that the night wasn't over yet. What was I going home to, I wondered? The hot, naked, possibly-celestial hunter, the scary fang-faced monster – or something else altogether? At that moment, all I really wanted was the cat on my lap and a mug of hot chocolate. Yes, I'm boring. So sue me.

In the end, when I reached my flat, I found neither friend

nor foe: instead, on my doorstep, there was a bunch of dark red roses; the colour, I couldn't help realising, a close approximation of blood. Attached was a note written in a beautifully – if flamboyantly – calligraphic hand. "You know where I live," it read. "Why have me followed?" It was signed with the initial, L.

I sighed. Well, that at least explained why there had been no sign of Cain. I wasn't sure how I felt about that yet: I was pleased that he was looking out for me, but something told me that having Laclos and Cain collide in my personal universe wasn't likely to end well for anyone. But I was too tired to analyse that now. Instead I just went inside, fed my cat, and fell into bed without even taking off my make up, and slept a restless night filled with dreams of burning houses. Then, in the morning, when I had decided my life couldn't possibly get any more complicated, along came the woman with the glowing sword.

It already hadn't been the best of mornings. It's the nature of my job that no sooner is one event out of the way than you're thinking about the next, and I arrived in the office to find Medea already in firefighting mode, as the venue we'd booked for our next party had cancelled, since an electrician doing some work in the building had uncovered asbestos in the ceiling. Obviously that wouldn't be a major problem for those of my guests who were already dead, but since I had no wish to give the rest of the attendees cancer, we had to scrabble around trying to find a replacement location. We managed that – Medea had already been making calls when I arrived – but the venue was only free for a different night, so we then had to spend hours contacting people to tell them of the change of both date and venue. This was a task made twice as difficult without my now-stolen desk diary to hand, as I had tended to keep all of my notes handwritten in that, a mass of scribbles and details scrawled in the margin which I never bothered reproducing in my online calendar. Medea, a woman like myself who sees the value in writing things down on actual paper, kindly forbore from tutting at my lack of digital organisation, as I started a new notepad and drew up a list. (I'm sorry, but there is a satisfaction to be had from crossing things off on a 'to do' list that can never be achieved by pressing delete on a computer). We were about three hours and a lot of cake and coffee into the task and finally making real headway when the door opened and Medea rose automatically to go and greet our latest visitor. And then had to spend several moments putting her eyes back into her head.

Now, I'm an OK looking woman. I won't be on Britain's Next Top Model anytime soon, but on a scale of one to ten, I'm a solid alright, and with the right lighting and make up, I can pass for attractive. And most days, I walk into the office, take one look at Medea, and wonder why I bothered putting mascara on. But the woman now standing in front of me made Medea look like Susan Boyle's frumpy sister. Tall, slim and athletic, with silver blonde hair that flowed to her waist, she radiated that sort of healthy, outdoorsy Nordic cool that automatically makes you feel like a lazy slob who eats too many pies, and she looked at me with a glacial disdain that had me glancing down at my top to see if I'd dropped food on myself. She looked, in short, like a freaking goddess. This appearance was of course reinforced by the fact that, despite being dressed in a well-tailored business suit that probably cost more than my annual mortgage repayments, she had, strapped to her back, a sword that was almost as tall as she was and which gave off a slight silver glow. My Sense went off like fireworks.

"You must be Cassandra Bick." She was looking at

Medea when she said this, and my normally unflappable assistant managed nothing but a stunned, throaty gurgle in reply.

"Um… that actually would be me…" I ventured, and she wheeled on me as if I'd insulted her, her nostrils flaring.

"*You* are Cassandra Bick?"

I didn't want to ask why that should be so surprising – it was my office, after all – but I said nothing. That was a *really* big sword. Instead, I merely nodded, and in that gesture Medea seemed to snap back to herself, and mumbled something about fixing us more coffee. Despite her flushed discombobulation, she didn't seem particularly scared by the arrival of a giant edged weapon in our midst. Perhaps she was too transfixed by the hotness of its carrier to notice. I gestured, helplessly, to my office, and the goddess gave a tiny nod of agreement and followed me. Medea, wide eyed, stared after us, and for a brief second I thought about trying to mime to her to call the police or cast a spell or something, but at the moment the scary warrior woman seemed quite calm, and I was wary of what would happen if I annoyed her. Perhaps best to just play this one out – but, I tell you, I was going to get Cain to bring me a gun to keep in the office, because this was just getting ridiculous.

"So," I managed, gesturing to a seat, which my visitor ignored, "What can I do for you?"

At this stage, Medea arrived with a tray of coffees – less from any hostessy instinct, I felt, that to get another look at the blonde hottie. But the woman watched her come in with icy indifference, only roused when she showed no sign of going anywhere once she had arrived.

"You may leave us, Wiccan," she frowned, and Medea gave a small, slightly distressed mewl, and hurried from the room in a most un-Medea fashion. I struggled to keep my composure, but as ever fear was making me outspoken.

"So, you're clearly not here to use my services, because if *you* can't get a date then frankly we might as well all kill ourselves now, so what can I do for you, Ms…"

The woman paused, not sure how much information she would deign to give me.

"You may call me… Val."

"As in Val the Valkyrie?" I blurted, possibly unwisely, but come on – tall, blonde, big freaking sword? All I needed was for her to start singing Wagner. Her expression became, if possible, even colder.

"You may consider it… a nickname from a mutual friend."

"Well, seeing as we're on a pet name basis already, Brunhilda, maybe you'd like to tell me why you're here?"

I mentioned terror made me stupid, right?

There was a sound like tearing silk and before I could even react the tiniest sting at my throat froze me solid. I glanced down – *very* carefully – to see the tip of her sword resting with deceptive gentleness against my skin. It actually did shimmer a little. I swallowed – again, very carefully – and she frowned at me, her beautiful face clouded with what looked like puzzlement. She flicked her wrist slightly, and the sword tilted my chin up so that I was looking directly at her, and she was examining me as if she'd found me under a rock. It felt, strange as this is to say, oddly unthreatening – at least as unthreatening as someone pointing three feet of glowing steel at you can get – as she regarded me with cool dispassion.

"I must admit," she mused, almost to herself, "I entirely fail to see the appeal."

My Sense tightened around me, and I struggled for a second to breathe, as I felt something stir behind me.

"That's because you don't know how to look," said a

voice, and I turned – not too much, and very slowly – to see Cain leaning against the wall. *Finally* he showed up at the same time as the bad guy. There was a long, drawn out moment as the Valkyrie and Cain looked at one another across the length of the room, her face unchanging, his expression as guarded as ever. I stood, spine-shakingly aware that I was perfectly positioned to get caught in the crossfire. Eventually, he spoke.

"I would consider it a personal favour if you were to put up your sword." His tone was as casual as if he were asking her to take her feet off the sofa, or to use a coaster to put down her drink. Of course, with Cain that didn't mean he wouldn't shoot her if she didn't comply, but her reaction was oddly the same as if he'd make some domestically polite request: a slight, 'oops, my bad' embarrassed nod as she slowly lowered the blade.

"I meant the child no harm," she protested, quietly, and he acknowledged this with a slight nod that seemed to say, 'yes, but all the same...' Freed from the blade at my throat, I stared at both of them, my head twisting like I was watching Wimbledon, but neither of these players were giving anything away.

"We have much to discuss," she said, eventually, as frustrated by his implacability as I usually was, and he gave a small shrug of agreement, prompting her to look at me with a glare more pointed than her sword. "But here is not the place, nor the audience."

Instead of saying anything, Cain simply stepped forward and then, in a gesture of courtliness that astonished me, held out his arm for her to take it. Even more astonishingly, she did.

"Husband," she nodded, allowing herself the slightest flicker of a smile.

Cain did not look at me, but acknowledged her with a bow. "Wife."

And then, as if I had simply vanished, they walked out of the room.

I sagged to a chair, my legs suddenly useless. Holy fucking crap.

"Let's look at things rationally," said Medea. We had decamped from the office to the local café, thinking that at least would give us respite from unexpected visitors, as well as unfettered access to more cake. The non-wibbly-with-terror part of me recognised that all of this stress eating was going to make me really fat, but part of me was thinking that, if I was going to die a horrible death at the hands of a marauding vampire/crazed demon/sword-wielding Valkyrie, then worrying about my weight seemed more than a bit pointless. Besides, I could diet for a year and still not compare with Scandinavian Barbie, so why bother?

Medea, at least, had returned to her normal, non-gibbering self, but since I'd only recently found myself reacting in a similar way to Laclos, I refrained from mocking her for her lapse. She was, though, staring at me in open astonishment.

"So that was your honey's *wife*?"

"It would seem so. But he's not my honey," I added, automatically, uncomfortable as always with any attempt to label Cain and my 'relationship'. Medea looked me up and down with open appraisal, then grinned.

"Wow, is he slumming it."

I should have been offended, but really she was so on the nail that all I could do was laugh, and she couldn't help but join in. In fact we laughed so much that people started to stare, which made me think we had perhaps tipped into hysteria, but honestly that was the least of our concerns. It took a moment for us to get a grip again.

"That's not the issue," I insisted, struggling to pull myself together. It was *an* issue, but not one I wanted to examine too closely any time soon. I was reeling enough from Cain's last revelation – I wasn't sure I had the headspace to deal with this one just yet. "The issue is, what's she doing here? What's Cain doing here? What the hell is going on?"

"Well, I'm guessing the fact that you've been having serious amounts of hot, sweaty sex with her husband might account for *her* appearance," Medea ventured. She paused. "And, let's face it, his as well."

I sighed. She had me there.

"At least he turned up before she ran me through, I suppose."

Medea looked at me, blankly.

"What do you mean?"

I returned her look. "Um, the enormous frickin' sword she was carrying? The one that glowed? The one she pointed at my jugular?"

Still the uncomprehending look, now tainted with doubt and confusion. I stared at her. "Mey, what did you see when you came into my office?"

A slight blush tinged her cheeks as she remembered. "A smoking hot Scandinavian in an expensively cut business suit…"

"With an enormous sword…?" I prompted.

She gave me an odd look, drawing out her reply. "*No-o-o.* No sword. I'm pretty sure that would have registered. Are you saying you saw a *sword*?"

I stared at her. Well, this was new.

Of course, we still had to go back to the office. Mysterious visions of possibly magic weapons, goddess-like and previously unmentioned wives, burglars – there were still jobs to do and bills to pay. I wondered if Medea was wishing she had just stayed at the occult bookshop I had poached her from, but she was as hard to read as ever, getting on with things with her usual graceful efficiency, only the occasional concerned glance in my direction betraying her consternation at this latest turn of events. As for me, I wasn't sure how I felt. Did I even have the right to be annoyed that Cain was married? It wasn't as if we had a proper relationship; we never talked about our lives outside the ridiculous little bubble of sex and drama we inhabited when we were together. He never asked about my romantic life – admittedly, if he had, I didn't have much to tell, but it wasn't a subject that ever came up. He must have known that I had boyfriends when he wasn't in town, and I couldn't assume someone who looked like Cain would ever stay celibate, so we'd tacitly decided early on to simply ignore the subject and enjoy whatever it was we had without trying to label or confine it. Unbidden, though, I felt the tickle of a memory: of nights when I lay in other men's arms and my Sense prickled with the presence of someone I couldn't see but knew was there, and I would wake with the bitterness of loss and disappointment in my mouth, never quite sure it was my own that I was Sensing. Only now did I ask myself how many times Cain had brought his own questions to my home, and left without an answer.

But a wife? All this time he had a *wife*? How could I be jealous of her, anyway? She was so far out of my league it would be like a matchstick envying a supernova. It might make me wonder what the hell he saw in me – not exactly a new question – but it didn't make me jealous. It was just I wasn't sure there was room in my head for a Cain who cared enough for someone to stand up in front of witnesses to say so; normally, witnesses were a concept Cain was careful to avoid. The thought of Cain making marriage vows – however fragile those vows turned out to be – was preposterous. Frankly, it was easier to accept Cain as some earthbound messenger of God than it was to think of him in love.

I half-expected him to have disappeared with her, never to return – I assumed that was why she had come, after all, to warn off the tart and reclaim her errant husband. So I was more than a little surprised that when I eventually left the office, after a long day sorting our reorganised party, I found him waiting for me, leaning against his monstrous motorbike as casually as a man whose wife *hadn't* been threatening his lover with a giant pointy magic sword only hours before. I walked up to him cautiously, not sure what I had to say.

"I imagine you have some questions," he said, which was somewhat of an understatement. He let out a long sigh, which was so weary I wanted to punch him. *He* was playing the long-suffering martyr card here? "Can we at least be drinking for this bit?"

I nodded curtly to the pub across the road, and we trooped silently towards it, neither of us speaking until we were sitting, our drinks in front of us. Cain took a very long swig of beer.

"Go on, then."

"So… you're married."

"Separated."

"Isn't that what all married men who sleep around say?"

"I haven't seen her in over four centuries. That's a fairly convincing separation, I would have thought."

OK, that was a fair point, but I was in no mood to be placated.

"So why haven't you divorced?"

"I married her until death do us part. Which, admittedly, in retrospect, was possibly a rash promise."

"So, what, you can't divorce her because that would break your marriage vows? What about the vow to forsake all others?"

He shrugged, infuriatingly calm.

"God asks that we try. Not that we always succeed."

"Wow, that's a pretty big get out clause."

A slight smile. "It works for me."

I wanted to throw my drink in his stupid smug face. Instead, I gulped a large part of it down, and steeled myself for his next answer.

"Were you in love with her?"

"Why else would I marry her?"

"For tax breaks?"

Another heavy sigh. "Does everything have to be a joke with you?"

"No, no, it's not, but I'm slightly thrown to find out the man that I'm sleeping with is not only trying to convince me he's a freaking angel, but now he's married, to boot. I didn't even know angels could get married! So excuse me for covering it up with a little nervous humour."

He fixed me with a steady stare, then turned away, suddenly fascinated by the view of the street through the window beside us. His voice, when he spoke, was almost wistful.

"Of course I was in love with her. She was magnificent. She *is* magnificent. In many ways I still love her. We were together for centuries. You can't erase that."

Wow, that is *exactly* what you want to hear from the man you woke up with. I suppose that's what you get for dating an immortal: they come with a lot of baggage.

"But it really is over between you?"

"Yes." He turned back to look at me. "Yes, it is."

"Forever?"

"No one who really understands the concept of forever can truthfully say that." I always ask one question too far, don't I? "But obviously, we're not together now, or I wouldn't be sleeping with you."

"Well, that's something, I suppose," I muttered, ungraciously.

"She would decapitate me with her sword if I were unfaithful to her when we were together."

I tried not to goggle at his matter of fact tone. *Of course* it would make sense that Cain married a woman as psychotic as he was. My, did I feel special. But I also wondered – could she decapitate him? Did this mean, although he couldn't die naturally, he could be killed? What would it take to do that? Did she actually have a magic sword, or had that been some new manifestation of my Sense, like seeing the intruder's gun before he drew it? But he'd seen it too, I couldn't have imagined it. I must have looked less than thrilled by his explanation so far, because that train of thought was interrupted when he took my hand, and frowned at me in confusion.

"Have I said something wrong?"

"You could have told me."

"Why? She hasn't been part of my life for hundreds of years. I assumed she never would be again. It has no bearing on us."

But it did, didn't it? And I couldn't explain to him why, because I couldn't articulate it even to myself. Instead, I answered with a question of my own.

"So what does she want?"

He sat back, his expression hardening.

"She declined to say. My wife…" (OK, that did sting a little) "..My wife is not a woman who regularly enters the mortal fray."

"The mortal fray?" I snorted. "Sorry, but can we dial down the swords and sorcery speak?"

He shrugged, unapologetic. "That is the realm she lives in. You saw her. What did you think she was?" That was clearly a rhetorical question. "She is a goddess of death, Cassandra, the legacy of a race who saw the only glory as that of war and conquest. She doesn't care about the Others and she's not here to save the stupid humans from themselves. She is all about the battle. She *likes* it when people destroy each other; she just wants it to be done with flair."

"Well, talk about your mismatched couples."

He totally missed my tone. "Early Christendom was very keen on swordpoint conversions and dying for your religion. There was a lot of overlap."

"Suddenly, I feel so much better about being single."

For a moment, an expression flickered over his face that, had I not known him better, might almost have been a look of hurt. Then he straightened up in his seat, suddenly businesslike. "That's not what we should be focusing on at the moment. I think it's more interesting to ask ourselves why a goddess of death has decided right *now* is the perfect time to come to London…"

Chapter 23

"SO LET'S recap."

We were in Medea's kitchen. Katie was hovering, making drinks and serving snacks, while a fat ginger Tom (presumably Timmy of the food bowl fame) curled around her ankles, begging affection. Katie and Cain were regarding one another warily, while Medea and I tried to pretend they weren't, giving the whole room an air of uneasy détente. We had enough on our plates to worry about without added hostility, as we were currently in the process of outlining. At least pushing the party had given us this unexpectedly free evening, so having a council of war seemed like a sensible idea, and having it at Medea's limited the potential for gatecrashers. Medea, as host, currently had the floor.

"We have a mysterious vampire show up at one of our parties, act gnomic and disapproving, and disappear. Then a henchman – presumably his – comes to the office to reinforce the warning. There are a bunch of killings in London – at least *some* of which we know are vampires – and Cain shows up. I'm guessing those last two things are related?"

Cain gave her a curt nod.

"Then Cass is attacked – twice – by unknown assailants, both of whom are clearly supernatural, given their reaction to metal…"

"Not forgetting the whole fangs and claws thing," I added, but she ignored me.

"Our offices are burgled and our files stolen, presumably to give whoever is behind the killings information on selecting more potential victims. Given the residue of power that I felt in the office, and the supernatural strength you'd need to conjure a demon – which we're assuming is what broke into your flat – we can surmise these things are also related?"

This time we all nodded.

"Then the Vampire Lestat shows up with a bouncer and a pair of leather trousers…" (Katie smiled at this – clearly hanging around me was rubbing off on her girlfriend.) "And they're blaming *us* for the murders… for what they see as our part in them, anyway. Then you find out your boyfriend is an angel and he's married to…"

"Separated from." Cain said, sharply.

"I'm sorry, *separated from* a Nordic war goddess who rolls into town to either check out the competition or take part in the fight." She paused. "Did I miss anything out?"

"I think that about sums it up," I conceded glumly. "The question is what can we do about it?" I glanced at Cain, who had opened his mouth to speak. "And I'd like an answer that doesn't involve burning down my city, please."

He grinned at me. "That's still my plan B."

"Please be joking."

His smile didn't falter. I sighed. "Sometimes I wish you were a bit less Old Testament, a bit more Highway to Heaven." He looked predictably blank at that. "Right… Any answers? Anyone?" We all looked at one another. "Jeez, where's Sherlock Holmes when you need him?"

"Actually he was a lot less reliable than you'd think," Cain said conversationally, and we all stared. "It was the drugs. Arthur really played it down for the books."

"Ohhhhhhkay, then," said Katie. "Moving on. What do we actually know? That there are at least two factions of vampires in town – Laclos and the gatecrasher. Right?" We all nodded again. "So, they don't seem to be working together, but that doesn't mean they are necessarily at odds, does it?"

She looked at Cain, who considered the point.

"No, as far as I'm aware the various vampire factions in London cohabit in the city relatively peacefully."

"OK. And someone is killing vampires. Possibly humans, as well, since we have no idea how many of the victims were Others, how many weren't, but let's stick with the vampire killer theory for now. And somehow Dark Dates – Meds and Cassandra – are involved in it. Maybe just for their information, or maybe whoever hates the vampires also hates anyone who has dealings with them – sees them as collaborators, or something."

"That still doesn't actually tell us what we should *do*," I pointed out, though that earned me a frown from Medea, who took her girlfriend's hand. Cain shook his head, impatiently.

"I keep saying, *you* don't do anything. You pack up, leave, and let me do my job."

"For how long?" Katie snapped. "We all have real jobs, for fuck's sake. I can't just tell my bosses I need to leave town because there might be a vampire apocalypse on the way. Do you know how hard it is to get a job in the NHS at the minute? I can't walk away from my career so you can play heavenly Rambo."

Medea and I exchanged glances: we weren't sure what was going on here, but clearly there was some weird animosity going on between Cain and Katie, and it was making my Sense ache. Though maybe I was reading too much into it, and it was just two strong willed, stubborn people butting heads. God knows Cain brought that out in the best of people. He glared at her then turned to me, not bothering to hide his exasperation.

"OK, then, you're the one in with the fang crowd. Talk to them, find out what they know. My sources have about as much of a clue as we do, no one knows anything."

"Maybe they just aren't telling you," Katie taunted, and he cut her dead with a look.

"Believe me, they'd tell."

Medea, warned by his expression, pulled Katie slightly back. The last thing we needed was these two fighting. Cain returned his attention to me. "All I know is what's already obvious – that this Laclos character, ridiculous as he is…"

"He's not *that* ridiculous," I muttered, which earned me another glare.

"…Has some serious say in this city. He's powerful and popular but he's not the only game in town: there are four or five clusters of older vampires in London, maybe a few more – a couple in the City, some over the river and a slightly looser band hanging around the outskirts. I have some possible names, and some leads on locations, but nothing for certain as yet – it's not like they want to advertise."

"I thought you were the big vampire hunter, though, surely you must know who all the big vampires *are*?" Katie scowled: which struck me as a valid question, but just made a nerve in Cain's neck jump.

"Like I said," he explained, through clearly gritted teeth, "The vampires in London have been relatively peaceful for decades. They represent a minimal threat here. Why would I waste my time investigating things I'm not going to hunt?" He flashed me a smile that had absolutely no humour in it. "Unless you think I *should* start hunting here?"

It was my turn to glare at Katie. That was an argument we really didn't want to resurrect right now. So I changed the subject back to what it was supposed to be: our incredibly well thought out plan. Or lack thereof.

"But what can I do, really? I mix with the lower levels – the younger vampires, the ones not in… clusters, or factions, or whatever you want to call it. I serve drinks and hand out canapés, Cain. No one is taking me to the secret vampire HQ."

"Yet they did, didn't they?" Medea pointed out. "Or at least *one* vampire's secret HQ. You know Laclos, now. You know where he lives. You can talk to him."

Cain pulled a face. "I'm not sure I like that."

"Or like him?" she challenged, mildly.

"Both."

"I'm afraid he's looking like our best option, at this stage, though. He may not know who is carrying out the killings – and we have to take his assertion on that point somewhat on trust – but he's our best chance of identifying our initial mysterious vampire, and how much of a threat to us he might represent, as well as helping us get a better lay of the land."

Did it thrill me a little to notice that Cain seemed less than delighted by that idea? I hid my pleasure with a sigh.

"You know what I really want to know?" I asked. "Why is all the scary stuff true, but none of the good stuff? There's vampires and werewolves and ghouls – many of whom are upstanding citizens of our community..." I added hastily, before Cain could seize on that, "And killers and demons and monsters, but where's the Slayer? Where's the Doctor? Where are the Winchesters? If we get all the crap why don't we get the FBI department staffed by hot people coming to investigate?"

"Honestly, how much TV do you watch?" Cain frowned.

"I don't understand," said Medea, more gently than Cain. "What do you mean?"

"Well, it's just..." I found myself trailing off, embarrassed by my outburst. "If there's all this horror, where are the heroes? Why do we get one without the other?"

Medea gave me her kindest smile.

"Maybe *we* have to be the heroes? Maybe we're the ones meant to stop this?"

I stared at her. "Now that really is depressing."

On that note, the landline in the hall rang, startling us all. Medea rose to answer it.

Cain patted my hand, unexpectedly tender.

"If it's any consolation, there genuinely is a secret department in the FBI…"

"Oh shut up," I snapped, grumpily, even though that thought actually *did* make me feel just a teeny bit better. At least until Medea walked back into the room, her face drained of colour.

"That was Lizzie, from the catering company," she said, her expression dazed. "We need to turn on the news."

Frowning, we all scrambled into the living room, while Katie fumbled with the TV remote, flicking channels until she found one that was 24 hour news. The BBC had interrupted normal news programming: it was running that rolling coverage that is the hallmark of the modern disaster, words spooling across the bottom of the screen. Even then it took us a few moments to realise what had happened: a shocked looking newsreader explaining there had been a massive firebomb in central London. No one had yet taken responsibility, though all the usual suspects were being talked about, and though property damage was massive – an entire building destroyed – luckily casualties had been limited by the fact that the place had been empty. The newsreader adopted an especially grave face to explain that this was sheer serendipity: had an event scheduled to take place tonight not been cancelled at the last minute, the casualties would have been in the hundreds. Never had a discovery of asbestos been such a lucky find.

Medea and I exchanged horrified glances. This was the

party that had been detailed in my diary, and on my computer. The one that we had spent all day re-arranging. This had been aimed at us.

Chapter 24

"THIS IS a bad idea."

I frowned at Cain.

"Yeah, I got that the first 300 times you said it."

We were both leaning on his motorbike, which he had parked across the road from the looming shadow of St Paul's Cathedral, which he was now regarding with wary eyes. I tried not to say anything about the fact that, as a supposed angel, he should feel right at home there. We'd been arguing enough already.

"At least let me come with you," he protested, for about the 10th time since we'd got there.

"We've been through this already. You know he'll be more open to talking if it's just me. He's had plenty of chances to kill me, Cain, why would he do it now?"

"Because he's an unpredictable bloodsucking freak?"

I sighed.

"Cain, can't we just leave it? You stay here. If I don't come out in half an hour, then you can ride to my rescue all guns blazing, but honestly, I'll be fine."

"It wouldn't take him half an hour to kill you."

"He's not going to kill me!" I snapped, my patience suddenly evaporating. "Honestly, Cain, *leave* it. I'm going in and there's nothing you can say to stop me. You're not my dad, and popping up in my life every few years for a fuck and a fight doesn't make you my boyfriend either!"

He whirled on me, equally angry. "Fine, but I'm also not an idiot! London suddenly becomes a playground for the vamps' own Jack the Ripper and now Lord of the Fangs here just happens to turn up for a little light flirting? That's not exactly a coincidence."

Well, *that* stung.

"Obviously, he couldn't actually be attracted to me," I pouted. Why the hell was I arguing? I knew what Laclos wanted, and I knew it wasn't me, but something about Cain's dismissing the idea outright made me petulant. He looked at me with utter disdain.

"Honestly, Cass? You really think you're *that* special?"

My mouth dropped open, and I felt like he'd slapped me. Clearly to someone married to a goddess who used me as a booty call to save money on a hotel, I *wasn't* that special. Did that mean I couldn't be to anyone?

"You know what, Cain? Fuck off."

He stared at me, astonished.

"What?" Realisation slowly dawned, but his reaction was impatience, not apology. "You know that I didn't mean…"

I was so angry I could barely answer him.

"But *I* do. Just… fuck… off…"

"Cassandra…"

"Wow, three times the charm with you, eh? Cain. Listen to me. I want *you*… to fuck *right* off. Right now."

He stared at me in sheer disbelief, but I really wasn't joking. And so, leaving aside my heavily armed, super tough immortal escort, I stormed across the road into the potentially murderous vampire's lair. See? Am I smart, or what?

Laclos didn't seem all that surprised to see me.

"I must say I *am* impressed your companion managed to track me down to the super secret hideout… that I had already invited you to," he greeted me, amusement heavy in his voice. I sighed, still too pissed off at Cain to be in any mood to defend him.

"I didn't know he was following you."

Laclos gave a dismissive half-shrug, as if the matter was

beneath notice. He was, need I bother to explain, once again shirtless, and the shrug did interesting things to his muscles. I tried not to look. At least there were no naked people on the bed this time, though I was annoyed at myself for glancing over to check, because Laclos saw me do it and gave me a smile that made my cheeks glow. Even the bodyguards – those statue-like vampires that had lined the walls of his chamber – seemed to have the night off, so once the unfamiliar young vampire who had shown me in retreated, we were completely alone. Perhaps that should have worried me more than it did. Laclos watched me take all of this in, his smile unwavering, but then his eyes narrowed, as if trying to place something, or bring back a memory he couldn't quite place. He leaned in towards me and breathed in my hair. I tried to stay upright.

"You smell... unusual today."

I flushed bright red. Was he saying I *smelled*? I'd showered, brushed my teeth, worn deodorant. Admittedly I was a little sweaty from the motorbike ride here, where Cain had driven so fast I had clung on for dear life but... oh my God. Could he smell *Cain* on me? The thought burned my eyes with shame, and I ducked my head to hide my mortification. I forced myself to glibness.

"Maybe you just don't like my perfume."

He made a small, curious, animal sound and leaned towards me again, then, with a snake-speed strike his head was buried in my neck, his hands in my hair, and I was blushing for a whole other reason. His icy tongue flicked briefly at my jaw, licking my skin, before he pulled away with a lascivious grin.

"And you taste... divine." He stared at me, as if trying to solve a puzzle. "You really are an enigma, Cassandra Bick."

He stepped away from me sharply and it took all of my

strength not to lean towards him. Yes, he was an evil, mind-bending vampire cliché in ridiculous leather trousers, but somehow my body hadn't got the memo that I was supposed to be laughing at him, and it was having a whole different reaction.

"Is this where you work your undead mojo on me and drink my blood?"

He cocked his head, smiling. "Is that what you'd like me to do?"

"Isn't that what you *do*?"

His smile tightened, and I sensed that his amusement with me was fast reaching its limits. I can have that effect on people.

"You know that's not quite true, though. Otherwise you wouldn't do what *you* do."

Well, he did have me there.

"Besides, Ms Bick, didn't you yourself once have a relationship with a vampire? Surely you don't need me to explain how we… work."

I stiffened, trying to hide my shock. Laclos' smile showed me how completely I'd failed.

"I do my research. You'd be surprised how easy it is to get even the most personal information about people when you are interested enough to look."

I hid my anger under a saccharine smile.

"And yet you've failed rather spectacularly in finding out who is killing your own people?"

A flicker of annoyance crossed his face.

"Which just shows how motivated they are to hide from me," he frowned, before rearranging his expression into a smile. "But that wasn't what we were talking about, was it? I was curious as to how little your vampire lover seems to have explained to you of our rituals."

"Well, I wasn't much *for* your rituals. And he wasn't much for explaining."

I had no intention of sharing this with Laclos, but it hadn't just been my unwillingness to let my ex bite me that had been a stumbling block to eternal bliss: he'd also actually been a monumentally boring guy. Though I suppose I at least had him to thank for inspiring my business: he had dispelled for me once and for all the idea that all vampires were charismatic. What can I say? I was young, and he was cute, and the sex had been great, and for a little while that had been enough – though it probably said something for how badly it ended that I went out and got some silver piercings in an act of petulant defiance straight after we broke up. Still, did I mention that the sex had been great? I frowned inwardly: thinking of being led astray by good looking vampires wasn't helping my current equilibrium.

Laclos watched me as if he could read my inner monologue, and my blush deepened. He smiled, then made a slight, conciliatory gesture, though he was clearly getting off on this whole fountain of knowledge routine. I put on my best awestruck and interested expression.

"Of course, there are still some vampires – more perhaps, than I would care to admit – who see humans simply as food, and would no more engage with one than you would with a hamburger. Then there are those who see your race as slightly high-maintenance pets. But you've seen what most of us are, now. What most of us want. We're as capable of affection, as capable of *desire* as you are..." as if to emphasise this, his reached out and traced a lazy line along my collar bone. I tried not to tremble. "We just manifest it slightly differently. Feeding is generally part of that manifestation. It's the ultimate consummation. I'd no more feed off a tramp in an alley than you would fuck one." He turned that dark gaze on me, and I knew that he could hear my heart beating. "I can't even begin to imagine how you can enjoy one another without that sharing. Drinking someone's blood… allowing them, perhaps, to partake of yours… it's an intimacy like no other. Sex pales in comparison."

He leaned in towards me, and I felt my mouth go dry. He was grinning, his fangs pricking those ridiculously full, kissable lips. "Of course, the sex is pretty fantastic, too."

I gulped, and tried to muster some level of coherence.

"How do you know it's real, though? That you're not compelling them to enjoy it?"

Laclos gave me an uncharacteristically serious look.

"Would you like me to be honest?" I nodded. "I don't. Most of the time. Most humans are open to compulsion. I could get almost anyone to do almost anything – no matter how repulsive or depraved. I could get them to invent new levels of depravity."

"Then how can you talk about love? It can't be real."

"I said I *could*. I didn't say I *do*." He paused, as if seeking a metaphor that I could understand. "Think of this. Most men are stronger than most women. And yet rape is a relatively rare crime – and it is almost always classed as a crime, an aberration. Even in realms where it is commonplace, it is still considered a horror. Because it's not the way it's meant to be, and at some level, we recognise that. Your myths of vampiric compulsion are there to scare you, to demonise us, but really, some of us are just very, very good at seduction." Again, that feline smile. "Sometimes it's just easier to say the bad man made you do it than to admit you really wanted to do it yourself."

"Then why don't the bites hurt?"

He shrugged.

"There's a narcotic in our saliva, of course, but how is that different from adrenaline, or endorphins? The body manufactures what it needs to protect itself while it does what it seeks to do."

I hesitated. Somewhere I was aware I had an actual reason to be here, real questions to ask, but suddenly listening to Laclos talk to me was the most important thing in my world. And he sounded so *sincere*. Didn't I agree with him, anyway? I spent half my time fighting with Cain, saying basically the same thing, only a lot less eloquently. But then a thought occurred to me, and I asked it before I could stop myself.

"How do I know you're not compelling me now, to believe you?" (Really, did I expect him to go, 'why yes, I am! Well spotted!' Like I said, my brain was being scrambled by my hormones.) But his delighted reaction threw me.

"Cassandra, don't you see? That's what's so marvellous about you. Your gift… whatever you call it… makes you impossible to compel. I could throw everything I had at you, and you'd be perfectly able to resist me…" at this he leaned in so close I could feel the lack of breath from his mouth. "If, of course, you wanted to…"

And right then, my God, I didn't want to. What I wanted was to throw myself against the cold marble of his chest, to be crushed in those lean arms, to feel his mouth again on my neck, in my hair. I felt myself tilt, and it took every last molecule of my strength to pull myself upright.

"That's not why I am here," I said, firmly, and Laclos' face settled into a pout.

"Well, that *is* disappointing." And he looked like he meant it. Ha, take that, Cain!

I took a calming breath and tried to sound like an adult.

"You know something bad is happening here. I want to know what. I want to know who I'm dealing with, and what's going on."

He frowned, abruptly serious.

"I honestly don't have any answers for you."

"But you know this world. You know how it's run, you know who the players are. You can't tell me you don't know at least some of the victims. Laclos, I'm sick of running around blind on the edges while I'm also getting blame from all sides. I need you to tell me what you know."

His gaze hardened, and he looked at me with an expression I hadn't seen before, and one I couldn't read. The he sighed, and clicked his fingers, and in a blur of speed a vampire came from nowhere and was gone, leaving a side table with a bottle of red wine and two glasses. So we had never been that alone, after all – I filed away that little piece of knowledge for later.

"Well," he sighed, filling each glass almost to the brim. "I'm going to need a drink for this."

Chapter 25

"ARE YOU sitting comfortably? Then I'll begin."

I scowled at him in the half-light, but Laclos simply smiled and gestured me to one of his ornately padded chairs. Reluctantly, I sat. He took a sip of the wine and pulled a face, as if wishing it were something else, then turned to face me. I tried not to notice how pale he looked in the dim glow of the candles, the flickering of light across the whiteness of his torso and face making him look like the better class of Greek statuary. I took a mouthful of wine, wondering if adding alcohol to this already heady mix was really the best idea. Hadn't I learned my lesson last time?

"Some of this you probably know already, but please bear with me, it's easier to just assume you know nothing."

I nodded – that was fine with me. I felt like I probably did know nothing.

"First of all, whatever you might have been informed, there is no supreme vampire overlord or court or council of ancients set above to rule us all," his voice dripped with sarcasm, as if this were a myth he regularly had to dispel. "At least, if there is, no one has deigned to tell me, and you'd rather think they'd want me to know. Old vampires are fairly rare, and often reclusive – I imagine everything gets tedious eventually, including the company of other vampires. How vampires are organised, if that is how you wish to describe it, varies enormously from country to country, the same as it does with humans. There are regions where the populace is in thrall to the oldest and most vicious of vampires, then there are countries where vampire affairs are almost all run by committee – the Germans are very fond of that, they do like their meetings. In more isolated areas, you may get small clusters, or even a lone vampire. We're as varied in our temperament as people so unsurprisingly we don't respond any better than they do to a one-size-fits-all template."

"And in London?" I asked, sensing he had reached a natural pause.

"Ah lovely, lovely London. It's a great place for us. An ancient city with a lifeblood of immigrants – it's been home to our kind as long as I remember, and was long before I arrived."

"Do you rule it?"

He laughed, flattered.

"No, as far as I am aware you have a mayor, and a government, ineffectual as they may be."

"You know what I mean."

He inclined his head in agreement.

"No one 'rules' London. There are perhaps half a dozen clusters of vampires, a little – if not exactly – like my own, and probably a couple of hundred families, where there is a sire and a handful of progeny. Then on top of that, a few hundred more, who are almost fully assimilated into the human world, and rarely mix with other vampires, or Others. They tend to be either very young or very old – and I imagine most of your clientele comes from that quarter, or from the smaller families."

"So who makes the decisions? The rules?"

"The head of each group, or clan, or family, mostly, either by consensus or force, depending on the nature of their arrangements. Again, much like humans."

I frowned.

"And what's the nature of *your* arrangement?"

He threw out his arms in that by now familiar Christ-like

gesture.

"Why, I manage everything on the basis of charisma and sexual magnetism, of course."

"Of course," I acceded dryly, and he flashed me a smile of such self-satisfied wickedness I had to cross my legs. "So how many vampires are in your... cluster?"

"Ah, now, Cassandra, I can't give away all my secrets."

I allowed him that. We looked at each other for a moment that was so drawn out it was almost uncomfortable, and I broke first, shifting in my seat.

"So what if one of the vampires causes trouble? Breaks the rules, draws attention to you?"

His smile stayed amused, but his gaze hardened.

"Well, there isn't some Bloodsucking for Beginners handbook that we give out, or some secret oath we swear, but yes, I will grant you that there are unspoken rules we are expected to adhere to. Most are simply common sense – we leave one another alone, we feed in moderation, we don't draw the attention of the hunters..." I flinched involuntarily at that, and he pretended not to notice. "If someone – usually what you would refer to as a ... "newbie"... usually one with an inexperienced sire... breaks those rules, then yes, we act, but it tends to be on a first come first served basis."

"What if it's someone stronger?"

"Stronger than one of our... families?"

"Yes. An ancient vampire or one of the Others or... " The words stuck in my throat. "Or a hunter."

Laclos leaned back, regarding me coolly.

"As I said, *really* old vampires are rare, and they tend to avoid attention. As for the Other races... we like to maintain a position of mutual wariness and respect, providing they comply with the same rules of the city as we do. There are few creatures who can cause serious harm to a mature vampire, and we live in a peaceful city, so there are even fewer who would try."

"And hunters?" I pressed.

"Again, why come here? We live harmoniously with the humans. Go somewhere else where you are needed. There are plenty of dark places in the world."

He sounded like Cain for a moment, and I was thrown by that thought. He was looking at me, though, waiting for me to continue, so I forced myself back to the topic at hand.

"Do you know the other vampire… heads, or leaders, or whatever you want to call them?"

"Yes. Not well, in most cases, but we are all aware of one another. This is not a big place. I know most of them by sight, and if not, by name and reputation."

I described my mysterious party crasher.

"Do you know him?"

Laclos shook his head, looking genuinely sorry.

"I'm afraid that 'tall, dark and handsome' tends not to narrow things down in vampire circles."

"Could you get me an introduction to the other vampires? The leaders?"

He spluttered out a laugh.

"Ah, no, Cassandra. I have seen the company you bring to people's doors. No one would thank me for that. Besides," he frowned, his eyes beginning to darken, "Why on earth would I want to share you?"

There was a weighted pause, and we both took a thoughtful drink. Eventually, as much to try and break the spell of his stare as to get an answer, I spoke.

"Do you know why this is happening?"

Laclos threw one long leg over the arm of the chair, arranging himself in a deliberately casual – and flattering – pose, running a hand through that insanely lustrous head of hair. He looked like an ad for aftershave, and again I was struck by the fact that though the effect should have been laughable, it was anything but. It was an effort to keep my expression neutral.

"You have to understand," he began, "For some of us, this is the best of times. Every teenage girl is growing up to want her own vampire, people are healthier than ever, so you can easily feed without killing them, and we live in a hugely populated city where nocturnal living not only isn't unusual, it's acceptable, perhaps even desirable."

"I feel a 'but' coming…"

He nodded. "Indeed. For some – for these very same reasons – we live in the end of days. Wanting to believe in something can turn into a willingness to believe and, to use a metaphor from your own age, the last thing we need is the Muggles storming Hogwarts. You may laugh at our clichés, Cassandra, but we are creatures of the night. We cannot stand up to the scrutiny of daylight." He sighed. "We're strong and we're fast but we're massively outnumbered in a world where science takes hourly leaps that only decades ago were unthinkable. Oh, if we were discovered, it would be rationalised – a disease, a psychopathy, a mutation – but the end result would be the same. Elimination, or cure."

I snorted in disbelief. "I think you're putting a little too much faith in the human race, aren't you? We can't find a cure for the common cold. Or cellulite."

"Perhaps. Perhaps not. But it would be foolish not to be on guard to the possibility."

"You honestly think it will happen?"

Laclos stretched backwards in studied languidness before turning back to me with an answer. I couldn't shake the feeling that this whole thing was an act.

"Personally? No, I don't believe we are any more on the

cusp of destruction now than we were when you discovered atomic weapons, or where half our number perished in the plagues that tore through Europe, or when this city itself was burnt to cinders by an errant hunter on a mission to be rid of us..." My Sense flared at that, and I tried to ignore the icy suspicion of who that hunter might have been.

"I don't think we'll ever live out in the open with your people – as much as some of my kind may wish or fear that – and I don't think you'll ever succeed in destroying us. I think our downfall, when it comes, will simply be a by-product of yours, of the human race's pathologically short-sighted and selfish disregard for any species but its own." He stopped, as if feeling he had perhaps gone on too far, and forced the carefree smile back on his face. "But I have no intention of living as if that is going to happen tomorrow."

I sat, sipping my wine, trying to take on board what he had just told me.

"But even if someone thinks those things... thinks vampires are in danger... why kill them? Why pick them off one by one? And why go through my business?"

Another artfully careless shrug.

"To cause chaos? To spread fear? To wipe out the competition? To imply the current system is flawed, the world needs changing? It's Machiavelli 101. Create a problem and suggest yourself as the best solution."

"You think it's vampires behind this? That all these people getting killed... it's just politics?"

Laclos rolled his head back in a gesture of ennui.

"Honestly, Cassandra? I have no idea. Vampire, human, Other – ultimately, some people are just cunts."

The sudden venom in his voice shocked me into silence. Again I got the strong feeling that Laclos was less laid back about these things than he was trying to appear. Then he sighed, and turned back to face me – though, ever the vampire, he had arranged himself at an angle that looked good. Then again, maybe he couldn't help that – maybe there wasn't one where he didn't.

"So do you really think you can stop it? You and your Wiccan and the mysterious man on the motorbike – who, I couldn't help noticing, drove off at some speed when you entered my building, leaving you completely alone?"

I scowled, not quite over that memory just yet.

"He knows where I am."

"And yet, apparently, he does not care."

I ignored that. It felt too true. "I'm involved in this, you know that. Whoever – whatever – is doing this has attacked me too, has targeted my business, has killed people that I know. I can't – won't – ignore it."

"You're only a human. What can you do?"

"I can try."

His laugh sounded genuinely amused. It also sounded very close, as he was crouched down beside me before I saw him move. He looked like a man who couldn't be more pleased with himself, so I tried my hardest not to look impressed – which wasn't easy, as up close he was actually rather impressive.

"I thought modern vampires were all about the angst," I pointed out, as he smiled up at me, a dog expecting to be fed. He lifted his hand to my chest, tracing one ice cold finger along a vein from my breast to my throat, staring at me as if he could see the blood move within it.

"I don't do angst very well, I'm afraid." And then he kissed me.

For a moment – alright, several moments – alright, several

long moments – I let myself give into it. The chill of his mouth on mine was strangely thrilling, the softness of his lips an exhilarating contrast to the stone solidity of his chest as he pushed his body against mine, his arms pinning me to the chair, his weight bearing down on me. Then, just as I felt I was about to swoon, to let myself get carried away on a tide I couldn't pull out of, my Sense flared a warning and I forced myself back to sanity, and gently pushed him away.

"That's not why I'm here."

"It could be."

"I need information."

"I've already given you that."

He was still leaning over me, his proximity making me giddy. I tried not to stare at his chest.

"I need more than stories. I need a name. A location."

He sighed, pulling himself upright, annoyed at a child that was being irrationally difficult.

"I have heard that the circle of Mallen is restless. "

"Mallen? And have you spoken to him? Done anything about this 'restlessness'?"

He stepped away from me, not wanting to answer.

"I have nothing but rumour, and without facts I cannot move against him. He has only been in London for a century or so but he is an old and powerful vampire, and he has many friends. It would be… bad politics."

Plainly annoyed, he waved a hand dismissively, and one of his flunkies – the Japanese vampire I had noticed on my last visit – appeared from nowhere. Whether Laclos had actually planned to seduce me or not, we obviously had never been genuinely alone.

"Taka will show you out."

And with that, I was clearly leaving.

Chapter 26

SO, ABANDONED by one man, dismissed by another, but at least with a solid lead to show for it, I trudged out towards the fresh air. I had plenty of time to examine Taka as he led me from the crypt, because whatever reason Laclos kept him around, it wasn't for conversation. He was a short, squat but handsome man, his hair that enviable poker-straight jet black curtain that only Asian people ever seem to manage, tied into a loose ponytail that hung almost to his hips. I wondered at his dress – the ceremonial costume of an ancient Japanese warrior, a leather skirt revealing muscled carves with some sort of tunic thrown over it, and couldn't help wondering if this was for a scary badass samurai bodyguard effect, or if he was simply wearing what he always wore, and hadn't changed his dress to follow modern fashions. Certainly, as I trooped up the stairs a careful distance behind him, my Sense told me he was old enough – power seeped off him like heat – and that was without the giant sword strapped across his back, which didn't look like it was only there for decoration. Honestly, I was starting to get a bit sick of the sight of big pointy blades. He showed me to the top of the stairs, and then bowed as I reached the main door. Silent he may be, but polite he certainly was. I smiled in acknowledgement, trying not to look nervous, and stepped past him to reach the doorway. It was then that he turned and shoved me down the stairs.

Stunned, I fell heavily and clumsily, my skin scraping stone as I tumbled down a flight of stairs and crumpled in an ungainly and painful heap on the first landing. What the hell? I looked up to see Taka grinning at me, fangs bared, and then I heard a noise that I'd heard only once before but was now terrifyingly familiar with – the torn fabric sound of a sword being unsheathed. Because clearly, when you are being attacked in a dark stairwell by a vicious vampire, having that vampire be a freaking samurai warrior with a fuck off enormous sword is just the icing on the cake. I tried to cry out, to scream, but the fall had knocked me breathless, so all I could do was fold up in a useless huddle as the blade swept towards me. For once, though, luck was on my side: swords are good for many things, but operating in confined spaces isn't one of them. There was a tooth-jangling screech as the metal struck stone, the vampire unable to extend his reach for a proper swing, and I used that second to scramble down the stairs away from him – distance seemed my only hope of survival, though I was grimly aware that going further down the stairwell was taking me closer to his master's lair.

Taka swung again, again caught stone, then let out a roar of frustration and leapt towards me, as agile as a cat, and far better able to see in this dimness than me. The force of impact threw me back, and my skull smacked against the brickwork with a judder that made me dizzy. The vampire grappled at my clothing, trying to secure a grip, and I thrashed and twisted in his deadly embrace, trapped against the wall but only too aware of the fangs snapping at my throat, the lethal edge of the sword only inches away from my face as we struggled in eerie silence. But while the combination of sword and fangs made his twice as scary, it split his focus: I felt him shift his grip as he tried to keep hold of the blade, and used that fraction of a second's inattention to lash out with a kick to the side of the knee that folded his leg beneath him and made him let me go. Made fast by terror and desperation I plunged up the stairs past him, but of course he was faster, and his hand grabbed at my ankle, bringing me down onto my hands with a breathless curse. I tried to keep my bearings but he was so, so much stronger, and he pulled me roughly back down the stairs towards him as if I were no more than a child.

And, oh, he was enjoying this. I twisted round to face him as he straddled my fallen body, his teeth flashing in a grin of triumph as he raised his sword above him to deliver the killing blow. He hesitated – just an instant, just long enough to feel my fear, to taste it, to savour the moment of the kill as I scrabbled around beneath him. Just long enough for me to pull my gun from my bag, shove it under his stupid ceremonial kilt thing and shoot him right in the balls.

The vampire let out an inhuman roar of agony, flailing backwards from the force of the shot and the impact of a bullet load of silver in the place that no man – inhuman or not – ever wants to be shot. As he toppled, screaming, I pulled myself to my feet and stomped down on his groin with all of my strength, hearing a sickening but satisfyingly liquid crunch in response. I looked around in a panic – surely someone had heard us, had realised what was happening? What would Laclos do when he knew that this little ploy had failed? The smart thing for me to do would be to run, and run as fast as I could, but, weeping and furious, I was in no mood to be smart. This… *thing*… had tried to kill me, and it was the latest in a long fucking line and I was just about done with it all. I landed another heavy stomp on that suddenly all-too-appropriate skirt and leaned down and tore the sword from the vampire's now unresisting hands. He looked up at me, whining, eyes blurred with blood, triumph faded into agony and the realisation that he had failed, but the only sound he could make was of pain. Did he want my pity? My mercy? It was a bit fucking late for that. Hefting the sword with all the strength my jellied-by-nerves arms could muster, I brought the blade swooping down on the fallen vampire's neck.

Which would have been wonderfully dramatic, had I actually

been some sort of warrior princess, and not a party organiser who never goes to the gym. Instead of delivering a clean decapitation, all I had managed was a ragged tear, which was now spurting Taka's last meal over the stairs and all over me in a bloody gush. Somehow that simply made me even more angry, and I took two more slashes, until the head was completely severed, and the vampire's gurgling finally ceased. Panting with exertion, I kicked the head like a football to the bottom of the stairs, where it came to a halt, with a pleasing sense of drama, at the feet of an astonished Laclos, who, presumably alerted by the noise, had just pulled open the door to the antechamber. He stood staring at me, his mouth flush with the blood of the willing acolyte lying limp in his arms, who had no doubt been wheeled in the minute I departed, me being so hard to replace, and all. Not that that was what I cared about right at that moment.

"This is your truce?" I roared, flourishing the sword at him with such ferocity that he actually stepped back. "You let me go in peace and have your fucking *MINION* try to kill me?"

Laclos looked at me in horror. The acolyte wasn't particularly pleased with me either, as Laclos was so shocked he dropped him like a sack of spuds, and he landed on Taka's head with a disgusted squeal, then fell with another dose of indignity as it crumbled to dust beneath him, as the ancient vampire's remains disintegrated.

"I... I knew nothing of this. I swear!" Laclos took a step forwards, reaching out to me, then froze as he realised my sword wasn't moving anywhere in a hurry. I Sensed, rather than saw, the Counsel appear on the stairs above me, and for a moment I stiffened, grimly aware he was between me and the exit, but I had a sword in one hand, a silver-loaded gun in the other, a shitload of adrenaline coursing through me and the righteous fury of someone who had been pissed off by one too many people already today. Let him just fucking try to stop me. Unless he already had, the sneaky little shit...

"Was this *you*? Did you send him?" I demanded, and Laclos and the Counsel traded glances over my head. I had to admit they both looked genuinely unsettled, but the Counsel recovered first.

"Of course not. This is... abhorrent." He struggled to keep his voice calm. "This is an aberration. We can... only apologise."

"How sorry would you be if I was dead, eh?"

"We did not intend this!" he protested, his hands raised. "You must believe us."

I glared at him, not sure what to believe. The sword was getting heavy, but I wasn't putting it down until I was out of there.

"I'm leaving, right now, so either get out of my way or I swear I will fucking cut through you."

The Counsel's eyes narrowed. He was an old vampire – older than Laclos, faster, stronger, and he was standing between me and the only way I was getting out of this building. He could probably take both the sword and gun from me before I even thought to use them, kill me before I could tighten my finger on the trigger. But instead, he simply bowed, and moved out of my way.

I checked the stairs above him, and then galloped up them as fast as I could, throwing open the heavy door and hurling myself into the open, staggering and gasping in the night air, trying not to retch, a blood drenched sword dangling limply from my hands. Obviously, everyone ignored me: this is London, after all – the only attention I got was from a couple of tourists, who presumably thought I was some sort of street theatre tied to St Paul's, and who asked to take my photo.

Dazed, I smiled and bowed in what I hoped was a suitably theatrical manner, trying to look as non-murderous as possible in the flash of a camera phone. But inside I was boiling with fury. I had just killed a vampire – killed another sentient being – and I didn't care. In fact, I felt exhilarated, anger coursing through my veins like caffeine and tequila. At that moment, I would have been willing to go back into that crypt and strike down everyone that I found. That thing just tried to kill me, and I was sick and tired of being a target.

Fuck Laclos. Fuck Cain. This was my fight now.

Chapter 27

"SO... WE have a sword, now, then," Medea commented, dryly, as we sat in the office and she listened to me recount my story which, let's face it, was becoming a bit of a habit. The look I gave her in response to that must have been fierce, because she held her hands up in a gesture of smiling surrender, then lowered them and pushed another plate of cake towards me before carefully changing the subject.

"I did as you asked. I cancelled the next few events. People didn't seem too upset – I think these murders are starting to worry everyone."

I nodded, tersely. I wasn't thrilled by the prospect of cancellation – or by the damage this could do to both my business and my finances – but I knew that in the short term it was the only option. I couldn't put anyone at risk until I knew what we were up against. Though, at the moment, part of me would gleefully have seen every vampire in London burn to a crisp while I stood by and held the matches, but that was a feeling I was desperately trying to get past. Medea was looking at me as if that sentiment was showing on my face.

"Are you sure you're alright?" She had asked me this half a dozen times since I arrived at work, but obviously none of my assurances were very convincing. I took a ragged breath and tried to cram my rage back into my chest, before I let it choke me.

"I can't keep being helpless, Mey. I can't be the girl who gets rescued from the bad guys all the time, the one pulled out of the burning building. I *won't* be that girl."

She looked at me like I was speaking Greek.

"So... what does that mean?"

I tapped the keyboard of my laptop.

"I have a name. I have contacts. And I have Google, so now I'm pretty sure I have an address. I know where Mallen is, or at least where I think he is."

She nodded, slowly, her face serious.

"OK. When do we go?"

I let out the breath I hadn't been aware I was holding, a surge of relief flooding through me. I'd spent hours last night – when I finally calmed down enough to speak – on the phone to every vampire I had an OK relationship with, dropping the name Mallen and gauging the reaction I got. These had mainly been nervous coughing or blank answers, but a couple of people had speculated that he operated out of a building in Canary Wharf, and a quick web search had brought up a Mallen Corporation with an address that fitted. It was thin, but it was a start, and if Medea was going with me, it was suddenly a bit less terrifying. I would have hugged her, except that even in our newly invigorated friendship, she struck me as not overly keen on being hugged.

"I'd like to do it tonight."

"OK. I'll tell Katie, she'll want to come with us." I was going to protest, but then the pessimist that lived inside me pointed out that we could do worse than having a nurse on board. She frowned at me, suddenly stern. "You do know I'm asking Cain to join us?"

I snorted. "Good luck finding him."

"He called this morning when you were on the phone, and left a contact number."

As opposed to calling last night when I had just nearly been murdered? His timing really had gone by the wayside, but then again his wife was back in town. He had probably been busy. I tried not to feel bitter, but I couldn't help thinking that in all the time I had known him he had never – *never* –

left me an easy way to contact him. So what should I be reading into the fact that he was now casually swapping numbers with Medea? Either the 21st century had only just caught up with his telecommunications needs, or he was really, really worried. That was another thought I needed to push away.

"Do what you like. If he wants to come, I can't stop him."

I was doing this, one way or another. And if it had to be in the company of a combat-trained, heavily armed killer immortal who may or may not have once burned down my city, well, then, so be it.

"Seriously? Vampires in Canary Wharf? Like the place isn't evil enough?" Katie muttered, as we assembled at dusk in the once vibrant heart of London commerce. I shrugged.

"Well, I suppose there's a shortage of castles in London," I paused. "Um, OK, actually, there's not, but these days they're probably better guarded." Though my mind flashed back to Laclos' lair, right in the centre of tourists' London, and I wondered how many of our landmarks held more than we realised. It was a scary thought. Katie looked unconvinced, raising her eyes to the towering structures that dominated the open square we were standing in, steel and concrete monstrosities that loomed above us as we tried our best to look like we belonged here.

"No, I approve of it," she decided, eventually. "It fits. Bloodsuckers of every sort together. Can we kill some bankers while we're here?"

I frowned at her, remembering that she was a public sector worker, so had taken the credit crunch – and the resultant attempts by our Government to dismantle anything approaching a welfare system – harder than most. I was suddenly worried she'd be taking a very personal interest in dishing out some payback.

"We're not here to kill anyone," I reminded her sternly. "We're here to see if we can find Mallen, and talk to him, and see if he's behind this."

Cain shot me a look mixing distain with amusement.

"Frankly I think the Scottish chick has the right idea."

Medea rolled her eyes – Cain and Katie clearly got along better when they were both having homicidal tendencies, but that wasn't a bond I felt we should encourage. I put a restraining hand on Cain's arm. Even after our argument – and we'd barely spoken the whole bike ride here, though given the speed he drove that was mainly because I'd had to concentrate on not screaming or throwing up – just touching him made my skin fizz. I might be angry at him, but I was still glad he was here.

"Let's just focus on getting some information from the vampires for now, eh?" I suggested. Katie cast a fierce glare up at the skyscrapers.

"OK, but if I see any bankers, I'm not making any promises."

It had been the work of minutes to find the building we were after: Canary Wharf wasn't exactly designed as a hiding place. This was a part of London that had been built as a naked tribute to wealth – the banks and law firms that had moved here from the City to create newer, bigger (and more affordable) offices in a new financial hub that, if it hadn't been entirely successful in replacing the Square Mile, had certainly relocated some of its money. Like so many other promises of the great capitalist dream, it had proved somewhat false – although it was still busy enough and there were plenty of sold out buildings, the crash had hit hard here, leveraged on nothing but paperwork and promises, and one only had to look at the abandoned Lehman Brothers building to see how illusory those had turned out to be. I'd been here before, and hated it: it was a mini-town built for one purpose only, and money has no soul. Having once seemed a monument to posterity, the giant office blocks now seemed a testament to folly. Built smack in the middle of one of the poorest parts of London, they'd preached 'regeneration' but in reality all these businessmen sneered down from their sleek steel and glass buildings at the peasants at ground level, who were only ever allowed inside their hallowed hallways to clean toilets and empty wastebaskets. Even at its busiest, it always seemed an artificial and sterile place, something about the way it was designed always trapping the wind and the shadows, so that it never seemed warm, and the denizens all moved in a hasty shuffle, heads down and huddled as they moved from the shelter of one building to the next, like mime artists playing at a gale. Now, at twilight on the weekend, despite the fact that the buildings were blazing their lack of ecological credentials by being fully illuminated against the encroaching dusk, the whole place was pretty deserted. At least this meant there was no one to stare.

Because honestly, I don't think anyone ever looked as out of place in this monument to money as our ragtag little bunch. Katie and Medea had arrived by tube, so looked relatively innocuous: Katie was dressed like she was about to go for a jog, clad in loose sweats and a hoodie, her hair tied back and her face set grimly. I'd wondered about the wisdom of bringing her – even now, my Sense buzzed at her presence, voicing my anxiety – but she seemed like she had a sensible head on her shoulders, and her presence couldn't do any harm. Medea, in contrast, looked positively exotic in full battle gear: her eyes were heavily kohled, her hair braided, and loops and chains of silver gleamed at her wrists, ears and throat, her only step to practicality being that she had changed into flat leather boots instead of her usual heels, and her skin-tight skirt had a kick pleat that freed her legs from their usual constricted sway. She looked like some ancient Hindu goddess you didn't want to get on the wrong side of, and the metallic tang to her aura told me she had already been working on some spells.

"How much magic are you packing? Do you think you could take down a vampire if you needed to?" I asked her, and her lips curved into a smile.

"I'm hoping we won't need to find out."

"Given the week we've had?" Cain muttered, giving her the once over. "What do you really think the odds are of this Mallen guy just welcoming us in for a chat?"

Despite myself, I couldn't help agreeing. Nobody seemed to be in the mood for a conversation lately – and having learned this lesson the hard way, Cain and I had come armed for a fight I had my purloined sword slung over my back, hidden in one of those long, ugly sports bags rowers use, and a Glock in my handbag loaded with silver bullets, figuring this was a combination that had served me well enough before, even though Cain had insisted on giving me a quick lesson in how to handle the sword before agreeing to let me bring it, arguing that it might hamper our progress if I accidentally lopped off a limb that belonged to one of us. Not that I had any intention of using it, but something about its ancient heft felt like power, and I suspected that unsheathed it would make a fairly effective deterrent to all but the most crazed of attackers. Even then, beside Cain, I looked like I was going to a tea dance. His jacket hung open, revealing a shoulder holster that held a seriously scary automatic weapon, and I knew for a fact he carried at least one handgun and a very sharp knife: I could only guess at what else he was carrying in his holdall, but it clinked heavily as he swung it off the bike. He had been sullen all day, and this showed no signs of abating. Having heard what happened at Laclos', he was annoyed at himself for leaving me there and – somewhat unfairly, I thought – annoyed at me, though he wasn't deigning to tell me how I'd offended him this time. Maybe all these lapses in his protection were starting to get to him: certainly, while I was still ambivalent about believing his so-called celestial nature, one thing was certain – if he was an angel, he wasn't my guardian angel, or if he was, he pretty much sucked. But whatever was bothering him, he was spoiling for a fight, that much I could tell, and I could feel his anger rasp against my Sense as we crossed the square towards our destination. I found myself hoping that bringing him was a good idea after all.

Still, too late to worry about that now, we were here. The Mallen Corporation wasn't even half the size of the biggest of the buildings, standing around 10 storeys high on the corner of the square, as near as huddled in a corner as one of these edifices could manage, though a vicious looking spike rose high out of the roof, as if compensating for the lack of height, trying to pierce the sky that was dominated by its much taller neighbours. Nevertheless we all stopped for a moment as we approached, staring at the blank, bleak façade, wondering if anyone inside there was looking back. Maybe the place wasn't actually oozing malice, but it certainly felt like it.

"Have you noticed?" Medea frowned as she squinted against the wind. I stared at her, confused, and she nodded towards the entrance. "All the windows are smoked glass. The sunlight can't get in."

Chapter 28

THERE WAS a doorman. Unsure of what we were walking into, we didn't want announcing, so Cain dealt with him – although, at my insistence, not fatally. He could be perfectly innocent, after all. Hell, *Mallen* might be perfectly innocent: Laclos might have pointed me at him for politics or amusement, and I wanted no irreparable damage done until I actually knew what we were up against. We were here to talk, I reminded myself, firmly, even though I drew the sword as I did so, ditching the sports bag behind the reception desk with the now unconscious clerk.

"Where do we start?" asked Katie, and it was a very good question. The floor that we could see beyond the entrance appeared to be virtually deserted. An expensive looking building directory provided no guidance – every floor simply bore the label "Mallen." The day was only now dipping, but inside the building there was no sunlight, only the unforgiving glare of artificial light – would we be finding a vampire just rising for the night, vulnerable and disoriented as we'd hoped, or were we walking into the presence of something that was awake, and alert, and waiting for us? I tried to reach out with my Sense but, already jangled with nerves and the presence of both Cain and a ramped up Medea, I couldn't get any handle on what was in here with us. Eventually, Cain leaned over the recumbent security guard, liberated a set of keys and strode towards the entry gates.

"Come on," he said, briskly. "We'll start at the top and work down."

We divided up into two of the lifts: Cain and I in one, Katie and Medea in another, hoping to split any potential target. After my tangle with Taka, I wasn't keen on tackling any stairs (plus, realistically, if I had to climb 10 flights I'd be fit for nothing at the top of them) but as the lift rose my skin started to itch and I was very aware that we were basically in a small, metal coffin. Cain, of course, was completely undisturbed by this – in fact, the prospect of some action had clearly lifted his mood, and he flashed a grin at my nervousness.

"We're here to talk, Cain." I reminded him. "Just to talk."

"Sure we are," he smiled, and pulled me into a brief, fierce kiss that left me more breathless than 10 flights of stairs would have. Before I could even respond, an electronic voice announced we had reached the top floor. So much for arriving by stealth – then again, as the doors slid open, it looked like we didn't need it. I felt Cain tense beside me, ready to spring... only there was nothing there.

The whole floor was deserted. One vast, open plan space, only a few glass-fronted offices tucked in the corners; there was simply no one around and no sign that there ever had been. Desks and computers stood untouched, eerily quiet, none of the signs of life that even a weekend office will hold: no personal mementoes, "comedy" signs or cuddly toys on desks, no empty mugs or abandoned crockery, none of the ambient noise you get from printers or computers on standby: this was a place that clearly wasn't in use. There are few things creepier than empty office blocks – and I say this as a woman who spends a fair amount of time in crypts – and this place reeked of abandonment. The only sound was the almost imperceptible buzz of the overhead lights, which made us all look pale and washed out in their glare. The hairs on the back of my neck rose, something telling me that this place wasn't like this because of the credit crunch.

"My God," I whispered, as Medea and Katie emerged

from their lift. "It's Wolfram and Hart."

Katie snickered but Cain shot me a stern look.

"You know, occasionally it would be nice if you could express yourself without referencing things the rest of us are unfamiliar with."

I pulled a face.

"And occasionally it might be nice if you got off your high horse and realised the rest of us watch television."

Cain rolled his eyes, casting an exasperated glance at Medea. I had the annoying sense that she reciprocated. Sometimes I felt unappreciated.

Now wasn't exactly the time for this argument, though. We inched forward, cautiously, weapons drawn: we might be here to talk to Mallen, but we weren't idiots – though I was feeling increasingly silly as it became apparent just how deserted these offices were.

"Hello? Um… Mr Mallen? We're here to talk to you! We'd just like to talk…" I called, nervously, earning myself a fierce glare from Cain and a worried glance from Medea and Katie. But what were we supposed to do? Wander around an empty building all night? I tried to stretch my Sense out farther than usual, see if I could pick anything up, but it was useless, disrupted by Cain and Medea, my nervousness adding to the blur. But we seemed safe enough: open plan offices might be the work of the devil, but here they were on the side of the angels – because nothing could sneak up on us in this exposed space.

Honestly, you'd think after being wrong so often I'd learn to shut up, right?

Nausea washed over me like a wave of filth and I stumbled, gasping, falling to my knees as if physically struck. Almost as one, my companions ducked to help me, and that stumble saved all of our lives, because, an instant later, out of nowhere – literally out of nowhere – the air where we'd stood had been torn open and we looked up to see a roaring, screaming wall of teeth and claws. So much for just coming here to talk.

"Behind me!" Medea cried out, crouching into a defensive stance, her hands thrown up in front of her. The air shimmered and her aura turned red, and the surging demons bounced off the protective shield she hurled up in front of her. Ducking into a crouch, Cain rolled out beneath it and came up firing, a gun in each hand, as Katie pulled out a fierce looking kitchen knife, ready to defend her lover if anything broke through the magical barrier. I rose from my stumble with my gun out but for a second the sheer spectacle of what we were facing stopped me. I couldn't even count the creatures in front of us: the very air was black with them, a horde of snarling, spitting demons, lashing out at us with long, muscled arms, claws leaving sparks as they slashed at Medea's shield. Were there a dozen? More? It was a blur of blades and scales; bodies that looked like someone had put bits of every kind of predator you are scared of into a blender and spewed out the results. And Medea's barrier was driving them wild – they flailed against it, screeching, furious, and my Sense could see the black scratches as their assault weakened her hold. Beyond that, barely visible, Cain was in the thick of it, guns roaring as he fired and elbowed and kicked anything that came within range. Then a space cleared, and I caught a flash of his smile as the monsters fell under the sheer kinetic force of his onslaught, only to be trampled under the advance of their compatriots. Bleeding, hurting, fighting for his survival – Cain was having the time of his life. Guns clicking empty, there was a blade in his hand and he was slashing forward, heads and limbs flying under the whirlwind of death. But there were simply too many, even for him, because for every one of them he killed, another appeared, and I started to worry that I was about to find out just how immortal this supposed angel would turn out to be. Terrified as I was, I couldn't just hide behind Medea's already weakening magic. With a curt nod to her and Katie, I ducked under the shield and dived into the fray.

Shaking and almost gagging with fear, I threw myself with more energy than elegance at the monsters. I emptied my gun into the creatures nearest to me, then, rather than waste precious time re-arming, lashed out with my sword and started slashing, figuring that in these close up quarters, even such an inexpert swordswoman as me could do a fair amount of damage, and trusting that Cain's well-honed survival skills would keep him out of the way of my blade. Behind me, I heard Medea's frantic chanting as she desperately tried to implement a reversal spell, sending these creatures back wherever they came from, no longer able to hold all but the sparsest shield against the unfailing onslaught. Katie stood crouched in front of her, knife raised ready against anything that might get too close. Powered by adrenaline and fear, my sword sliced clean through the legs of a monster that had been hurling itself towards them, but that didn't stop it: crippled, it turned on its assailant – which would be me – dragging itself along the ground, howling and snarling, inch-long claws gouging tracks in the flooring as it went. Well, goody for me, that got its attention. Maddened with pain, it lunged at me, and I staggered backwards, tripping over its fallen brothers in an ungainly heap, the sword knocked out of my sweat-slicked grip. Clearly I wasn't cut out of this superhero lark. I fumbled in the bag I had strapped to my hip, desperately searching for bullets, clumsily but quickly reloading. The force of my bullets threw it back, but it wasn't enough – one swipe of an enormous arm struck my gun arm and the gun went flying into the melee, leaving me unarmed and helpless.

I closed my eyes, some primal, childlike belief surfacing that if I couldn't see the Bad Thing, the Bad Thing couldn't see me, though as I could feel the hot saliva dripping from its jaws onto my legs and smell the stench of its breath, there was no getting away from the terror. So I took a deep breath, and opened my eyes to see the thing that would kill me. But instead I saw a blur of fur and claws as a giant golden cat seemed to appear from nowhere, a streak of solid muscle and sinew that moved with an eerie speed and silence, knocking the monster aside, tearing through what was left of its torso like a lion with a gazelle. I watched, stunned, as the cat – which looked, to my non-David Attenborough eyes, like some kind of pale leopard – grabbed the monster's neck and with one shake of its mighty jaws tore clean through it: the creature might have managed to move without its legs attached, but nothing lives when you've ripped out most of its throat. Around us, even some of the other creatures backed away, some primitive instinct recognising a predator in their midst. Then the air shimmered, and standing, bloodied and naked, was Katie. She looked at my stunned expression with the slightest of smiles.

"You thought I was Tara to her Willow, Cass. But I was always Oz."

Then with a grim, gory smile she dived back towards the monsters, muscles rippling and changing as she went, so that where our attackers had seen the leap of a pale, freckled girl, they felt the impact of a giant, snarling leopard. Holy fuck. I barely had time to laugh in disbelief before realising the fight wasn't over, and grabbing up my sword and my gun and getting back into the battle.

But we were still losing. I could Sense it as well as see it:

there were just too many of them, and they weren't stopping. There were three of us fighting – and one of those was me, so it was probably nearer to two and a half – and leopard Katie's attention was still focused on protecting Medea rather than attacking, so even with Cain's unstoppable carnage, we weren't coming anywhere close to beating them. They outnumbered us 10 to one and we were barely slowing them down. If Cain was really an angel, now would be a good time for a miracle.

Then the whole floor shook as a wall of windows exploded, and the goddess of death flew in. She landed with a grace that would put Katie's leopard to shame, ditching the harness she'd swung in on in one smooth movement, shaking herself free of broken glass and drawing not one but two swords from behind her in a single stroke. Only this time, they might not be glowing, but everyone could see them. She was upon the monsters even before they could react to her arrival, and within seconds she was at her husband's side. It was all I could do not to stop and stare, suddenly aware of what a clunky, useless amateur I was, being schooled in how these weapons looked in the hands of a professional. I might have been doing the odd bit of damage, but she was mowing through them as if they were made of paper. Whatever my personal jealousies – and my relief that I was well out of reach of those blades lest she 'accidentally' hit me – the woman could handle herself. Cain had been right. She was, not to put too fine a point on it, magnificent. Admittedly, as she slashed and hacked her way through flying limbs and heads, it was a brutal, gory magnificence, but it was still awesome, in the truest sense of the word. Cain, his back to hers, matched her blow for blow, alternating between blade and bullets, as they protected one another's flanks with practised ease, an unstoppable machine of slaughter. Before them, the creatures staggered and fell, and we could see the tide was turning – and whatever these monsters were, some part of them knew death when they saw it coming. Some of them simply fled, vanishing into noxious clouds rather than face this unholy nemesis, fearsome predators reduced to scrambling, fleeing prey.

"How did you find us?" Cain couldn't hide his delight at this turn of events, of being reunited with a lover as dangerous as he was. She didn't even turn to him to answer, but I saw that she was smiling, too.

"Husband, do you think I do not always know where you are? This is merely the first battle it has been worthy of me joining."

He turned and shot her a look.

"If that's the case, I could have used you for that takedown in the Congo."

She shrugged, pausing to disembowel an attacker before answering.

"I have no desire to waste my time in minor skirmishes."

He almost lowered his weapon in shock.

"That was a whole army unit…!"

She looked unmoved. "And yet, you survived. Which you may not if you stop paying attention, now. I have them at bay here." As if to prove it, her boot lashed out, crushing the windpipe of a staggering monster foolish enough to keep struggling once he was on his way down. "Go, do what you need to do."

Cain looked at her for a moment then, in a movement so fast I wondered if I'd really seen it, he laid the slightest of kisses on the back of her neck and, with a final grin at his warrior wife, kicked a monster out of his path and dived towards me, holstering his gun as he grabbed my wrist, his hand hot and sticky with whatever passed for monster's blood.

"Come on, then."

"What?"

"We need to get past them while they're busy, find out whoever is controlling them. We have to find Mallen!"

"We can't leave them!" I protested, but Cain looked back at Val, who was now clearly stemming the tide of monsters, leaving Katie little to do but pick off the stragglers.

"Trust me, she can handle this." He gave me a grim smile. "This is her idea of a good time."

He half dragged me to the nearest stairwell. It was quiet here, and part of me couldn't believe that we were only metres away from such carnage.

"Where are we going?" I demanded, breathless and shaken.

"I think you're the one that needs to tell us that," he said. He put his hands on my shoulders, and looked me straight in the eye. Even splattered with gore and his eyes gleaming with some dark death lust I had never seen in him before, the solid weight of his grip was oddly reassuring, and I felt my thudding heart start to calm.

"You need to concentrate, Cass. It's clear these demons have been summoned to protect something, but what? Where's the vampire? Use your Sense. Find him."

I was about to protest – when I was this rattled my Sense was virtually useless – but Cain was right. Val the Valk's arrival – well-timed and fortuitous as it was – hadn't been subtle, and even in the semi-deserted Wharf it was likely someone had heard the windows smash, or would soon enough notice that one of the buildings wasn't looking as well fenestrated as it should be. We didn't have the time or resources to do a proper sweep of the building: if we wanted

Mallen, we had to find him now.

I closed my eyes, allowing the steady presence of Cain, the warm solidity of his hands, to soothe my addled mind. I felt the wall of his aura in front of me and my Sense skittered away from him, knowing the pain that getting too close would bring, but I could also Sense him closing himself down, protecting me against exposure to whatever his nature really was. I could feel the glowing mass of the battle, shrinking as Val took us closer to victory, though her presence burned like a firework in the dark, eclipsing the paler fire of Katie and Medea. At least I knew now why Katie always set my Sense off, I realised, before shaking the thought away as distracting. I could think about that little development later. Now, I needed to focus. I allowed my Sense to roll out like a mist, seeping through the building: this was more than I had ever tried before, but I could feel Cain's steady, expectant gaze on me, and I couldn't bear to disappoint him. After all, the woman in the other room had given me a lot to live up to.

Then I felt it: a cluster of power. My eyes snapped open and I saw that Cain was frowning at me in concern. No wonder, I was shaking from exertion, and when I tried to speak my voice wobbled.

"He's here. I can feel it," I managed, shakily. "He... they... are in the basement."

Cain sighed and drew his gun again.

"Should've known we were starting at the wrong end of the building. Come on, then. You up for a few stairs?"

I thought I might actually die. Honestly, I think I would have preferred being back with the monsters. Cain, of course, was taking the stairs with the brisk step of the born athlete, only his cautious air and raised gun giving the hint that this was anything but a nice little work out for him. I, on the other hand, out of shape and already exhausted by the fighting, was one step away from collapsing in a heap of jelly, and wishing Cain had dragged me out of the fight towards one of the exits that housed a lift. He sighed with barely hidden impatience as I gestured to him that I had to stop when we finally reached the first floor, bending over and taking deep breaths to stop myself retching all over the landing.

"Come on, we're nearly there!"

"We don't all have angelic superpowers, you know!" I snapped, leaning against a handy fire door for a moment, my body crying out for more permanent rest.

"Mm, the angelic superpowers that come from taking regular exercise?" he smirked, and if I'd had the energy I would have swore at him. Then suddenly his smugness was the least of my problems, as the door I was leaning on gave way, and I felt strong arms grab me and drag me backwards, and the cold steel of a gun barrel press sharply into my face.

"Put your weapons down, or the girl dies."

I couldn't see my assailant, but I recognised that voice – it was the thug who had come to my office to warn me off. A small part of me triumphed in the thought that I had been right – this *was* all connected – but that was quickly drowned out by the far more immediate fear that he was going to blow my head off. Because the way Cain was looking at him made me realise with cold certainty there was no way he was putting down any weapons. Thug boy must have seen that to, because he gave my body a fierce jerk, the gun digging deeper into my face.

"I'm not kidding!"

I felt my eyes prickle with tears, but Cain looked unflustered.

"I don't care if you're kidding."

"I'll kill her!"

Cain took one look at my trembling, shaking form and barked out a laugh that was pure ice, his face settling into a scowl. He didn't look either worried or angered by my predicament; he looked, for want of a better word, insulted.

"I said put your gun down!" the man was shouting now, thrown by Cain's nonchalance.

"Wait... you're actually serious?" Cain couldn't hide his amusement, now. "You're threatening me with this... human?"

I felt the thug's grip tighten, and could Sense his growing confusion, even as my own face grew hot with shame.

"You don't actually think she means anything to me, do you?" he gestured upwards. "I have a goddess up there fighting for me... an actual *goddess*, no less, and let me tell you that fighting is only one of the many, *many* ways in which she is physically incredible, and you're threatening me with some human bimbo I occasionally fuck? She's recreational, you moron. You think she actually *matters*?" He laughed, and it was a cold, hard laughter. "Wow, does your research suck."

My mouth fell open.

"You bastard!" I cried, and he turned on me with a look of genuine bemusement.

"Oh, hell, apparently she thought so, too." Cain looked back at the gunman. "Well, you'd better kill her now, or I'll never hear the end of it."

I felt the gun wobble against my cheek as my assailant struggled to cope with this sudden revision of his script. Cain leaned back now, almost casual, and made an impatient, "come on, get on with it," gesture. I squeezed my eyes shut, expecting at any second to have my face blown off. The fact that it wasn't was greeted with a weary sigh from my supposed guardian angel.

"Go on, then." He twirled a hand in the universal sign for

'let's hurry this along now.' "Kill the infant, and let the grown ups talk."

There was a split second hesitation from the thug, and then the gun exploded. I felt a hot spurt of blood and I fell to the ground, my last breath cursing Cain. Only… I wasn't dead, and the blood and gore that covered my face wasn't mine. Dazed, crying, my ears ringing, I was pulled roughly to my feet as Cain holstered his smoking weapon and kicked the body back into the doorway.

"Come on, there's probably more of them!"

Stunned, half blind with tears, I could do nothing more than stumble after him, as he led me down into the bowels of the building. But my relief at being alive wasn't the only reason my heart was pounding and my limbs shaking. Because I couldn't help thinking that Cain had meant that. He'd meant every word.

Chapter 29

IT WAS, to say the least, an anti-climax. Having shot and slashed our way through half the inhabitants of hell, when we reached the basement, on seeing my confirmation nod that this was where my Sense was leading, Cain pulled out his automatic and kicked in the heavy wooden doors and we found ourselves in... an office. I was at the very least expecting a lair.

But no, sitting there, casually as you like, as if he were waiting to interview us for a not-very-important job vacancy, sat my mystery gatecrasher, the vampire I could now assume was Mallen. Dressed in a dark, well cut business suit, dark hair slicked back smoothly, his features no longer blurred by that slight but constant movement he had deployed at my party, he looked like a handsome, well to do but otherwise completely ordinary businessman. He also seemed remarkably unfazed by the arrival of two armed intruders: his face bore an expression of slight amusement that the night had not turned out as he expected, but nothing more. But for all that, I could Sense his coiled power, and I felt Cain tense up beside me, as if he recognised it too.

"So, you bested my sentinels, I see."

"Sentinels? Really, people say that?" I asked, though couldn't help scanning the room with my Sense to see if there were any more such 'sentinels' nearby. Cain rolled his eyes in a 'shushing' gesture at my remark, but he could fuck right off, I was in no mood to take his orders. Mallen lifted his eyes ceilingwards, as if listening for where our friends were still fighting, and I wondered if his vampire's hearing went that far. To me, it felt like we had left them a universe away.

"I have to say," Mallen went on, with maddening calmness, "I think you are over-reacting."

"You're killing people! You're blowing up my city!" I protested. "How the fuck should I react?"

"Like the businesswoman you're supposed to be?" he suggested, mildly.

"*I* came here to talk," I pointed out, peeved at this. "You're the one who turned this into a supernatural smackdown."

Mallen looked at Cain, his mouth twitching into a smile.

"Ah, but Ms Bick, the company you keep is not famous for his conversational skills. Besides, we *have* talked. I gave you a warning, you chose to ignore it."

"But… you're killing your own kind!" I was aware of how feeble that sounded, but I was floundering in the face of his implacability.

"Which is something your species does all of the time." He gave the slightest of shrugs. "My species is over-proliferating. Youngsters, unappreciative of the old ways and the old hierarchies, asking too many questions that, frankly, I have no desire to answer. I am doing your race a favour, Ms Bick. I am simply cleaning up. I would have thought your celestial consort, at least, would approve of that, even if he dislikes both my motives and my methods."

I felt Cain give a low growl, but he remained otherwise silent and unmoving at my side. Having abandoned the talk option when we got jumped by the demonic horde, we were both a little unprepared to switch back to conversational mode, no matter how seemingly rational the vampire in front of us. Besides, something was… wrong. I felt it nagging at my Sense, like a sound on the edge of my hearing I couldn't quite identify. But Mallen was still talking.

"However, there's really no reason for you to be any more

involved in this than you already are. You have desisted in your activities, you can leave me to mine, and we can put the casualties you have inflicted today down to unfortunate collateral damage. I have what I need from you, now. You may go."

"You'll call them off?" Cain nodded upwards, and the vampire inclined his head in assent. So, wait, that was it? We'd come all this way for... what? A pat on the head and a dismissal?

"Of course, I should warn you that any attempt to interfere further with my interests in this city will have... severe consequences," Mallen was saying, but he was smiling, still smiling, even as the movement of the air beside me told me that Cain was raising his weapon, ready to bring matters to his own kind of conclusion. Then I realised, finally, what my beleaguered Sense, drowning in fear and adrenaline, was trying to tell me.

"Cain! He's not really here! He's *not here*!"

The words were barely out of my mouth when Cain grabbed me and, moving faster than I had ever seen him move, slung me over his shoulder with a force that knocked me breathless and was pounding up the stairs two at a time, racing towards the exit like a man possessed. I saw stars as we smashed through the main doors and Cain hurled me to the ground, throwing himself on top of me heavily, his hand pinning down the back of my head so that I could barely breathe, never mind lift it to protest. And he was still holding me tightly as all the air was sucked out of the world and the building behind us exploded.

Chapter 30

FOR A moment, there was nothing in my universe but noise and pressure: a giant 'whoomp' of air that felt like it would tear my skin off and crush me all at the same time, even covered as I was under the protection of Cain's body. He lay face down on top of me, his hand over my scalp, and I could feel him panting into my hair, but I was deaf and blind and Senseless. Then life came back in a great rush, like the volume switched back on a TV, and I could hear glass and rubble falling even as I could feel the ground shake, and above me Cain's body was wracked with a hundred tiny, terrifying shudders as he bore the brunt of the impact of debris, until his taut grip on me loosened as he slumped into an unconsciousness that scared me more than the explosion. I had never seen Cain hurt: ambivalent as I might be about his claims of origin, I realised I never believed him as anything but invincible. The thought that he actually might not be brought tears to my eyes.

For what felt like a long time I simply couldn't move, pinned by the weight of an unmoving Cain and whatever else was on top of him. A loud buzzing filled my ears, and my throat was burning with acrid smoke, and I was filled with the terror that I would die here, trapped beneath the rubble and the dust. Then I felt movement above me and my eyes blinked, even the night seeming bright compared to the darkness of being buried. I turned my now-free head and saw Val, terrifying and beautiful as she tore the debris off us with her bare and bleeding hands, throwing aside rocks as if they were made of papier-mâché. Behind her, stunned and shaken, stood Medea, magic streaming off her like steam, as she leaned on the shoulder of Katie, who was naked, bruised, covered in the black goo of demon blood, mixing with the red from her own cuts and scratches. Both of them looked blank, frozen with shock.

"Help them!" Val barked, and Katie, trained for emergencies, snapped into action first, heading towards me like an automaton, ducking to examine me as Val hauled Cain off me and pulled him, not particularly gently, to his feet. I released the breath I wasn't even aware I was holding as I heard him groan, and saw his eyes flicker into consciousness, as Katie helped me stand. Back to herself now, she was unembarrassed by her nakedness as she briskly checked me over for injuries, her voice soothing and calm even as I couldn't make out her words through the swarm of bees in my ears. I must have passed muster, because she nodded at Val, who was looking at Cain expectantly. He shook himself like a wet dog, and when he looked up his expression was plain enough to read. We had to get out of there, and we had to go now.

By the time the sirens arrived, Katie, Cain, Medea and I had made it to a greasy spoon transport cafe, near enough to the main square of Canary Wharf that we could keep track of what was happening, but hopefully far enough away that our bedraggled band couldn't be connected to the explosion. We had shuffled and stumbled our way back to Cain's bike, where Medea had left her backpack, from which Katie procured a t-shirt and leggings (presumably stored for such an eventuality), and we had used almost industrial quantities of wet wipes to clean off the worst of the dust and blood, Cain and I averting our eyes as Medea hastily applied some kind of foul smelling balm to the worst of Katie's injuries. Luckily Cain's leather jacket had borne the brunt of the falling debris, and the disarray of the rest of his clothes and the tears in our jeans could presumably be taken for fashion choices. We weren't going to be winning any catwalk competitions any time soon, but at least as we sat, still dazed and disbelieving, we didn't look like terrorists. Val, of course, had simply vanished, racing off with a gazelle's grace to wherever warrior goddesses go when the fighting is over. I couldn't help notice that she gave Cain a brief kiss goodbye before she left: a mere peck, but on the mouth, and Cain's words in the stairwell came blazing back into my mind. I noticed he didn't turn back to me until her retreating form had vanished from his sight, and when he did, his expression was unreadable.

He had said nothing much so far, though as the only one of us currently capable of coherence, he had taken it upon himself to order tea and biscuits all round, and he watched us as we tried to calm our nerves with sugar, pretending not to notice that our hands were shaking. He, of course, had returned fairly quickly to his preternatural calmness, but his movements were slightly sluggish, and if I hadn't known him better, I would have thought he was in pain. I couldn't help but wonder what this was costing him. He'd said he conserved his strength because it had limits – a finite supply of power stretched over an infinite amount of time. How much had he used to survive a falling building? To heal himself now? How much, a tiny voice in my head was asking, had it cost him to save my life?

The cafe was sparsely peopled, but already there was a buzz of chatter, as the staff and clientele went outside to watch the police vans and fire engines roar past, the TV above the food counter hastily switched to a news channel. Two explosions in London in as many days: it was the tube bombings all over again, and we could see familiar footage of a grim-faced anchorman wondering aloud whether this was the work of Al-Qaeda, pondering whether the fact that only deserted buildings were being targeted meant it was some other, newer threat. Tonight's explosion, he assured us, had not yet been proved to be a bomb, and the only confirmed casualty was the sole nightwatchman. I felt a surge of guilt at that – another man who might not have been dead had it not been for my interference.

"So," I began, turning my attention away from the TV and trying to keep my voice steady. "That went well."

Medea let out an uncharacteristic skitter of nervous laughter, and Katie put a steadying hand over hers. Cain shrugged, unconcerned, but when he spoke his voice was hoarse and raw.

"We're alive, relatively unhurt and we know more than we did this morning. I'd call that a result."

I thought of the dead watchman, and the smouldering pile of what had once been a building, and realised I would hate to see what Cain considered a loss. The fact was that had Val not been there, Medea and Katie would most likely be dead: there's no way Medea's shield could have withstood that level of damage. As it was, as soon as the building started to shake, Val simply swept up the pair of them, grabbed her abandoned harness and swung out the way she came, spooling down the rope to slow their descent as the building fell after them, allowing Medea's shield to cushion the latter part of the fall, whereby Val's supernatural sturdiness and Katie's ability to always land on her feet took over and they had a safe if scary landing. All jealousies aside, I had to admit the woman had style.

"I'm just disappointed I didn't get to kill any bankers," Katie muttered. I think she was joking. Medea shot her a mildly worried look which I suspect mirrored my own, and held up her hands to get the attention of the group.

"So, let's think about what we know," she suggested, always one for a recap. I think it's the Wiccan fondness for ingredients that makes her one of life's quantifiers. I frowned.

"Well, we know that on top of all the usual things that go bump in the night, there's a Secret Squirrel cadre of evil magic vampire traditionalists plotting to take over London, or at least blow big bits of it up, and they know who we are, and they know that we're onto them, and they probably want us all dead."

Cain flashed me a smile of grim satisfaction.

"Insane, right? I mean, you're so famous for making their lives difficult." I glared at him. Now was *so* not the time for a rehash of this argument.

"So," Medea went on, deliberately ignoring this exchange, "what do we do about that?"

Cain sighed heavily.

"Do I have to keep saying this? *You* do nothing. You leave. You were useful enough in there, sure, but now it's time to leave the field to the professionals."

If I weren't worried it might break my hand, I would have slapped him.

"Excuse me? 'Useful enough?' I'm the one bringing the witch and the werewolf to the party."

"Wiccan."

"Shapeshifter."

Both Medea and Katie spoke in unison, and I gave them a nod of apology.

"And I'm the one who Sensed it was a booby trap while you were all ready to go all Bruce Willis on an astral projection. I think we more than pulled our weight."

"You were nearly taken hostage!" Cain protested, which drew alarmed looks from the women, but I was too angry to explain.

"As if that would have bothered you! You'd have stepped over my body and carried on!"

Cain looked at me, shocked and angry.

"What, so now you're unhappy about *how* I saved your life? I'm sorry, I wasn't aware that not hurting your feelings was more important than not getting your fucking *head* blown off!"

Medea, ever the peacemaker, stepped in quickly before I could answer, which was good as his last comment rendered me a bit speechless.

"In Cassandra's defence, the last three bad guys that have come after her have taken their heads home in their handbags." Her sternness was bringing out her Scottishness. "She's not exactly a helpless damsel in this."

I could have kissed her for that. Only not in front of her scary shapeshifter girlfriend, maybe. Cain looked at her, unconvinced, but also with a newfound respect, as if now finally getting that he wasn't dealing with some useless girlie who cast charms in her bedroom.

"I don't mean to offend you or disrespect your opinion," he said, which was more courtesy than he ever gave me, "But that was more luck than anything else. You're amateurs. You're not entirely without abilities and resources, yes, but you're way out of your depth. You're spunky," (Spunky? Did he just call us 'spunky'? What were we, the frigging girl guides?) "But mainly you've just been lucky, and that isn't enough to keep you alive."

"Perhaps it has to be," she rejoined, and I could feel her how her calmness irritated him. Just as his was infuriating me.

"Look, Cain, I appreciate that you saved my life back there…"

"Again."

"Again."

"Twice."

"Yes, twice, thank you. And I appreciate and that you want to protect us wee helpless women against the scary monsters and you'd be happier if we kept our pretty little heads down and let the big strong bloke take care of us, but the fact is we're in it now, and we're not getting out till it's over. I'm not some useless, stupid fuckpuppet you get to play with every time you drop into town for a little R & R. This is my city. Our city. The public transport sucks, the weather is shitty and the people aren't very nice, but if you think I'm going to sit idly by while you and the bad guys carve it up between you, you've got another think coming."

Cain was staring at me, and I realised that raising my voice to a man who'd just slain half of the army of darkness wasn't the smartest thing I had done today, but it had been a long night and I was more than a little sick of how everyone was treating me. Then I noticed that his mouth was twitching, and he was trying not to smile.

"Um, fuckpuppet?"

"Oh, shut up."

Medea and Katie were suddenly enormously interested in their biscuits.

"You do know that's what I'm going to call you from now on, right?"

He grinned. Medea let him have his moment before turning back to the subject at hand.

"I think we're rather losing sight of the bigger picture, here," she frowned. "Cassandra has rather eloquently stated her case for involvement. And while she did rather volunteer us both without asking..." I flushed guiltily. "But since we can, clearly, be of some use in this and we have the same concerns as she does, we're not planning to sit out on the sidelines either." I nearly pointed out that she had just volunteered Katie without asking, but since Katie was holding her hand and nodding supportively, I kept silent. This must be one of those relationship things. What did I know?

"So," she went on. "I suggest we come up with a plan. Can we assume the continued assistance of... your wife?"

Cain looked slightly awkward, an unfamiliar look for him.

"I don't know. I can try and find her again, and see what she says."

"Why did she help us just now?" I asked him, trying to keep the accusation out of my voice. I'd seen those kisses.

"Honestly, I have no idea. I like to think it's because of my warm and friendly personality or that she still bears me some residual affection after all the centuries we spent together, but realistically it's more likely that she just saw an opportunity to kill things."

"Well, you're clearly better matched than I thought you were," I muttered, but Medea cut me off, impatiently.

"That's not helpful, Cassandra."

I ducked my head, feeling like a reprimanded child. It didn't help that Cain seemed more amused than anything by my jealousy, and was mouthing the word 'fuckpuppet' at me. I really needed to learn to shut up.

"OK," she continued, sounding very used to this 'take charge' malarkey. "Plan B it is, then. We just need to think of one, now. But first, I think, more tea."

She rose to go fetch some, and I went with her to the counter.

"So..." I ventured. "You didn't tell me your girlfriend was a... wereleopard."

"Shapeshifter, technically."

"It's optional?"

"She can control it, yes."

"Impressive."

Medea smiled warmly, for the first time that day. "It's actually one of the least impressive things about her."

I thought of Katie, calm and capable in the aftermath of the explosion, coolly assessing our injuries as we stumbled our way to escape, and could sort of understand what she meant.

"So, a week ago, I didn't know your magic was this strong, or that you were gay and had a girlfriend, or that she was a wereleop… shapeshifter."

She smiled at me.

"I didn't know you were dating a so-called angel who was married to a pagan war goddess."

"Maybe we should go for after-work drinks more often."

She laughed at that, and I couldn't help but join in.

"So, is that all of your secrets?" she asked me, and I nodded.

"Pretty much. Yours?"

Again, that laughter, a bell chiming.

"Oh, Cassandra. I couldn't even begin to tell you all of *my* secrets."

OK. Well, *that* was reassuring.

Chapter 31

SO, WE had a plan. It wasn't much of a plan, and Cain once again didn't like it, but this time he was coming with me, and this time we were going in prepared.

Of course, we needed to rest first. Cain might have superhuman powers of resilience – albeit he had possibly pushed them to the limit – but the Wiccan, the werecat and the plain old human were all knackered after a night of battling demons and dodging falling masonry, so we agreed that no plan of action would start until we'd managed to get a few hours kip. Medea and Katie headed off to their place, texting us as soon as they arrived safely, established their home was monster- and assailant-free and Medea had re-created her wards, and Cain came home with me. I had half expected him to take off as soon as things had been decided – perhaps vanish off to wherever his ex-wife, sorry, *current* wife, had disappeared to – so was both surprised and not exactly pleased to have him accompany me, although I must admit it was nice to have him be the one to check my flat for bad guys. I felt like what had happened in that building – with the Valkyrie, with the gun thug – had changed things between us, and I wasn't sure I was ready to examine how. He'd saved my life, after all – again, and, as he had reminded me, twice, both by shooting the thug and by taking the weight of a falling skyscraper on top of him, which wasn't exactly nothing. But his words had stung me, tapping into some primal fear inside me that what he said had been the truth; that *was* how Cain felt about me. I was a convenient body, providing somewhere to rest his head and his penis whenever he was in town, but nothing more than that. And every time I closed my eyes I saw him and Val fighting, side by side in perfect unison, glorious in battle, and I felt my face flame as I remembered him leaning in to kiss his goddess softly on the back of her neck. How could I even kid myself that I could compare to that? As Cain had so bluntly informed me before my meeting with Laclos, I wasn't that special.

But I was here, and she wasn't, which probably accounted for his invitation to join him in the shower when we were safely ensconced in my flat. Any port in a storm, I suppose. I demurred, fed the cat and, not even bothering to clean myself up, stripped off my clothes and slid straight into bed, my aching, exhausted body sagging in relief as I slumped into that old, familiar comfort. Sensing my distress, Dante curled up beside me, his purring a steady buzz as I stroked his fur, and I was already dozing when I felt Cain, warm and still slightly damp from the shower, slide his naked body in beside mine. I lay there, for a moment, feigning sleep, not wanting to deal with whatever was happening between us. But then Cain put his arm around me, and pulled me closer to him, his body leaving me in no doubt that sleep wasn't upmost in his plans. I should have just shoved him away, got out of bed, or maybe even insisted that we actually have a conversation about the night's events, but instead I simply let him pull me on top of him as if I weighed nothing, my treacherous body already responding to the heat of his touch. I looked down at him for a moment, trying to read that inscrutable face, wondering if what he had told me was true, if he had seen even half that he had hinted at. If so, how many women had been where I had been, how many women had he looked up at with that half-smile of desire? But then he reached up and pulled me into a kiss, and I found myself unable to think anything at all.

"Just so I know. We *both* agree this is a bad idea this time?"

Cain was frowning at the enormous edifice of St Paul's as it loomed in front of us. We were leaning against his bike, his arm slung around my shoulder with a casual possessiveness that I couldn't help find rather pleasing, but also wondered if it was for effect: after all, they had to be watching the outside of the building, and know that we were coming.

"He sent us into a trap. I think that at least warrants a conversation."

Cain looked at me sceptically, since we were both painfully aware of how well our last attempt at 'just talking' to a vampire had gone. I shrugged, a movement which felt oddly heavy, mainly due to the enormous Samurai sword once again strapped to my back. I might not be much good at swordplay yet, but I felt like it made a useful point, if you'll pardon the pun. Cain, too, had made no effort to hide how well-armed he was, an automatic weapon tucked inside his jacket, a blade tucked into his belt – and that was just the visible firepower. I'd spent the entire bike ride here terrified we'd be pulled over by the police – I suspected Cain wouldn't take such an interruption well – and wondered if he was putting out some sort of angelic mojo that meant he went around unnoticed, or if he just looked like too much of a headache even for the boys in blue to deal with.

"Come on then. Let's see if we can put him in a talkative mood."

With that, he took his arm from around me, and strode towards the entrance to Laclos' crypt.

We were unsurprised to be greeted at the main door by the Counsel, though I nodded slightly to Cain, tapping my hand twice against his lower back in what looked like an affectionate touch but was really to confirm that my Sense had picked up at least two other, younger vampires hanging around in the gardens outside, shielded by the darkness. Whether the ramped up security was because of us or whatever had infiltrated and turned Taka – if Laclos' version of events was to be believed – I wasn't sure, but it was clear that the vamps were on high alert. The Counsel nodded at us coolly, his gaze taking in our weaponry, though his eyes narrowed when they met Cain's, as if he were trying to read something from his expression.

"If you come to seek vengeance, I can assure you that none of your recent travails are the work of any who remain here, so you are on a futile mission."

"What if we don't care and we've just come to see a whole lot of bloodsuckers burn?" Cain asked, with an uncharacteristic cheeriness. I goggled at him. *That* hadn't been part of the plan.

The Counsel inclined his head.

"Then you will find us well-prepared to deal with any such assault."

"You think?" he grinned, and for a second the Counsel actually looked unnerved. I stepped forward, thinking I better stop this before they dropped their trousers and got to comparing manhoods.

"We're just here to see Laclos. To talk." I said, firmly.

"Then you will not mind leaving your weaponry at the door."

Cain just laughed at that. Something about the way he was smiling was scarier than the guns.

"Yeah. That's going to happen."

He took my hand and simply stepped towards the Counsel, forcing him to step aside or have us walk into him. The vampire gave us a look that summed up the weary resignation that Cain does tend to induce in people, and he moved out of the way. Then, with a vampire's fastness, he

was in front of us again, opening the door with a smooth bow.
"If you would care to follow me."

By now the room was starting to feel familiar. We had taken the stairs as carefully as if they'd been a rope bridge over a canyon full of crocodiles, but my Sense picked up nothing but the vampires beyond the door to the lair, the faint buzz of the ones outside, above us, and the strong, steady glow of the Counsel as he guided us deeper down into the earth. He pushed open the door and stepped back to let us in, vanishing into the blackness behind us as we stepped into the dim light of Laclos' chamber, though I could Sense he didn't go too far.

"A crypt. How original," Cain muttered, casually scanning the room as if judging the decor, though I knew him well enough to know he was counting exits and adversaries, and seeing what, if anything, could be used as a weapon or a distraction if he needed one. Again I grabbed his belt, my hand tapping a quick tattoo that let him know the room held more vamps than we could see – as ever, one end was cloaked in darkness, and my Sense felt a huddle of power in the shadows.

One thing that was not in darkness was Laclos. He lay sprawled on the giant bed, clearly having arranged himself for best effect, the candles casting shadows off the muscles of his chest, his long hair curling down over his shoulders. I must admit, posed or not, it was a very nice picture. Not that that was a thought I wanted to give headspace right now. He sat up as we came further into the room, his movements as languid as a lion after a big meal – you knew he had the power to kill you, but you sensed you had caught him at the one time he'd rather not. His smile broadened when he saw me, but when his eyes flicked to Cain his reaction was almost alarming: he sat bolt upright, his pupils flaring. Oh dear. I realised for the first time this might not go well for a whole different set of reasons from the ones I had anticipated.

"My dear Cassandra," he purred, delighted. "What *have* you brought me?"

I tried to keep my voice from shaking.

"After last time I thought it wouldn't hurt to have a little muscle on my side."

"And *what* muscle, indeed…" And as if he had simply appeared there, Laclos was standing inches in front of us, staring at Cain with a look made sharp by hunger. Gone was the sated lion, here was a predator smelling blood. To his credit, Cain didn't even flinch, though I saw a nerve in his jaw flicker as Laclos' gaze swept over him from foot to face. It took the vampire an almost visible effort to drag his attention back to me. Which was, let's face it, in keeping with my week.

"I cannot apologise enough for Taka's uncouth and inexplicable behaviour…" he began, but I was in no mood for his games.

"That's not why we're here, and you know it. You know where we've been, and you know what happened, or at the very least you can give it a bloody good guess. And believe me, we aren't happy and we're more than ready to take it out on you, so you damn well better tell us what exactly you know about what's happening and exactly what you're willing to do to stop it."

Laclos' face brightened into a broad smile.

"That's quite the speech, Cassandra."

"I'm getting a lot of practice," I scowled, though frankly I could have said anything at that point, because Laclos was no longer looking at me. His eyes had gone back to Cain, pulled as if magnetised, and he stepped forward, an inch or two closer than was polite, and was staring at him with frank scrutiny. He stood slightly taller than Cain, his lean, marble paleness a stark contrast to Cain's well-muscled solidity and olive skin. The fact that Laclos was, as ever, only half dressed and Cain was layered with clothes and bristling with weaponry made the effect all the more marked. And, ashamed as I am to admit to it, it was actually pretty hot. Scary, obviously, but also... very hot. I blushed, and tried to banish that unworthy thought. Laclos, of course, wasn't having any problem with the same idea.

"So, you're Cassandra's little friend," he reached out with those long, slender fingers, lightly tracing the pulsing vein that now stood out along Cain's throat. Cain just looked at him, coolly, immobile, as if Laclos was of no import at all. Laclos' fingers ran up to Cain's jaw, and paused, fascinated. I admit the unworthy thoughts made another appearance, making my stomach lurch and parts of me several inches lower than my stomach react quite strongly indeed. Cain simply smiled a tight smile, though as Laclos tilted his head to examine him more closely, I noticed Cain's hand was resting on his gun.

"Mm, I must admit, I see the appeal."

"For her or for me?" Cain asked, calmly.

Laclos flashed a grin that made my blood fizz.

"I suppose both of you at the same time would be utterly out of the question?"

To my surprise, Cain let out a bark of laughter, genuinely amused. Laclos' voice deepened, seduction phasers clearly set on stun.

"I don't know what you are, Cassandra's friend, but I can smell the centuries on you. Don't tell me in all that time, it never once appealed?"

His hand had moved to Cain's chest, where it rested with

deceptive lightness just over his heart. A vampire of Laclos' age could punch through a man's chest wall as easily as through paper and pull out his heart before we knew he'd even moved: I wondered if Cain would be able to fend off any such attack? Just how strong was his body? I hoped we weren't about to find out. He was still looking directly at Laclos, as if not bothering to notice he was being quite openly felt up by his host.

"Maybe I was just waiting for you to make me an offer," he said, his voice clipped, and Laclos head actually lolled back for a moment in delight.

"Perhaps you were."

And then *my* heart almost stopped as Laclos leaned in and kissed Cain full on the mouth, his eyes closing as his lips touched Cain's, his hand closing into a fist, Cain's t-shirt clenched within it. The kiss only went on for seconds, but it felt like a very, very long time, and when Laclos pulled back his expression was transformed. He looked almost stunned – sated and starving all at the same time, his eyes wide and his mouth hanging open. To be fair, Cain had that effect on me a lot of the time, but it was odd to see it reflected on someone else, especially when that someone else was a centuries old vampire. And, yes, it was *more* than a little bit hot.

Cain just continued to level his unwavering gaze at Laclos, as if this whole thing were one colossal bore and his patience was starting to thin. Laclos, however, was too far gone to notice. He blinked a few times, rapidly, as if forcing himself back to lucidity, and finally tore his eyes away long enough to look at me.

"Well, I see that Cassandra's tastes are as extraordinary as she is," he murmured, which Cain acknowledged with a curt nod. Then, dazed, Laclos reached back for him again, almost unconsciously, and in a movement as fast as any vampire's Cain had grabbed his hand and was holding it firmly in his grip. His voice, when he spoke, was as calm as if he was reading out a weather report.

"I have to tell you, vampire, if you touch me again I'll rip your hands off and burn the stumps."

Laclos looked down, as if surprised both by his own movement and by Cain's reaction, and when he frowned I realised that Cain was actually hurting him. Cain watched him for a second, letting that realisation sink in with the shocked vampire as well, and then finally dropped his hand. Laclos stepped back, shaking his fingers as if to get the blood back into them, staring at them like they didn't belong to him.

"Duly noted." The feeling restored to his errant digits, he looked back at us, his smile only slightly less certain. "I should, however, point out that we are in fact on the same side here."

"I really doubt it," Cain scowled.

Laclos lowered his head slightly in what could have been a nod.

"Whether you choose to believe me or not, neither of us wants London to become a playground for monsters. You, because you believe us all to be hellspawn, and me... well, mainly because it cramps my style. As I have already explained to your lovely companion, peace suits me. It suits my people. We don't prey on this country. We feed on it a little, of course, but really, no more so than its human inhabitants. Even if you think us merely parasites, you have to accept that it is a foolish parasite that destroys its host."

"What about killing the other fleas?"

"Not to overstretch the metaphor, but I happen to believe there is enough dog for everyone." Cain looked sceptical, but Laclos simply shrugged. "Killing people hasn't been profitable for centuries, and killing one another has rarely been required. As soon as those things stopped being necessary or useful, I made sure they ceased."

He made sure? I stared at him, wondering how much clout Laclos really wielded in London.

"You should be on my side," he went on. "My kind and I are all that stands between this city and carnage."

"Look around you," Cain snarled, his temper finally showing. "You need to do a better job."

Laclos tilted his head, in sorrowful agreement.

"You are right, of course. Current events have too plainly illustrated the limits of my influence. So I am suggesting that we… join forces. Get into bed together, if you will."

Honestly, he couldn't help himself. I could feel Cain's patience evaporating off him like steam, even as I could Sense how excited Laclos was, both by Cain's proximity and, perversely, by the prospect of him losing control in front of him. Not that I needed to Sense it; I could actually see it. Let's put it this way, some of Laclos was moving closer to Cain of its own accord. My own patience thinning – not least because I was starting to feel more than a little invisible in all this – I stepped in between them, putting a hand on both of their chests. For a moment I almost started, feeling like I'd earthed some electrical connection, completed some circuit, and if I hadn't known better I would have sworn I felt Cain's heart jump, just a little, when I touched him. Clearly all these hormones were driving me a little crazy here, too.

"Look, knock off the cheesy metaphors and the demonic seduction routine, would you, Laclos? We've already seen that at least some of your people are involved, unless you think Shogun just went rogue because he didn't like my perfume. The last tip you gave me nearly got me and my friends blown up and left a fucking big crater in Canary

Wharf, so frankly I think you owe us some straight answers. I'm not having a bunch of Others barneying in my hometown as if the humans don't matter, and at the moment you're the best option we have other than my "lovely companion" here going nuclear on the whole city. So enough of the Hugh Hefner of the Dead act and actually help us, or admit you're completely fucking useless in this whole thing and we'll be out of here before Cain loses what little is left of his temper and we find out just how fucked you can be."

Then I stepped back, out of their way. If it was going to kick off, I didn't want to be in the middle.

But Laclos spun to face me, seeming delighted by my defiance. He went to move towards me, only to be barred by Cain's suddenly outstretched arm. I would have been flattered by the gesture, had it not just felt like more macho posturing in what was becoming a slightly tedious pissing contest. Laclos looked down at Cain's arm, as if debating just how much force would take to move it, then took a careful step back.

"As ever, Cassandra, you have stated your case with enviable eloquence. I am starting to think that if your mythological counterpart had possessed any of your persuasive skills, she may well have had her prophecies taken more seriously."

"No, she was pretty much just a nut," Cain muttered, not quite under his breath, and both Laclos and I goggled at him for a moment. But evidently, Cain had reached the end of his tether.

"We're done here. We've delivered the message. Use your people. Your sources. We need to know if Mallen is the only one behind this, because we fully intend to stop him. We want to know where we can find him – and the real him, not the bullshit astral wizard projection."

For the first time, Laclos looked actually rattled.

"I told you what I knew. It is all simply rumours, tales of the street. Now people are even more scared. You think we are any better equipped to deal with an ancient vampire who possesses magical abilities than you are? Everyone fears his reprisals should they speak. No one is talking. Trust me, I have asked."

Cain's expression was pitiless.

"Ask harder. And don't worry about reprisals. Now we know what he is, we'll find a way to stop him. *You* find out where he is. Find out who's helping him. We can do the rest."

Which was rather news to me, but I didn't dare say anything. Cain gave Laclos a withering look that somehow managed to encompass the entire chamber, hidden, silent bodyguards included.

"And we know where *you* live. We know what you are. Don't forget that."

And with that he grabbed my wrist and almost dragged me from the room, opening the door with such force that even the Counsel stumbled in his hurry to get out of the way.

Chapter 32

I'D RARELY seen Cain so angry. His face was set like stone and his hold on my wrist had gone from firm to painful as he pulled me up the stairs behind him, hoisting me up impatiently when I tripped in my struggle to keep up with his furious pace. I wasn't sure what exactly was making him so mad. I suspect being French kissed by a bisexual lord of the undead hadn't been high on his to do list for the evening, but he seemed to be taking it a little too personally. I flinched as he kicked open the door – which was a tad over dramatic, as it wasn't locked – and I blinked as we were suddenly out in the bright lights that illuminated the cathedral against the night. Cain released me and stalked over to his bike, leaning against it as if struggling to control himself.

"Well, not entirely sure if that achieved anything," I admitted, which clearly did nothing to improve his mood. He glared at me, his expression so fierce that I backed away from him.

"It gave you something to look at, at least," he snarled.

"There is that," I tried for lightness, but my tone floundered in front of his fury. All this because of a kiss? Cain didn't strike me as a man so insecure about his sexuality he'd be this angry about what was surely not much more than a clumsily executed pass. Confused, I reached out and touched his shoulder, ready to flinch away if he shook me off – which he went to do, before visibly stopping himself, his hand clamping down on mine.

"I know that can't have been... fun for you." I began, tentatively, and he raised eyes to mine that were so full of rage I had to exert an effort of will not to pull back from him.

"He was trying to get into my head."

"It's just mind games," I said, with a reassurance I didn't feel. "It's how he operates. It's just for show."

"No, you don't understand, Cass." Cain's voice was uncharacteristically hoarse. "While I was in there, someone… was trying to get inside my head. Into my mind. I could feel it. It was like my brain was being skewered on meat hooks."

My mouth fell open.

"It wasn't the vampire sticking his tongue down my throat that bothered me, Cass." He shot me a grim look. "Though I think I'll need a couple of bottles of mouthwash to get rid of *that* particular memory. It was that one of the other vampires was trying to rape my mind at the same time."

Cain wanted to leave straight away, but I was worried about him riding a motorbike in his shaken condition: hell, he'd been in better shape when the building fell on him. So we stashed the weapons on the bike, pushing it away from where we'd left it to a different part of the road, further away – hoping that Laclos' cronies wouldn't bother looking for us to steal them, or, let's face it, cut our brake lines and kill us. I was all cheery thoughts today. Cain must not have felt well, because he let me take charge of moving the bike, and sat quietly where I left him at the table in a nearby pub, while I squeezed through the midweek work crowd to get us a drink. He swallowed the shot of whisky I brought him straight down, following it with a long gulp of the pint. I slid in beside him, gingerly aware I was watching him like you might watch a fire near a petrol pump, wondering if he was getting ready to explode. But the drink seemed to calm him, and he smiled at me, looking almost like himself.

"Nice friends you've got."

"They're not…" I began, but didn't bother finishing.

"Did... did it get you?" I thought of the wave of shock and terror that had greeted me when I'd reached my Sense out to read him, and wondered what kind of creature could survive that and keep digging. Cain looked almost amused at my question. If he was treating me like an idiot child again, clearly he was feeling better.

"No, Cass, it didn't 'get' me. I don't think there is an Other alive that could successfully mount that kind of attack on me. But it was strong, to make me feel it. To make it... hurt." He pulled a face. "Gah, I feel like I need to wash my skull out with disinfectant."

"You think it was Laclos?" For some reason the thought horrified me, and it wasn't for Cain's sake. Cain gave an abrupt little laugh.

"No, it wasn't Laclos."

"Are you sure?"

He gave me a tight little smile. "Laclos is barely a millennium old, Cass. If he'd tried that kind of stunt, we would have been picking bits of him off the crypt floor."

That wasn't exactly reassuring.

"So it was someone... something older than Laclos?"

"Significantly so."

"Mallen?"

He shook his head in frustration.

"I don't know. It's been centuries since I've faced that kind of attack, and it's not like I wasn't otherwise occupied at the time. I couldn't tell where... or who... it was coming from."

I felt rather guilty now about how much I'd been enjoying his discomfort at Laclos' attentions.

"Why couldn't I Sense it?"

It was his turn to look a little guilty.

"I'm afraid I rather shorted your Sense out when it comes

to me."

"That's probably the least of what you've done to me," I muttered, which at least made him smile. He leaned in and kissed me, uncharacteristically gently, and the trace of Laclos lingered beneath the alcohol on his lips. I tried not to notice how oddly erotic I found that idea. When he pulled away he was frowning, and for an awful moment I thought he'd read my mind.

"You do know it's going to get worse, right? We've only just seen the start of the damage."

I felt my stomach plummet. That wasn't what I wanted to hear right now. Then I blurted out a question that was a shock even to me.

"How many people have you killed, Cain?"

He looked as surprised as I did, but recovered quickly.

"Define people."

"It scares me you need to break it down like that."

He sighed, and took another long drink of his beer.

"I've been alive a long time, Cass. You've been in this fight a week and how many corpses have *you* stacked up? And, no offence, but you're a total amateur. So trust me, you don't want me pulling together numbers. You won't like the answer."

I took a swig of my own drink, unhappily. "I'm not sure. At the moment I might find it reassuring."

His expression softened by my obvious misery, Cain reached out and put an arm around my shoulder, pulling me into a comfortingly tight embrace. Part of me didn't care, then, about all the violence and the trouble, I just wanted to be crushed against the rock of his body forever. But it was a child's wish for safety, and I forced myself to pull away, my eyes meeting his, as if in explanation. Undeterred, he raised a hand to my face, gently pushing back my hair.

"I know you hate this. But you were right, and I was wrong. We're all in this, now, and we can fight this fight. We can win."

Stupidly, I felt my eyes start to blur.

"And then what? We don't know even what we're really fighting. How do we know when we've won?"

"Maybe we won't. Sometimes you don't. You just move onto a different fight."

"And that's it? That's life? That's not what I want, Cain. I throw parties for a living. I don't want this life."

Cain looked at me with an expression it took me a second to recognise as pity, because I'd never seen it on his face before.

"Sometimes we don't get to choose."

"But I don't even like horror movies!" I protested, in what came out as a pathetic, needy wail.

"Then you pretty much chose the wrong job."

I couldn't help but pout at him. "That doesn't make me feel any better."

This time he smiled at me.

"Babe, so far you've beaten off an inhuman mugger with a handbag, scared a demon with a frying pan, taken out half an occult army and shot a vampire Samurai in the nuts. I think you've got plenty of fight in you."

Chapter 33

"I THINK I may have issues," I said, into the phone. I swear, I could *hear* Medea roll her eyes in response.

"I think you may have to narrow that down a little."

It was later. Cain had delivered me back to my flat, checked for monsters – and paused to pet the cat, who he seemed to have developed an unlikely affection for – and then gone off on the one mission I really wasn't keen on him taking: to find his wife.

"She can help us. You've seen what she can do," he had reminded me, when he saw my reaction to this casually delivered announcement. "If we can get Val on side…"

"Really, you call her Val?" It was an odd thing to seize on, admittedly, but somehow I couldn't imagine that scene of domesticity. "Val" somehow didn't seem how you'd address a warrior goddess over breakfast. "That really can't be what you called her when you were together."

Cain's expression snapped closed like a trap.

"You don't want to hear me call her any of the things I called her when we were together," he informed me, brusquely, which was a great note for him to depart on.

So, taking advantage of the fact that we were officially friends, now, I had phoned Medea, and was currently conducting this conversation while sitting in my kitchen, eating ice cream from the tub, feeling like a scene from the unreleased Bridget Jones movie: the one where she not only has to fend off hot competition for her emotionally unavailable man, but defeat the encroaching army of supernatural evil while she was at it.

"What *particular* issues are you talking about tonight?"

Medea prompted. I swallowed a mouthful of strawberry cheesecake ice cream.

"Cain. Laclos. Mallen and his mysterious evil powers. Cain's ex-wife. Sorry, very *current* wife. Why don't I know any normal people?"

"Why, thank you."

"You know what I mean. I don't mean you," Wiccan werecat lover, I added mentally, but very quietly, even in my head, because the last few days had taught me I really had no idea the extent of Medea's powers. She sighed, and rolled her eyes. Honestly, I could hear it. Or Sense it, maybe.

"You run a dating agency for vampires. Maybe you aren't actually interested in normal people?"

"What?"

"Well, people generally attract what they want, consciously or subconsciously. So maybe this *is* what you want."

"Then how come I haven't attracted Johnny Depp?"

Another sigh.

"OK, something you want *and* believe is possible."

"So you're saying, somewhere in my consciousness, my psyche, I don't want a normal, 'let's rent a DVD and get a curry' relationship, I want a gun-toting homicidal God freak or Iggy Pop's undead bisexual lovechild?"

At least she had the decency to laugh.

"I'm not saying your subconscious is that… articulate. It's just that since you have discovered your… gift, I bet you have never felt normal. So I'm assuming that on some level, you don't feel that your lovers…"

"Laclos isn't my lover!" I protested, my face flushing hot at the thought.

"Although he is rather being included in that context," Medea pointed out, gently, which made me go even redder, before she conceded, "Alright, your... admirers... to be normal. It's up to you to decide whether you think that is a good or a bad thing."

I paused, and not just to take a mouthful of ice cream.

"That's very profound. Is that some sort of Wiccan philosophy?"

Medea chuckled, suddenly sounding very Scottish again.

"Well, that and Katie bought me the DVD of The Secret for my birthday."

"Oh, well that's just great," I scowled, but my disapproval was interrupted by a knock.

"Is that your front door?" Medea asked, instantly alert.

"Yes. But you're the only person who would be coming to my house this late."

"It might be Cain?"

"Cain never knocks."

"OK... I'm holding on here until you tell me it's OK." I heard a muffled conversation in the background, and she came back. "I've got Katie on her mobile with the first two nines dialled."

"Right. I'm going to see who it is." I wanted to tell her not to worry, but it hadn't been that kind of week, and I couldn't help thinking this whole back up thing was actually pretty cool. But back up halfway across London, cool as it might be, was one thing: I picked up my gun as well, just to be on the safe side.

My treacherous Sense, though, rolled over like a puppy as I went to the door, a reaction I'd never had before but wasn't exactly unpleasant. I couldn't help the surge of colour that came to my cheeks as I looked through the spy hole to see Laclos standing there, looking as louche and pleased with himself as ever, though at least being outdoors had meant he'd put on a shirt. Which was a good thing, obviously. Really.

"It's Laclos," I told Medea.

"Shall I stay on the line and listen in?" She sounded slightly keener than she should be at that prospect. I saw Laclos – who could of course hear us both – raise an eyebrow in amusement.

"No, I'm pretty sure I can handle this," I assured her, and hung up and opened the door. But I didn't put the gun down.

Laclos smiled at me, ignoring the weapon in my hands, and held his arms out wide in that now familiar gesture, half surrender, half inviting worship. Even fully dressed as he was, there was something about the way Laclos wore clothes that suggested he was only ever seconds away from nudity. It was remarkably disconcerting.

"I suppose it would be too much to expect you to invite me in?"

I struggled to keep my hands and my voice steady.

"You suppose right."

"Your neighbours might talk."

"This isn't exactly a high end part of town, Laclos. I could murder a tramp on the doorstep and no one would say a thing."

He inclined his head in agreement, and lowered his arms.

"Cain isn't here, if you're after a re-run." I was alarmed by how petulant that sounded. Dear God, was I jealous? I was jealous. From his broadening smirk, Laclos had picked up on that, too.

"It isn't Cain I'm after."

"What, so now he's not in your eye line, I'm visible again?" OK, I knew how that sounded, and I didn't care. Laclos looked more puzzled than offended.

"Yes, he did have rather an odd effect on me," he mused, curiously, as if not entirely clear on how that had happened. "I realise that came across as rude, but he was rather *exceptionally* distracting. But only… *temporarily* distracting." He paused, as if this was something even he struggled to articulate. "He is… quite extraordinary. Whatever he is."

That was deliberately pointed, but I didn't rise to the bait. If Cain's real nature was hidden to Laclos and his fangy band, that might be an advantage, and one I wasn't in a hurry to throw away. Realising he wasn't getting an answer, Laclos smiled at me.

"Now, however, I am quite returned to my senses. And so it is you I came here to speak to."

He reached out to touch me, but the threshold of my flat held him back like a solid wall. He gave a slight tut of impatience.

"I'm just as disturbed by this situation as you are, Cassandra."

I wasn't sure which situation he meant, exactly, so I said nothing.

"You may mock Taka, but he was faithful to me… in a number of ways…" I had a vivid flash, there, that made me blush even more. "For centuries. *Centuries*. To find that Mallen, or those he is affiliated with, have infiltrated that close to my inner sanctum," Yes, he actually said 'inner sanctum', with a completely straight face. "… that is horrifying to me. I do want to help you stop him."

"Then why don't you do something?"

He let out a sharp sound of frustration.

"Did it ever occur to you that Mallen is more powerful than me? That the forces at his disposal significantly dwarf my own? We have been at peace for generations in this city, Cassandra, and so have had no need of an army. But Mallen has clearly been assembling one. He has been in London less than a century, but he already has allies, and they are obviously powerful, and on top of that he is both bold and reckless. That is a dangerous combination. We have spent years making ourselves invisible and he unleashes murder on the streets and then blows up not one but two buildings? He wants a battle, patently, and he wants it to be seen. We must find a way of fighting him without our very engagement in the fight being the thing that secures our own downfall." His hand twitched towards me, again, and he lowered it, annoyed. "That is why I have come here – at considerable risk to myself and my people – to tell you that I will try to help you. I am not being deliberately opaque about Mallen – I have had little to do with him, ever, and we have managed to rub along in this city for decades by the simple expedient of virtually ignoring one another's existence. He disapproves of me, apparently," he added, and couldn't hide a smirk of self-satisfaction at that.

"I can't imagine why."

"But clearly I was wrong to assume that that would mean he would simply keep his distance from me, as I have from him." He sighed, and for a second a look of tiredness flashed over that ridiculously handsome face. "I am realising that I am not as skilled at politics as I thought I was. I really should have paid more attention to Machiavelli. But honestly, I thought it was just fairly tedious pillow talk."

I goggled slightly at that: he was as bad as Cain, and I could never tell if they were joking. Maybe they should get together, they could compare notes. Which was exactly the wrong thought to think when standing next to a vampire who can hear your heart speed up: Laclos flashed me a knowing look and I coughed, trying to resume some control of the conversation.

"Ahem… OK. So, thanks. Message delivered."

"I really would like to come in."

"I really would like to look like Christina Hendricks, but we don't always get what we want."

His eyes dropped unmistakably to my cleavage.

"You look perfectly fine to me."

My blush deepened, but I said nothing. His smile evaporated.

"You know that if all I had wanted to do was to deliver a message, I could have sent someone else."

"Then what do you want?"

His voice sharpened with impatience, his usual routine suddenly abandoned.

"You know what I want."

"Why?"

It was such a genuine question that it shocked him. He stepped towards me, and it took him an almost visible effort to calm himself from being repulsed again by threshold.

"Why do you find it so hard to believe that I am actually sincere in my suit? That I do genuinely want you. More than that, that I…" he floundered, as if seeking an unfamiliar word. "That I like you."

I frowned at him.

"But… why?" OK, I do know how pathetic that sounded. But Laclos paused, realising that his answer was important to me.

"I have been alive a long time, Cassandra. Most people… whether dead *or* alive… bore me in seconds. Honestly, sometimes I find myself having sex with them just to shut them up. But… you fascinate me."

"Yeah, because I'm *that* fucking special."

He looked at me, frighteningly sincere. "Why would you refute that? You're unreadable and impossible to compel. You are fierce in your defence of yourself, your friends and, even more impressively, Others – the very same creatures that tore your adolescence in half." He saw my eyes widen at that, and he nodded slightly in acknowledgement of my shock – he hadn't been kidding before when he said they'd done their research on me. "These are the creatures that are currently running amok in your city, and yet you cling to your belief that we be judged as individuals, not a species. You are... remarkable under pressure. Your best friend is a Wiccan and your lover is... clearly not of this realm. Why do you insist on thinking of yourself as mundane?"

I felt tears prickle my eyes and my gaze met his, searching for any hint of a lie in his face. But he wasn't lying.

"Cassandra, why can't you see how intoxicating you are to me?"

I couldn't help myself. I stepped forward, out of the safety of my threshold, and into his arms. Because he had just described the woman I always wanted to be and known I would never measure up to: brave, and principled, an alluring woman with amazing friends. Hearing it from him made me think that, for that moment at least, it could be true.

Also, I think I may have mentioned this earlier: he was really, insanely freaking hot.

Then he was kissing me. This wasn't the gentle tease of last time; this was a fierce, passionate embrace that crushed me against him, a kiss that I felt surge through my whole body like fire. The chill of his lips and his skin met the blaze of mine and I wanted to warm him, to heat that frozen flesh with the force of my desire. His arms tightened around me and he gave a moan of pleasure as if drinking in my warmth, and then I felt the sharp sting of his teeth on my neck and smelt blood and I buckled, startled, pulling back only to see that he looked as alarmed as I did.

"I... I'm sorry. I didn't mean..." he looked like a puppy caught peeing on the carpet, so unlike his usual confident self it startled me. He was fumbling for words as if he was speaking a language he had barely learned. "I… it's the effect you have on me. I got carried away."

I felt myself ache at the pain in his expression, and shook my head, sounding almost as apologetic as he did.

"I'm sorry, Laclos. That's just… too much for me."

"But you have been with a vampire before…" he protested, uncomprehending.

"And it was too much for me then."

He looked uncharacteristically crestfallen, and reached out one pale hand, stroking my face.

"Will it always be?"

Unbidden, I had a flash of memory, and I saw Cain, and the look on his face as he casually told a man to kill me.

"I don't know."

He forced a smile, his voice returning to its usual teasing cadence.

"Well, the only thing sweeter than blood is hope."

I laughed.

"And on that note, Edward, I am going back inside."

He at least had the grace to chuckle at that.

"What if I wait around here and look soulful? Will that encourage you to invite me in?"

"Well, you *are* immortal. You have plenty of time to find out."

I stepped back, smiling, and closed the door in his face.

It took less than 15 minutes for him to get bored of waiting and knock again. It had taken all my strength to hold out that long myself, the only thing stopping me letting him in straight away was the fact that I had no earthly idea what would happen when I did. But I couldn't just leave him out there.

"OK," I laughed, swinging open the door, "For the sake

of the neighbours at least, you can come in."

Then my Sense finally overcame my hormones, too late screaming for my attention. A fist made of solid brick hit my face and as the world went black I realised it wasn't Laclos that I had just invited in.

Chapter 34

I WAS scared before I was even awake. My Sense was howling, railing and thrashing like a trapped and wounded animal, and the discomfort in my body was only a distant contender for my attention over this almost primal wave of fear. I cursed my Sense and my own stupidity – I'd been too distracted by Laclos to pick up on what my Sense had been trying to tell me, and so I had left myself wide open to attack. I grimly made myself a promise that in the unlikely event I survived whatever was waiting for me when I opened my eyes, I would learn how to nurture my Sense, to direct it better, not let it flounder when I was under pressure, only ever using it when there was nothing real at stake. That promise gave me something to cling to, as I tried to gauge my injuries without alerting my captor to the fact that I was awake.

My face throbbed where I had been punched, but now I calmed my Sense enough to listen, that pain was joined by a litany of complaints from the rest of my body. I was sitting on a hard, cushionless chair: without opening my eyes it was difficult to tell what kind, but it felt like just an old-fashioned wooden dining room or schoolroom chair; judging from the way it wobbled slightly as I stirred, a fairly cheap and elderly one at that. I was tied up: my arms by my sides, each wrist fastened tightly to the back of the chair so that my arms were forced straight down, my ankles tied to the front legs of the chair, my feet flat on the ground. My limbs screamed out a protest at being locked into one position, although how long I had been unconscious, I had no idea. Tears came instantly, and I blinked to try and stop then, and the slightest of coughs from the other side of the room made me realise the gesture had been noticed. Having nothing to hide, now, I opened my eyes.

The vampire Mallen stood, watching me, his body frozen with a vampire's preternatural stillness as he leaned against a tatty, metal framed desk, the only other furniture I could see in the room. Beleaguered as it was, my poor Sense could tell it *was* his body I was looking at, not an illusion – the one time I actually wanted the bastard not to be there, of course he showed up in person. He wore the same well-cut suit he'd worn before, and pulsing from him came that same throb of power that I had noticed that first time, our first meeting, so long ago. To think I'd actually been attracted to him: I had *wanted* to see him again. Careful what you wish for, I suppose. To be fair, though, he didn't look any more pleased to see me than I was to see him.

"I thought it would be easy," he scowled, speaking the minute I opened my eyes, as if this was a complaint he had been saving up and couldn't wait to tell me. I couldn't help but notice that the Eastern European accent seemed to have been discarded: he sounded as English as I was. "There's nothing in this town but low levels and poseurs, a bunch of stupid vampires who overdosed on Anne Rice and Twilight and wouldn't know real power if it bit them. And Laclos, of course, who has plenty of power but fritters it away on rock star fantasies and blood groupies and the idea that, 'hey, why don't we all just get along?' And what else?"

He looked at me, but plainly wasn't expecting an answer, having obviously decided to give me the entire evil egomaniac speech in one go.

"A few Others. Nothing significant. And people. People! People too soft and stupid and self-obsessed to see what is happening in front of their faces. And on top of that, one of them..." here he gestured to me. "Makes me a shopping list!

All of the new ones, the young ones, with their lack of protectors and knowledge and their idiotically integrationist ideas. Could it actually get any better?"

"Do I need to be here for this conversation?" I asked, putting as much boredom as I could into my voice. "I'm happy to step outside while you get the rant out of your system."

His eyes flared, and when he smiled at me, it was more a simple baring of fangs than anything else.

"So what stops me? A human? And even then I'm thinking, she might be gifted. She might be... what is that word? *Spunky*? She might be slower to take a hint and handier with a frying pan than I anticipated, but really, what harm can she do to my plans?"

Clearly, I wasn't meant to have any input on this. He was getting well into his stride, the veins in his face bulging, coursing with the blood he had recently consumed so that they stood out, blue red, against the paleness of his skin. But in his anger he was losing control of damping down his power, and it felt like I was being repeatedly smacked in the face. I realised with a spurt of panic that he might not even have to deliberately hurt me: being exposed to this much power head on might fry my Sense for good, and whatever that meant for the rest of me, I couldn't imagine it would be fun.

"I have resources. I have skills. I have allies more powerful than you could possibly imagine. While others of my kind have wasted the centuries indulging their basest desires, I have put the time to profit. I have tapped into magic so dark it isn't spoken of. I have unleashed legions of hellspawn. And I am thwarted by a... girl?"

He spat the word at me like an insult. I thought this would be exactly the wrong moment for my inner feminist to correct that to 'woman', but I couldn't help myself. Sensibly – or luckily – he ignored me.

"And how does she stop me? Because she is friends with a witch! Whose lover is a werecat!"

"Shapeshifter," I muttered, clearly determined to annoy him further, because, hey, that seemed like a good plan.

"And she is fucking a psychopathic hitman who turns out to be an angel!" I couldn't help notice his speech was getting decidedly more 21st century the angrier he got, the Dracula impression he'd affected when I met him receding. Was anything about this vampire actually as it seemed? For a supposed traditionalist, he was sounding awfully modern. "And he turns out to be married to a frigging Valkyrie." He let out an almost-hysterical laugh. "Are you kidding me? Did I pull out the losing hand at Supernatural Top Trumps?"

OK, that actually made me laugh, which turned out to be a mistake, because that finally got his attention. He turned his bulging, bloodshot eyes at me, and as always when terrified I retreated into cockiness.

"You know, I think the real problem here is you're a little too fond of the supervillain exposition speech."

He flashed me a grin that somehow managed to be all fangs, his face far too close to mine for comfort.

"He did say you were amusing."

He?

"So amusing that killing me would be depriving the world of much needed laughter?" I ventured, and his smile broadened.

"Not that amusing, no."

I sighed, theatrically. "It's a sexist world. No one likes a funny woman."

"If it's any consolation, I can think of some very entertaining ways to kill you."

I tried to ignore the tremor in my voice. "Well, if you're

going to do it, can you get on with it? I think I'd prefer to be killed than listen to you go off on another one."

His face twitched in anger and I desperately tried to stop my heart thudding: a ridiculously pointless exercise in a room with a creature who could probably hear my hair grow. And fear must have been coming off me in waves: he could probably taste it. It was certainly clear he enjoyed it. He leaned in even closer, and the lack of breath when he spoke was oddly disconcerting.

"Oh, Cassandra Bick. Killing you is the last thing I want to do to you." He paused, for proper super villain effect. "Of course I *do* plan to kill you. But there is an awful lot I want to do to you first."

He moved with inhuman swiftness, tearing my shirt open even before I registered his movement, my bra snapping like gossamer as he ripped it away from me. I felt rather than heard myself cry out as, his hand wrapped in my torn clothes, he grabbed the silver cross that hung from my nipple and yanked it free in one brisk pull, dropping it and the now-tainted cloth like it was toxic.

"I don't think your trinkets will do you much good, now. It's over for you. You might as well enjoy it. I certainly intend to."

Then he ducked his head and took my bleeding breast in his mouth. I felt the stab of his teeth and for a second the almost animal sound of him suckling made me want to heave. There was no room for jokes, now, for cocky comebacks or plucky defiance. Everything fled beneath a wave of terror that hit me like a tsunami and left me shaking, unable even to struggle as his hand pinned my throat, as in some grotesque perversion of sex his free hand caressed my other breast. And then slowly, gradually I could feel it, the narcotic in his saliva flooding my system like the drug it was, soothing me, calming me... exciting me. Ravaged as it was, my nipple hardened under the lapping of his tongue, the pain fading into a sensual blur. Why shouldn't I let him take me? This was divine. Now I was straining against him for a different reason, pushing my chest forward into his mouth, and I giddily heard him utter a low, guttural moan of pleasure as he drank deeper, my entire being focused on the sweet, sharp delight at my breast.

So who was that screaming? It was there, nagging at me, pulling at my mind like a wayward child, and the small part of my brain still functioning realised it was my Sense. I squeezed my eyes shut, and let my Sense flow, and as the world came into focus I could see the vampire and his drug now for what it was: a poison, a pollutant. It was pestilence, not pleasure, that was sweeping through my system. But recognising this didn't mean I could stop it. Replacing the dull glow of joy came humiliation and shame and terror as I realised just what he was doing to me and how completely helpless I was to prevent it. His hands moved down my body, pushing my skirt up past my hips as he slid his palms between my thighs, easing them apart. And though I felt tears stream my face as the flimsy cotton of my briefs was snapped away from me, and I felt him pull back long enough to unfasten his belt, releasing his erection, his hands beneath my hips as he lifted me, all the better to rape me properly, a bitter smile formed on my face because I knew Mallen, distracted by his own desire, had just made his first mistake.

Almost the instant he touched me he roared away in pain, his hands cupping the genitals that had been scorched by the two tiny silver studs embedded in my own.

"You fucking bitch!" he howled, but in that instant I was on top of him. Using my weight to pitch the chair forward, I hurled myself at him, my head ducked so that, as he rose to attack me, I caught him squarely once again in the very area he'd just made vulnerable. Being nutted in the nuts is no fun for anyone – especially not a vampire recovering from a serious burn – and he toppled, screaming, back to the floor. For a moment, I knew how Cain must feel. I wanted not just to kill him, to obliterate him, but to kill them all, every single one of them. Driven by that fury I rocked back on the hind legs of the chair, so that the front legs rose off the floor. For a second I thought I would topple backwards, as Mallen scrabbled under me to grab at my ankles, but I swung the chair forward just before it tipped over, bringing the front legs down with as much force as I could muster. It was only as both wooden legs speared his body that Mallen realised, belatedly, he had effectively tied me up on top of four stakes. He let out another cry, barely human now, twisting his impaled body to try and get away from me.

Again, I tipped my full weight back on the chair, and though it took a couple of attempts – both of which were greeted with satisfyingly agonised screams from the vampire – I managed to wrench the chair legs free of his flesh. Hunched over my bindings, I gripped the back of the chair tightly and managed to get all four legs of the thing off the ground enough to let scuttle around on tiptoe. Not a huge amount of mobility: but then I didn't need to go far. I launched myself backwards at the edge of desk, this time allowing myself to fall. I struck the side so hard I felt my teeth jar, and a burning sensation told me at least some of my back had been scraped raw by the impact, but I got the splintering sound I needed as the chair cracked against the metal. The backrest of the chair was sheered straight off: I raised my still tethered hands and brought it crashing down again, this time splitting the flimsy wood into two jagged halves. I might still be tied up, with half a chair strapped to my ankles, but my arms were free, I could just about stand, and the splintered shafts of wood strapped to my wrists were weapon enough. I turned to face the fallen vampire, my fury giving me strength, because I knew now that I would kill everything in this world before I would let this creature touch me again. But Mallen suddenly didn't seem so terrifying.

"No... it wasn't... it wasn't..." he gurgled, his eyes rolling in his head, no power about him now. "I can tell you..."

But I really wasn't interested in anything he had to say. I threw myself onto him with an incoherent howl, and his body jolted as I plunged one arm down, my hand and the makeshift stake attached to it striking his chest with a blow made fierce by rage and adrenaline. Gasping, crying, I pulled myself free, and my face jerked back as the spray of my own blood that hit me, suddenly freed from his veins. I sagged to the ground beside his corpse, half-hobbled by my restraints and weak with relief and exhausted by my efforts. Yay for all that extra cake, I thought, and allowed myself a small, hysterical giggle. But that was OK, I was safe now. Except of course I was locked in a room, God only knows where, with no idea how many of Mallen's cronies were outside the door waiting for me.

Then the door splintered off its hinges and I realised I was about to find out.

Chapter 35

THE VAMPIRES swarmed through the doorway like a plague of locusts, fangs bared and faces distorted, screaming bloody murder at the death of their leader. I raised my makeshift stakes with a desperation borne of knowing that I was hopelessly outnumbered. I was going to die here, half naked, bleeding and violated, and no one would ever find me, but I was going to go down fighting, and I would take as many of those bastards with me as I could. All of which I thought in the flicker of a second, before realising I was utterly, utterly wrong. The vampires weren't attacking. They were fleeing.

I threw myself back down to the ground simply to get out of their way as they pushed and shoved one another in ungainly haste to escape whatever was behind them, as if the very fires of hell itself were nipping at their heels. Though of course, I saw, it was the opposite, because there stood Cain, his face set in grim fury, a flamethrower – a freaking flamethrower! – roaring death from his hands. He stood, braced against the doorframe, barking out short, controlled bursts of fire that scorched everything they touched. Confined in a small space of this bare room, panicked, the vampires had no chance, and I felt myself rejoice as screaming, writhing and scrabbling in terror they met their brutal fate. Then beside Cain – and then, in a blur, in front of him – was Laclos, diving through those vampires lucky enough to escape the flames, inhuman in speed and strength. Those that didn't fall beneath his slashing stake were simply torn apart by his bare hands, tossed aside like rags, and I could hear the sound of their bones splintering as they smashed against the walls. It took mere seconds, and what had been a teaming mass of terrified vampires became a blackened and broken heap of bodies, the air choking with the smell of scorched, inhuman flesh.

"Cassandra!" Laclos cried, instantly at my side, but as he knelt towards me I flinched away, my Sense too brutalised to distinguish between members of the undead. Even through my fear and shock, I felt a grim satisfaction at the look of hurt that crossed his face.

"It's OK. You're OK," he soothed, taking off the long coat he was wearing and gently draping it over my exposed body, taking care not to touch me, as if aware I couldn't bear the thought of a vampire's skin near mine. Then there was a final, cleansing roar of flame, and Cain stepped through the carnage, his flamethrower dropped, discarded, because he had simply run out of bodies to burn. I had time to notice that his face was shiny with sweat and there was blood on his clothing before he reached down past Laclos and scooped me up into his arms as if I were a child. I turned my face to the familiar warmth of his chest and let my tears flow.

"It's OK," he murmured, echoing Laclos' words. "I've got you now. You're safe."

And even without my Sense, I could tell that he was lying. I knew in that moment that I would never be safe again.

Everything was softness. I opened my eyes to consciousness and my mind flared into panic before my Sense – and then my senses – kicked in, and I remembered where I was. I sank back into the comfort of my own bed. I barely remembered getting here: the frantic dash crammed with Cain and Laclos in the back of the latter's ridiculous limo, though I noticed – in the way the mind will seize on the most irrelevant detail in times of stress – that its interior was far shabbier and more battered than I would have imagined for such an owner; I only had the blurriest of memories of Medea and Katie's concerned faces waiting for me. I remembered that Katie had examined me with the brisk, no nonsense manner I was growing accustomed to and found, now, oddly reassuring. She applied salve to the raw skin at my ankles and wrists, and cleaned the blood from my torn breast, pronouncing it unharmed: I wasn't going to be wearing another nipple ring any time soon, but there was no permanent damage. She tactfully enquired after more intimate injuries, but when I outlined, in faltering terms, the extent of my contact with the vampire, she nodded sagely, patted my hand and handed me a supply of anti-septic wipes, leaving the room as I scrubbed myself until I stung. And as I tried to wipe myself clean of the taint of his touch, I wept again as I thought of how close Mallen had come to raping me, and wondered if I would have managed to come back from such a violation.

I must have, eventually, cried myself into exhaustion, because now I was awake again and Medea, tactfully absent during Katie's examination, sat at my bedside, one hand gently folded over mine. The other rested gently on the fur of my cat, who had curled up against me as if he could ward off further distress, and who, in my sleep, I had thrown an arm around, unconsciously grateful for his comfort. Without speaking, Medea nodded her acknowledgement that I was awake, and rose to leave the room, returning moments later with a steaming mug and a large slab of chocolate, from which she patiently snapped off a chunk and handed it to me, expectantly, watching me eat it like a mother bird feeding her chick.

"Now this… sip it, though."

She held the mug to my lips, as if not trusting me to be able to hold it. The drink was sweet and hot and tasted so vile it must have been good for me, and I managed only a few mouthfuls before gesturing for her to put it down. But it had restored me, slightly, and I pulled myself up so I was sitting fully upright. Dante, alarmed by my movement, shot me a look and then, content I wasn't going anywhere, rearranged himself on my lap. Medea was frowning at me, her large, dark eyes more sorrowful than I had ever seen them, her lovely face gaunt with worry.

"Are you alright?"

There were a thousand answers to that and none of them good, so as ever I tried for levity.

"I'm still recovering from seeing Cain and Laclos working together without killing each other," I grinned, and she gave me a slight smile, acknowledging both the feebleness of my joke and the reasons behind it.

"Cain came back to the flat and couldn't find you, but he saw Laclos outside the building in his car… it apparently took each of them a little while to believe that you hadn't been spirited away by the other…"

"I would have paid to see that conversation," I laughed, and this time Medea did smile.

"Well, I don't think Laclos' car will recover quite as speedily as you, let's put it that way." Ah, that explained the trashed looking limo. But it didn't explain much else. "How did they find me? Where was I?"

I had been so thoroughly bundled up in Laclos' coat and Cain's arms I'd seen little as we left my place of captivity, too shocked to take in any details of my locale.

"You were in a warehouse in Docklands. Another of Mallen's holdings – it seems he is… was… quite the property magnate. His real lair, too, presumably, given that there were dozens of vampires there. They were all fairly fledgling, apparently, but it looks like he was gathering quite a following." I thought of those screaming, dying fiends – their bodies not disintegrating at death, like the ancient ones, only reduced to ash under the fury of Cain's fire – but I couldn't muster anything but dark joy. They were monsters, and they deserved it, young though they might be.

"And Laclos helped kill them?"

"I believe most of the… damage… was done by Cain, who it seems has some previously unrevealed skill with a flamethrower." I nodded at that. Add one more tick to the scary list. "But yes, Laclos acquitted himself fairly admirably in your defence, by all accounts." She paused. "And considering where that account comes from, he must have been fairly impressive."

She wasn't kidding. I dreaded to think how vicious a killer you would have to be to get Cain to admire you. There was clearly more to Laclos than stupid leather trousers and an over-developed flirt gland, but I couldn't let my head go near that thought, just yet.

"But how did they find me? I searched for Mallen's properties, remember, and this one wasn't listed anywhere, and none of the vampires I spoke to knew about it – they all thought he was based in Canary Wharf."

Medea looked uncomfortable.

"Ah. That would be me."

"What? How?"

Her dark skin flushed slightly, and she wouldn't meet my eyes.

"I put a tracker spell on you. I hope you don't mind. It's not very intrusive and I was just worried with everything happening and…" she stopped, aware that she was gabbling, and flashed me a nervous smile. "I know it's a little invasive… but I'm not stalking you or anything, I promise."

I reached out and took her hand, only to be alarmed for a second by how pale mine was compared to hers. Even given the natural difference in our skin tones, I looked like a ghost beside her.

"Since you just saved my life, or at the very least stopped me from being turned into one of our clients, I'm very happy to be stalked."

But it was another stark reminder that I needed to train my Sense better, and use it more: that someone could put a spell on me – even a friendly spell – without my knowledge should have been unthinkable. I was clearly letting my Sense get flabby, and it needed a serious work out. But that was for another day, I had too much else to think about at the minute.

"Where are they now?"

She rolled her eyes.

"Out-machoing one another and wearing holes in your carpet." I must have looked puzzled, because she explained. "You invited Laclos in when they brought you back, remember?" I didn't, but that was hardly surprising. "If you hear someone coughing, that'll be Katie, choking on the clouds of testosterone."

I laughed, but that made *me* cough, so Medea handed me the mug and encouraged me to drink some. I took a mouthful before remembering how bad it tasted, and gulped it down with an unclassy swallow, my eyes stinging from the evil brew. But Medea wasn't satisfied with that, and held the mug at me disapprovingly until I managed a couple more mouthfuls.

"Will this make me feel better?"

"It'll help you sleep." I was about to protest that I had just woken up, but she held up a hand to stop me. "You need to rest, Cassandra, you've been through a lot – physically and emotionally – and you need to give yourself a chance to recover, at least a bit."

She leaned across and kissed me softly on the forehead in a gesture that was almost maternal, and made to stand up. For a moment her aura enfolded me, that familiar scent of cinnamon and spices, the sense of Christmas and comfort that she carried around her.

"Will it all be over when I wake up?"

"It *is* over, Cassandra. You killed the bad guy. His followers are dead – whatever army he had at his disposal is, quite literally, toast. We've won. It's over."

I nodded, smiling, comforted by her words and the warm, golden glow of her aura. But as I sank back into the bed and began to drift off, something was nagging at me, a thought I couldn't place or shake; and a tiny voice inside me was telling me she was wrong.

Chapter 36

SOMEWHERE INSIDE me, my Sense was purring, as if stirred by some wonderful dream. It was almost with reluctance that I pulled myself out of sleep, and as I dragged myself towards consciousness the feeling cohered, so that I knew it was Laclos sitting beside my bed before I became aware of the slight chill of his hand, resting gently over mine. I opened my eyes and was surprised to see him frowning down at me, his face creased in an entirely unfamiliar expression of concern.

"I'm pleased to see that you are finally awake. You gave us both quite a turn, your boyfriend and I."

"He's not my boyfriend," I protested, automatically, without quite knowing why. Laclos gave me a brisk, 'all the same' nod, and continued to stare at me as if scared I would vanish if he turned his eyes away. His intense scrutiny made me uncomfortably aware that I must look a bit of a state... which made it all the more surprising when he suddenly leaned forward and kissed me, softly – but before I could help it I reacted to the coolness of his touch with a start, turning my face away. He let out a rasp of frustration and sat back, scowling. I got the feeling Laclos didn't have a whole lot of experience with people turning away from him.

"Why are you faithful to him?" he snapped, which seemed a rather wilful misreading of the situation to me.

"Have you ever thought my reluctance might not be about him? It might actually be about you."

He looked almost shocked for a moment, then arranged his features in a pure-Laclos smile.

"Honestly, no, that hadn't even occurred to me."

"You don't think what you are bothers me? Especially now. Especially after... this."

His smile vanished as quickly as it had appeared, replaced by an uncharacteristic seriousness.

"I think at this moment it does, and I... apologise for my insensitivity. But I think that when you have recovered, when you are calm, you will realise you have constructed your entire life around the belief that what we are, we cannot help. It is who we are, and what we do, that matters."

"I'm not sure I much like what you do right now."

"Do you like what your current lover does?"

I looked away from him, not sure how to answer that, and not entirely sure how comfortable I was with that 'current'.

"Cassandra, you had half of your life wiped out – and that of your friends extinguished – by a creature so scared of the potential of your power that he wanted you dead." I looked up sharply at that. It wasn't the first time Laclos had referred to knowing about the fire; I was shocked enough by that, but how could he possibly know who or what caused it? I had always believed that was something only Cain had known, but was now faced with the uncomfortable thought that the real story was out there for whoever knew where to look. Laclos ignored my startled expression, and went on. "And what did you do when you recovered from that attack? Did you use that power, that knowledge, to wreak vengeance on our world? No. Admittedly your lover exacted... appropriate revenge, and he can hardly be faulted for doing so. But you? You spent time and effort and a considerable investment of money creating a business that facilitated harmony between our kinds. One person is not a species, you know that. I am not the vampire who killed your friends, or the one who assaulted you. Although, yes, I concede that my actions – and my inaction – contributed to your harm, and I am truly sorry for that." His voice hardened. "But before you judge me too harshly, I would remind you that I am not the one who has lied to you. I am not the one who leaves you for years without a word, who has kept the existence of a spouse a secret. Who, whatever he is, is clearly not what he pretends to be, because he is no more human than I am. If you accept nothing else, you know you have to accept that."

I frowned, and though my brain was still foggy I couldn't help but wonder how Laclos could know so much about Cain without knowing that one key thing? Though he was right, wasn't he? But equally I wasn't sure I was ready to trust this new, sincere version of Laclos.

"So, you're the upstanding and loyal romantic hero now?"

A flash of that familiar grin.

"No. No, I am not. But at least I won't ever pretend otherwise."

That elicited a bitter laugh.

"Well, I can put your mind at ease there, because Cain never pretends otherwise, either."

Laclos' smile broadened.

"Then he can have no objection to me doing this," and he leaned in and kissed me again, just as gently, and this time I didn't turn away.

"I'm sorry, I didn't realise you were busy." With his usual immaculate timing, Cain was standing at the doorway. I pulled away, guiltily, but frowned at Laclos, wondering how long he had known Cain was there – sneaky as Cain could be, I couldn't believe he could fool a vampire's senses at such close range. Cain scowled at us, looking, it has to be said, less like an avenging angel and more like a petulant teen. Laclos, in no hurry to pull back from me, smiled, an almost lazy expression of self-satisfaction crossing his face as he turned the full wattage of his charm on Cain.

"No, it is nearly daybreak. I must be going. I am glad to see you recovered, Cassandra. I look forward to continuing this… discussion."

He stood up with his usual fluid grace and gave me a small, polite nod before leaving the room, managing to brush ridiculously close to Cain in doing so, even though Cain had stepped back to let him pass.

"It's not…" I began, helplessly, even though I had no idea what I was going to say.

"I'll let you rest," Cain said, tightly, his face unreadable.

He closed the door and was gone. Then I heard my front door slam and wondered if he would ever come back.

Chapter 37

IT SEEMED unfair, somehow. Cain had a massive, kick ass motorbike, and Laclos had a limo big enough to fuck or feed in – though, admittedly, that was now in for repairs and he was having to make do with a slightly more sedate BMW – and all I had was a travel card and less than sensible shoes. Still, I wasn't going far, and I wasn't in any hurry to get there.

Cain had, of course, come back, but it hadn't been the funnest of reunions: several terse exchanges where there was not so much an elephant in the room as an entire wildlife documentary, and we carefully avoided any acknowledgement of the fact that Laclos had kissed me, or Cain had kissed his wife, or the inevitable truth that it was only a very short matter of time before Cain took the aforementioned kick ass bike and roared back off into the sunset, and how I felt about that. So now, after the teeth scraping hell of that happy chat, I was off to have another conversation that I would have cheerfully postponed for a root canal.

"Laclos is not here."

The Counsel stood, solid and sneering, managing to put an eternity's worth of scorn into his expression as he greeted me in the crypt. He waved a dismissive hand at the young vampire who had shown me down the stairs, and she melted away like mist, not even daring to meet his eyes.

"I must say, Ms Bick," he went on coolly, his voice dripping distain. "You severely misjudge him if you believe that he will be taken by you turning up on his doorstep like one of those swooning teens your modern writers are so keen on. You amuse him at the moment, but his attention is fleeting and his affections are transient – you only do yourself a disservice if you see them as more than they are."

I fixed him with my brightest smile. "I bet you say that to all the girls." I paused, remembering who we were talking about here. "And boys."

He didn't smile. Tough audience.

"Would that I did. I get no pleasure in puncturing your illusions," which, even without the flare of my Sense, I could tell was a big fat lie. "But, by way of illustrating your folly, even as you arrive to continue whatever flirtation you believe you enjoy with him, he is out securing his evening's companions."

He watched me carefully for my reaction, and I saw his composure flicker slightly when my smile brightened further.

"I suppose I'll have to settle for talking to you then," I sat on one of the armchairs, not waiting for invitation, and was gratified that when he frowned at my rudeness. "Perhaps I can seek… Counsel."

Something in my tone startled him, and he raised a hand, and the two vampires I had Sensed standing guard at the back of the room simply vanished, moving at inhuman speed to whatever chambers lay beyond this one, the only mark of their departure the click of a wooden door closing. Clearly, the Counsel didn't want this conversation overheard.

"I am of course happy to advise such a friend of our species in any way I can," he said carefully. I nodded, as if pleased by this sentiment, and waited a nicely dramatic moment before I continued.

"OK, so you must be… what, twice the age of Laclos? Maybe more?" I kept my tone conversational, but it was clear that beneath that placid expression he was wary. "I mean, you damp down your power – your *significant* power – but it's clear you have it, right?"

He paused before answering, as if searching my words for

a trap.

"And?"

"I just wondered why, with all that power – powers, even – and all that wisdom, you aren't the leader here? Why aren't you the one being driven around in a limo with the hot and cold running humans? Instead you're being French kissed for show in front of a bunch of fledglings. Clearly Laclos isn't exactly Mr Sensitive Boss of the Century. It's hardly surprising that Taka went dark side, is it? Years of being Laclos' funboy then he gets made to stand guard while his former BFF gets all Charlie Sheen with the humans. The big shock there is he didn't do it sooner."

"Your point?" The Counsel frowned.

"My point is you're strong enough to rip Laclos' fangs out if you wanted to. So why the hell do you put up with him?"

He gave the slightest of shrugs.

"We live in shallow times. We need a flashy figurehead. I have no interest in such gaudy show, but it is an area in which even his enemies would admit Laclos excels."

I nodded in agreement.

"True. That's very true. Sex and charisma and just a bit of ridiculousness. All that shine on the surface, it can be very distracting."

I could Sense the effort it took him to keep his voice calm, but he finally sat down, facing me with that steady gaze.

"I'm afraid I'm not sure what you are implying."

"Well, leaders get the attention, don't they? That means they also draw the fire. Laclos, Mallen – both showy bastards, when it comes down to it, all dramatic and mysterious appearances and messages, fancy lairs and flash tactics. But leaders come and go. Even in my world, politicians get voted out. Regimes change. But it's still the same people ruling the country, isn't it? The businessmen, the bankers, the spin doctors, the captains of industry, all keeping quiet about their power, knowing that whoever is out there taking the flak, they're the ones with all the influence, with their hands on the strings."

"I'm still not entirely clear on your point. Are you comparing me to a banker? I believe in today's parlance that is a significant insult."

"No, I think you're more a senior civil servant. One of those people with the gold-plated pensions and fingers in every pie. It's in your very name, isn't it? You're the advisor, the influencer, and it doesn't matter too much who you're actually steering. And I imagine there's a whole lot of leverage available when not only do you know where the bodies are buried, but you put a lot of them there yourself."

He sighed, wearily.

"Immortal I may be, Ms Bick, but I am beginning to fear that even I may not live long enough for you actually to reach a point of some sort."

I smiled. He might be a sly bastard, but he certainly had a way with words.

"My point is, all that power, all that influence, and yet civil war nearly broke out on your watch and you did nothing to stop it. Why the fuck not?"

For the first time in the evening, the Counsel smiled.

"Quite honestly? Because I really wouldn't care if it did."

We sat, looking at one another in a parody of drawing room civility, even though every inch of my Sense was telling me to flee. Undistracted by Laclos' presence, I felt like I was really seeing the Counsel properly for the first time. He was actually quite an enormous man: I'd noticed his size before, of course, but I felt like it was only now I was really appreciating it. He was tall as Laclos but even broader than

Cain, and as solid and unmoving as the ancient stone that surrounded us, and I felt that, like the stone, he could remain there, silent, waiting for me to speak. Which, never being able to handle silence, I did.

"But you had enough information to stop it, didn't you? You knew about me, about Medea, about Cain and his wife. You clearly have contacts beyond the vampire community."

He didn't deny it. "It is my job to be informed."

"And to share that information?"

"As appropriate."

"So my big question would be, why share it with Mallen rather than Laclos?" I saw a muscle twitch in his face and saw that I'd scored a hit. "Laclos still has no idea who Cain really is – it's not exactly common knowledge – but Mallen knew *exactly* what he is. The same way you do. In fact, he even used the same words to describe him. 'Celestial consort', wasn't it? Not a phrase you expect to hear bandied about from two different sources."

The Counsel said nothing, but I was on a roll.

"You serve Laclos, but you hate him, because you think he's a preening fool – and, y'know, there's not a huge amount of evidence to contradict that. It would suit you enormously to see a power struggle in town – and that's what would happen, wouldn't it? Prove Laclos can't control his own men – and I can't imagine it was enormously difficult to turn Taka, not with your influence and his existing resentment. Vampires dying – handily, all those young ones with their new fangled ideas to whom you seem like a relic. And you knew my files helped identify the young ones, too, didn't you – which is funny, because how could you have known that unless you were the one who stole them? You knew it the same way you knew how Laclos would react to Cain, to what he was – giving you a chance to try a bit of mind rape. Pity *that* one didn't work out so well for you."

He didn't answer, so I went on, letting that point hang there. I'm not above a petty triumph. "And if Laclos can't protect the vampires from the bad guys, can't stop the slaughter, what use is he? He talked about the other vampire nests in town, but he was... well, not lying, shall we say, but exaggerating, not wanting to show his full hand, let the human see how much power he really wielded, especially the human with such... aggressive friends. Because if there had been any other major players in London, they would have stepped in to stop this too, that much is obvious to me now. Vampires haven't stayed safe here for centuries by letting this kind of chaos go on. But really there is just Laclos, isn't there, and a handful of lower level clusters – not without power, but nowhere close to Laclos or Mallen, nowhere strong enough to challenge what I assume they all knew at some level was going on. So it suited you to start up a war."

"That's an interesting theory."

"Oh, but it gets more interesting. Because I couldn't help wonder – if Mallen really was successful, how would *that* suit your purposes? You could take over Laclos' cadre but you'd have helped create a new bossman in town, so you'd just have replaced one Big Bad with another. And you are way, *way* cleverer than that, aren't you?"

"You seem to be under that impression, at least."

"Oh, I know so. Because Mallen was a little too convenient. An ancient vampire with exactly the same traditionalist views as you, ready to do the wet work on your behalf and then just step out of the way when it's over? Really? I bet you're not even sorry he's dead. But I tell you this, you're going to be sorry it was me that killed him."

At this, he actually looked surprised, and I couldn't help but sound just a little bit gloating.

"Because that was what tipped me off. He wasn't an ancient vampire – he'd been in London less than a hundred years, and I'm guessing that's because he'd actually been alive – or, rather – dead for less than a century. Maybe you actually sired him, I'm not sure, but you bloody well *made* him. You're the sorcerer, the one who helped him summon the demons, and cast his fancy illusions, the one who created that veil of power that he carried – it's you that has spent the years stocking up on black magic, not him. It's a long game you've been playing, but then vampires are nothing if not patient, right? You've been watching the tide turn for a while now, but always known you had a player in hand – ready to kick off if things started changing in the way you didn't want them too, but ultimately disposable if it all went wrong, because nothing could be traced back to you. But when he died, when I killed him, the link you had with him broke, and the illusions vanished. So he didn't crumble. Ancient vampires – ones as old as Laclos, or Taka, or as old as Mallen was supposed to be, they crumble to dust when they die. Younger ones don't. Mallen didn't."

I sat back, exposition dump over, and waited for his reaction. If I'd expected the Scooby Doo reaction of guilt unmasked, I was sorely disappointed, because he said absolutely nothing. But that was OK, I had more to say. Or at least to ask.

"So where do *I* come into it? Why drag me into the mess?" Then I laughed, the answer appearing even as I asked the question. "Of course, Mallen told me, didn't he? You hate what I'm doing. You hate what I stand for. I wasn't just collateral damage, I was part of the target."

"You seem to be doing an admirable job of holding this entire conversation without any input from me," The Counsel said calmly, "but while I find your wild speculation entertaining, I find myself once again puzzled by what exactly you expect to achieve by sharing it."

I took a deep breath, because this was what I came for.

"I want to be left alone. That's all. My friends, my business, my life – stay out of them. Fight your power battles all you like, but leave me be. After what Mallen tried to do to me, I'm done caring about what happens to the vampires. I'm not a fighter. I'm not a hero. I just want to get on with my life knowing that I won't find a demon in my kitchen or a gunman in my office. If you promise me that, if you promise to leave me alone, then I will stay silent, and I won't tell Laclos or Cain what I know."

"Ah." I saw the belated realisation dawn on him that it had never been about me coming here to see Laclos: in fact, I had waited outside until I saw him leave. Tonight had always been about this moment, about me, not him. "I suppose in the circumstances, you are being very reasonable."

I stood up, and nodded, and walked to the door.

"But of course I can't possibly let you leave."

Well, that wasn't entirely unexpected. I turned back, slowly, to see the Counsel had also risen to his feet. He smiled at me, looking worryingly unperturbed by the gun I was now holding in my hand.

"Really?" he raised a sceptical eyebrow. "After all you have just said I am capable of, you think you can stop me with a gun?"

"Ancient or newbie, a silver bullet will hurt you."

"If you can hit me."

He moved his hand in a sweeping gesture and the gun was ripped out of my grip at the same time I was hurled back into the wall, so hard that the air was thumped out of me. All the dampers on his power had gone, now, dropped like a veil, and the pressure of it was crushing me almost as completely as whatever force he as using to pin me, suspended inches above the floor, unable to move.

"Of course, you are right. I was the one behind Mallen. I am the one with the power – some of us have chosen to spend the centuries doing more than simply exploring the limits of our own decadence. I hope that gives you some satisfaction before you die. Though I am surprised, I admit, that given your extensive and well-documented love of popular culture, you decided to come here, the lone female baiting the villain in his lair."

I nodded bitterly at his satisfaction. He was right. A thousand different cop shows, dramas, and every horror movie I had ever seen had proved the perils of being the plucky heroine who thinks that confronting the bad guy alone in some deserted spot is a smart idea. It never, ever is.

I looked up at the Counsel, and he was shocked to see me smiling. "That's why I brought help," I told him. "I didn't need to defeat you, Counsel. I just needed to distract you."

And then, for about the tenth time in a week, the world around me exploded.

Chapter 38

I MIGHT be getting used to the sight of Cain smashing down doors, but it never stopped being impressive. The entire wall behind the Counsel – where whatever hidden exit the bodyguards had made their soundless disappearance through had been – seemed to buckle, and a wooden door, now reduced to planks and splinters, skittered across the room propelled by the force of Cain's kick as he emerged into the crypt. He was carrying enough weaponry to start a small war, and wore a smile of pure, malicious joy. If Cain truly was an angel, it was for a very dark god indeed.

If the Counsel had attacked him straight away, perhaps he could have felled him, but he had been made lazy by power. He made a gesture to summon assistance, and then looked stunned when no one came. So clearly the first part of my plan had worked; distracting him with my wordy confrontation while Cain led Medea, Katie and Val the Valkyrie in subduing the vampires in the lair. Val had been lured back by the prospect of more action and whatever private promises Cain had made to her, though now was not the time to be thinking about what those may have been. I just hoped that she had kept to her agreement to stick to laying down suppression rather than committing wholesale slaughter – the soundproofing provided by the thick stone had served our attack well but was also stopping me from knowing its outcome, but that was also a concern for later. Right now I was a lot less worried about a load of collateral damage than I would have been a week ago. Concentrating, I could Sense Val, standing guard at the exit, the same way I could Sense Katie and Medea, now just outside the main door upstairs.

Never having been able to pick up on how many vampires there had been in the building – my Sense damped by the psychic resonance of such an old and sacred structure – I had no way of knowing whether the dull glow of their presence had been drastically reduced. But right at this instant, it didn't matter. Now, all I could do was watch the real battle play out.

Cain cast me a quick glance and, if I hadn't known better, I would have sworn that he winked. Pissed off at me he might have been, but he'd listened to my suspicions and – eventually – agreed to my plan. The plan which unfortunately currently saw me stuck to a wall by a magic vampire, but I prayed that this was only a temporary setback. Now, more than ever in my life, I needed Cain to really be the cavalry.

"Do I even have to tell you to let her go?" he asked the stunned Counsel, his tone surprisingly reasonable.

The Counsel took a moment to recover himself. I realised that, for all his power, a man who fought through proxies was unused to such direct confrontation.

"And if I do? Do you just let me walk unhindered into the night? Somehow I suspect that is not part of your agenda."

Cain shrugged, as if this didn't matter to him either way, and I had a horrible flashback to that stairway in Canary Wharf. I felt suddenly very exposed, suspended and helpless as I was.

"You can go. Get out of London."

"You would just let me leave?"

"Oh, I'd track you. And find you, eventually, and wipe you off the face of the earth like the worthless vermin that you are." That was Cain, ever the diplomat. "But at least this way you get a head start. Maybe a few more days of what passes for life in your species. Maybe even a couple of weeks."

The Counsel, sangfroid restored, looked almost amused.

"It's a tempting offer."

"One time only. Expiring fast."

For a moment, I thought the vampire was actually thinking about it. Then he smiled, his fangs bared, and raised both hands, and a surge of energy hit me like a blow. Cain's weaponry was torn from him, every last scrap of it, and flew towards the wall as if someone had turned the masonry into a giant magnet, the metal hitting with such force that it bent and flattened with the impact. I saw Cain wince and stagger, struggling to keep his feet. The Counsel gave him a small nod.

"I think, this time, I shall pass."

He was now almost grinning: he could see the same thing I could, that the strength of his magic was pushing Cain so hard his boots were scraping against the floor as he tried to resist the force that had stripped him of his guns. But there was also something in that look that told me the Counsel was finally, really angry, and my Sense curled up in terror at the thought of that unbridled rage.

"I am almost disappointed in you, celestial. You come at me with guns? You have no comprehension of the magics I wield. I have seen millennia turn, and I have used the centuries well. You have been earthbound too long, angel, and become too dependent on mankind's toys. You have forgotten what real power is."

As he spoke, each word clipped with fury, I felt him ramp up his energy: it radiated off him like heat, and the pressure in the room felt like it might suffocate me. But now it was Cain's turn to smile. He stopped struggling, suddenly, because there was simply nothing he had to struggle against, and I saw the Counsel's eyes widen as a man who had been flailing in a storm stood tall, and straight and unmoving.

"You talk about centuries, about millennia?" Cain spat, his eyes blazing. "I was alive before the filth that spawned you even existed. I watched the humans you feed on crawling bloody and muddied from the swamps. I saw the seas themselves form. I am older than the very earth you walk on, and I saw it torn from the universe itself by a simple act of will. So don't for one single fucking minute think you get to lecture me about the meaning of power."

And then Cain laughed, delighted, and the ground beneath us shook. I stared, horrified, as first dust and then stones started to fall as the foundations of the building shifted, and, released from the Counsel's hold, I tumbled heavily to the floor. The two men faced one another, a frozen tableau, neither seeming to know or care that the world around them was buckling and twisting. The force in the room was almost crushing. Whimpering, terrified, I huddled in the corner, my arms over my head to shield me from falling masonry, though it seemed an even bet whether a brick or the pressure in the room would get me first. Somehow when I had suggested we confront the Counsel, this hadn't been what I had had in mind. But Cain's eyes were gleaming, luminous, and his smile was demonic; even with my eyes closed, I could Sense him, almost gleeful with the joy of finally unleashing a power he had so long kept in check.

"You think you know the world, vampire? You think you know what I am? You know *nothing*. You are merely a child, having a tantrum." He held a hand up, and my Sense whined as I felt the whole city around us tremble. "And, old as I am, I have very traditional ideas on discipline," Cain grinned. "So I think you need a bit of a slap."

He smacked his palm forward, the smallest of distances, and the Counsel... simply exploded. One minute he was standing there, magic and energy and flesh, and the next he was no more than dust, mingling with the clouds that were falling from the ceiling. The pressure in the room vanished, and Cain swept me to my feet, his face lit with dark delight. I stared at him, beyond stunned.

"I can see why you don't need a flaming sword."

Chapter 39

THEY REPORTED it as an earthquake. Luckily the actual structure of St Paul's was remarkably unscathed, despite the wreckage now beneath it. Maybe there was a god, after all, and he liked his churches, or maybe Chris Wren was just a *really* clever builder. The rest of the city also came out of it relatively fortunate. Besides a few cracked buildings, a lot of scared people and a whole bunch of annoyed tube passengers – who had been stranded underground when the very rails beneath them cracked – there were only minor injuries and minimal damage. There were dark mutterings, of course: London wasn't exactly known for earthquakes, and coming on the back of two terrorist attacks and a spate of murders, it had the whiff of conspiracy about it. In fact there was a story that the tremors were the result of an SAS attack on a terrorist cell, and despite the fact there was no evidence to substantiate this – mainly because I made it up in the pub over a boozy lunch with a journalist contact of mine – it soon became an accepted reason. After all, the authorities – who had been helpless in the face of the bombings and the serial murders – were in no hurry to explain to people that it *wasn't* them that had caused them to stop.

We had told a stunned and disbelieving Laclos the truth, of course. How could we not? He had returned home to find his vampires restrained and unconscious – a peaceful bunch not used to anything trickier than styling their hair without a mirror, most of them had fallen easily enough to the combination of Medea's magic, Katie's growled threats and the brute force of Cain and his goddess. On top of that his lair was half-demolished and his second in command now able to fit neatly in a dustpan. He was shocked, hurt and angry – both at the Counsel's betrayal and at the fact that we had tackled it without him; he was unconvinced by my explanation that we felt we had to validate our suspicions (and, it remained unsaid, prove that Laclos knew nothing of what his right hand man was doing) before involving him. But, as he looked around the battered remains of his home in dismay, it was the first time I had ever seen him lost for words. Knowing we couldn't help him, we left before he had the chance to find them.

Now we were back in my flat. Val the Valk had, of course, once again vanished the minute the action was over. I didn't see what farewells she made to Cain – anymore than I had seen whatever deal he'd struck to get her here – but she evidently didn't consider me worth saying goodbye to. Perhaps she was disappointed I had survived. Katie and Medea, both exhausted and almost as shaken as the building they'd been standing next to, and neither of them entirely clear on what had taken place in the crypt, had hugged me and made for the sanctuary of their home. This left only me and Cain, the only other person who knew what had really happened. I looked – and felt – like I had been hit by a train. He looked like he had been for a light jog round the park.

He smiled at me gently. I was aware that I was staring.

"I told you that I rationed my power. I never implied that meant I didn't have it." He shrugged, lightly, and I saw him try to hide a wince. I wondered how much that confrontation had really cost him – and how long it would take to recover.

"I never got the chance to thank your wife."

He turned his eyes away from me. "The battle is always reward enough for her."

"Well, be sure to pass on my thanks, anyway, if you see her."

"That isn't very likely," he answered, but he wouldn't look at me when he said it. Suddenly weary, I sagged back into my chair.

"Do you think it's really over?"

Another shrug, and this time the wince was unmistakable.

"There will always be monsters. We have beaten this particular one. So it's over for now, I suppose."

I bit my lip, not wanting to ask this next question, because I knew how desperately I needed the answer.

"And what about us?"

He finally turned back to me.

"What do you mean?"

"Are you just going to vanish again?"

He didn't reply, which I suppose was answer enough.

I sighed, frustrated. "What am I to you, Cain?"

"What do you want me to say to that?"

Now that's never a question that makes a girl feel good.

He scowled at me in frustration. "I just saved your life. *Again.*"

"Against a bad guy you've wanted to kill from the moment you got here. I'm grateful and all, but let's not pretend that all those heroics were just about me."

He looked at me for a long, long moment, and when he spoke I could feel him trying to keep his voice from shaking, though it was anger, not anything else, he was trying to hold in check. "What do you want from me, Cass? I like you. I enjoy you, and I thought that you enjoyed me. But if you want some declaration of eternal love… I couldn't even manage that with an *actual* eternal. Do you want to hear some romantic claptrap about how I've waited for you through the centuries? Because I've actually been pretty busy. And I've been alive a long, long time, Cass. Nothing – *nothing* – is new to me. No one surprises me. No one is that unique."

Hating myself for it, I felt my eyes fill with tears.

"Well, I guess it takes a lot to be special to you."

He let out a tired sigh.

"You *are* special to me. Here. Now. Why can't that be enough?"

I stood up, and tried to keep my voice from wobbling when I spoke.

"I think I need to be alone for a while. I'm going to go for a walk, get some fresh air. Thank you for saving my life. Again."

He scowled, suddenly accusing.

"Are you going to him? Back to Laclos?"

"Would that matter to you?"

"He's a monster!"

"He's not human. But neither are you." I leaned down and kissed him, gently, on the forehead. He lifted his face towards me, but I stepped back, moving away from him in a way I had never done before in my life. "Goodbye, Cain. Maybe I'll see you in heaven."

I was at the door before he spoke, in a voice so low I could barely hear it. "You don't believe in heaven, Cassandra."

I didn't look round. Now it was my turn to leave.

Epilogue

MEDEA WAS leaning against the doorframe of my office, her familiar, mysteriously lettered mug in her hand, regarding me with a mix of curiosity and suspicion. The taint of her magic still clung to her, mixing with the hint of Katie's supernatural nature, obvious now I knew how to Sense it. The magic she had done over the last few weeks seemed to have changed her aura, and I wasn't sure whether it was permanent or not. But then, I suppose, what had happened had changed us all. Though mercifully one thing that remained the same was her ability to stand there patiently while I let my mouth run on. She had been listening to me rant for the best part of 20 minutes, all of the frustration I hadn't been able to take out on Cain being vented now, her dark gaze unwavering and calm.

"Honestly, what have I been doing all this time? How much time have I wasted waiting for him? And waiting for what? He doesn't care about me. He's *married*. He disapproves of my life. I need to move on."

Medea raised one perfectly shaped eyebrow.

"To Laclos?"

"No! Maybe. Don't you start!" I flushed, the memory of that doorstep kiss still hot and fresh in my mind. Medea smiled, gently.

"I'm not saying *not* Laclos," she said. "I'm not saying Cain. I'm just saying… perhaps you're being a little unfair. To him, and to yourself. You say he doesn't care about you… but he nearly pulled down half a city to save you."

"To save himself as well."

"He's immortal, isn't he? I don't imagine he needs a huge amount of saving."

"He wanted to take down the bad guy." I knew I sounded petulant, but her reasonableness was annoying me.

"Perhaps. But the 'bad guy' was precipitating a war that he approved of. Had he wanted to, he simply could have let the battle rage and then picked off the victor."

"So, you're saying he cares but what, he's emotionally inarticulate? I know men mature later, Mey, but he's had eternity to get his act together."

She kept her voice soft and patient.

"Exactly. Eternity. You complain that he only sees you every few years – have you ever thought that, for him, those years may pass in the blink of an eye? It's hardly a long time for him – and how can either of us ever really understand that perspective? Given how long he has lived, how long he will live… how can we understand what he feels? What he has felt, or what he has lost?"

I scowled at her, not at all liking where this was going.

"So basically, you're saying I should stop being such a bitch about it?"

She laughed. "No, I'm not saying pin your girlish dreams of the future on him, Cassandra. I'm just saying… give him a little more credit. Perhaps his actions speak louder than his words. And think about what those actions have been."

I stared at her, as a creeping sensation of horror crawled over me. Crap. Maybe she was right. What had I done? I put my head in my hands and groaned. I had helped save my city, that was true, overcrowded, smelly and bad-tempered as it was. But had I pushed away my guardian angel, and in the process given my heart to the very thing he saw as a devil? You go, girl, Cassandra.

What the fuck was I going to do for an encore?

Acknowledgements

Thanks to all of my 'beta testers' for their time, feedback and encouragement (although any mistakes that are left are, of course, entirely mine): Kathryn Allen, Clare Ault, Lori Frecker, Rosalind Galt, Leo Goldsmith and Clare Thompson. Special thanks must go to Caroline Goldsmith for her unwavering support, and for creating the cover of this book, and Laura Harris for her thorough annotation, without which the book would be even more rife with errors than it no doubt already is, and an apology to the other Caroline for usurping her surname for one of the bad guys. As ever, gratitude to all my friends for listening to me burble on about my writing and never giving in to what at times must be an overwhelming urge to brain me with my own laptop.

Cover design by Caroline Goldsmith, copyright 2012.

About the author

Tracey Sinclair is the author of the novel Doll and short story collection No Love is This (both Kennedy & Boyd). She is a regular contributor to the theatre site Exeunt and has been published widely in both print and online magazines. She is a performed playwright, with the short play Bystanders produced at Baron's Court Theatre in 2011. You can follow her on Twitter under the profoundly misleading Twitter name, @thriftygal, or keep up with Dark Dates via darkdates.org or www.facebook.com/darkdates

The Dark Dates – Chronicles of Cassandra Bick series so far

Dark Dates
A Vampire Walks into a Bar (short story)
A Vampire Christmas (short story)
Wolf Night
A Vampire In Edinburgh (short story)

Disclaimer

All characters and organisations in this book are fiction, and any resemblance to any person living, dead or undead is entirely unintended. Although many of the locations do exist in London, I have taken some liberties to facilitate the story, or simply because my own geography sucks. As far as I am aware, there is no nest of vampires in St Paul's Cathedral, but it's still beautiful and worth a visit, and they really do have a very nice gift shop.

Printed in Great Britain
by Amazon